"… the text is full of humour, elements. I think this is a splendid piece of work."

—Peter Snell,
editor, Vine Leaves Press.

"Excellent comedic control and turns of phrase."

—Laurence Edmonson,
Storgy Magazine.

"A weird and wonderful place that's a perfect setting for a modern-day fairy tale or a Fellini film."

—Kim Conklin,
All Write in Sin City, podcast.

THE BANK STREET PEEPER

I am a Ford City author.
I hope you like my book.

Twitter: @ErmaOdrach

The Bank Street Peeper

A novel

by

ERMA ODRACH

Adelaide Books
New York / Lisbon
2021

THE BANK STREET PEEPER

A novel

By Erma Odrach

Copyright © by Erma Odrach

Cover design © 2021 Adelaide Books

Published by Adelaide Books, New York / Lisbon
adelaidebooks.org

Editor-in-Chief
Stevan V. Nikolic

All rights reserved. No part of this book may be reproduced in any manner whatsoever without written permission from the author except in the case of brief quotations embodied in critical articles and reviews.

For any information, please address Adelaide Books
at info@adelaidebooks.org
or write to:
Adelaide Books
244 Fifth Ave. Suite D27
New York, NY, 10001

ISBN: 978-1-955196-83-3

Printed in the United States of America

This is a work of fiction. All names, characters and events are fictitious or used fictitiously. Any resemblance to actual persons living or dead is purely coincidental.

This is for you Rho, Tanya, Christina, and Michael

Contents

Chapter 1
The Telling of Reginald Rutley   **13**

Chapter 2
The Pregnancy   **22**

Chapter 3
Noble Knives   **32**

Chapter 4
Carlito and His Three Sisters   **48**

Chapter 5
I Killed Him!   **64**

Chapter 6
The Cabbagetown Jazz Band   **79**

Chapter 7
The Writer Sholomitsky   **89**

Chapter 8
Mamma Mia   **100**

Chapter 9
Christy Throws a Housewarming Party **114**

Chapter 10
The Wet Dream **127**

Chapter 11
Elevator Shoes **130**

Chapter 12
Lily's Antiques **137**

Chapter 13
The Bootlegger **148**

Chapter 14
Nick the Dick **164**

Chapter 15
Cats **177**

Chapter 16
The Mouth Painter **191**

Chapter 17
Margarida **202**

Chapter 18
Murder on Bank Street **216**

Chapter 19
Fancy Feast **236**

Chapter 20
The Drunk **248**

Chapter 21
The Red Mustang **260**

Chapter 22
Reginald at the Art Gallery **269**

Chapter 23
The Street Party **286**

Acknowledgements **299**

Credits **301**

About the Author **303**

Chapter 1

The Telling of Reginald Rutley

Reginald Rutley was a man of limited growth barely four feet tall but his body was corpulent. He was grotesque-looking with a hunched back, a balding head, and eyes that stuck out like that of a frog. Some would say he even looked like a frog with that greenish tinge to his complexion, those bow legs, and that pushed-out heart-shaped chest. When he spoke his voice often broke with croaking sounds, and if one didn't know any better one would swear he was saying, *"Ribett, Ribett."* Reginald was an excellent jumper too, even for a man of forty, and just like a frog he hid behind trees, sheds, rocks, in all sorts of unsuspecting of places.

Reginald lived on Bank Street, in one of the largest cities in North America. What he liked to do most was spy on his neighbors, peep through their windows when the sun went down. As unlawful as it was, he was good at it, so good hardly anyone ever noticed. He even developed a system of reading people's minds, where he could tell what they were thinking at any given moment. Reginald was weird and he was as much weird on the inside as he was on the out.

It was hard for Reginald to come into contact with other human beings, as he was very shy. He had no family and he was alone, estranged from those around him. No one ever came to visit him and neither was he invited out. Sometimes he liked to drink, especially red wine or scotch, though he was never seen drunk. Usually, he spent his days in his own thoughts, where life had a rather bitter taste to it. People knew he was suffering long and deeply, but no one ever bothered reaching out to him, and the odd time they did, it was either by accident or out of pity. These are the sorts of things they would say, "Oh, you poor thing," or "Is everything all right?" or "If only I could do something." On such occasions, like a famished animal, he would devour the crumbs of warmth and kindliness thrown his way.

Being the little person that he was with his little arms and little bent shoulders, his insufficiencies were more than apparent. People never missed an opportunity to disparage him. When they talked amongst themselves, they all agreed there was something unappealing about his appearance, even repugnant – the twist of his mouth, that strange look in his eye, that croakish-sounding voice. His small size made him a lesser man than other men. A few laughed behind his back, some to his face, and little did they know or care it was the laughter that brought him the deepest anguish. They came to believe his condition was a result of some accident at birth.

Not a day went by that Reginald didn't struggle with himself and try to get away. He conveyed a quiet despair that always seemed to be there and the neighbors wondered if he had dreams or if he ever hoped for anything. He was not a sociable man, and if there was one thing they knew about him, it was that his life was not regular like theirs. He lived by himself very quietly and he seemed on the sensitive side with low self-esteem.

His way of living was strange and his world was his own. He did not have a wife.

Prone to bouts of depression, Reginald found ways to atone for any onset. He designed a life for himself that was ideal, where he convinced himself he did not need friendships. He developed his mind with solitary pleasures such as reading, music, art, and when he found the need for company he turned on the TV or put on a video and pretended someone was there with him. Yesterday, for example, when watching a news episode and the broadcaster said, "Welcome to the six o'clock news", it was as if a visitor had come to call. It's a good thing Reginald was smart so smart he was even able to outsmart himself.

But it was spying on people that gave him the greatest form of pleasure. By looking through the windows of others he imagined himself at home in all of them, even though he knew it was far beyond his reach. Life for him was harsh, forever pushing him out and casting him aside and making him into the lonely figure that he was, but in the spy world everything was possible. It took care of all his needs and gave his life meaning. He could nestle into living rooms, kitchens, even bedrooms of strangers and be at the center of it all, if only for a little while. By keeping what he saw for his own, he was able to hide his bitter struggles and his need to fit in. And his neighbors couldn't have been more accommodating – the things he didn't see! A cheating wife, a bootlegger, an armless painter, a murdered sex-trade worker, and the list goes on. If anything, the people on his street covered every aspect of everyday life and not a day passed that something didn't happen.

(Allow me at this point to briefly interject. Though Reginald was a window peeper and found a kind of perverse excitement in all that he saw, in no way was he a peeping Tom, at least not in the Lady Godiva sense. Never did he go out of his way to pruriently spy on people, no, that was just not his way, but if he accidentally stumbled upon something of a prurient nature, then, it was like hitting the jackpot.)

Bank Street was part of an immigrant working-class neighborhood with no more than fifty houses on it, modest, eclectic, some of the Victorian era, some pre-World War Two. There were also a couple from the 1960s, box-like in shape, giving the street a bit of a suburban feel. The houses were set close together and all stood near to the road. Along the way were shade trees, namely oak and acorn, several grape arbors, and bushes of various assortments. At one end was a variety store filled with last-minute items such as bread, milk, cheese, and eggs, and at the other, a park with a rather large community center, where teenagers hung around all hours smoking pot and playing loud music. Bank Street had some vehicular traffic but it was predominantly local and went one way, from east to west. Connecting up with other small streets much like it, if one were familiar with the area, driving, one could turn left on Bank Street, right, another right, and end up on Dundas one of the city's main arteries. But most who passed by Bank Street didn't notice there was a street there at all.

Though Reginald wasn't on familiar terms with any of his neighbors, he knew most of them by name – there was Joe from Number 19, Mamma Mia from Number 35, Christy from Number 3. Normally, when he would pass them by, he would exchange a few words or nod a polite hello, and they in return would offer their own kindly salutations. Reginald would say to them, "Good day, how do you do?" and they would say back, "Fine, thank you, and a good day to you too."

Over the years many changes had occurred on Bank Street with people moving in and people moving out, and Reginald, being the longest residing resident, had seen it all. Bank Street had always been a lively place full of people all wanting the same thing – to carve out a decent life for themselves and their families.

Number 25 is where Reginald lived and it was one of the biggest houses on the street. Built in the late 1800s of red brick, it came with a spacious veranda, a steeply-pitched roof, and vergeboarding in the gables. It was three stories high and on all floors were large bay windows with wooden sills and ornate cornices. Reginald loved the house where he had lived all his life and where he was born. Being the persnickety type, he kept it in perfect cleanliness and order, and routine for him came as second nature. For example, he scrubbed the kitchen floor every second day, he polished the furniture every third, and every fifth day he made sure his bed sheets and pillow cases were stripped and changed. Outside the hedges were neatly trimmed, the grass perfectly mowed, and a dwarf plum tree carefully pruned.

Reginald's parents had come from Ireland and had bought the house only a few years after arriving in their new homeland. His mother at the time was pregnant with him, her only child. When she prematurely went into labor one cold winter day, his father, all excited, rushed outside to bring the car around to take her to the hospital. But it was too late, Reginald's head was already showing. After three strong pushes there he was born in the middle of the living room on the brown upholstered sofa. But something was not right with the newborn. The father noticed this at once and cried out:

"Good Lord, Nellie, if he isn't the tiniest thing I ever did see!"

Reginald owned and operated a small hardware store on Dundas Street, which was a block and a half away from his house. There was a sign over the front door in bold black letters: Rutley's Home Hardware. Every morning he opened at nine and closed at six, except on Saturdays when he closed at five and on Sundays when he didn't open at all. It was a very busy store cluttered with garden tools, building supplies, and all sorts of kitchen gadgets and small home appliances. He had inherited the business from his parents, who had passed away several years before in a freak car accident while traveling to some warehouse on the other side of town to pick up inventory. They had been t-boned by a transport truck and had died on the spot. The news had devastated Reginald, as he had been close to his parents and he didn't know life without them. For the longest time, he was unable to come to terms with the fact that they were gone and forever. At night he often woke up with his head full of memories.

The hardware store had always been a lucrative business, servicing customers in and around the neighborhood and sometimes even commuters who were changing from bus to streetcar because the streetcar stop was right in front of the store door. Reginald regularly had sales on and posted them in the window as a means of drawing people in – water hoses in the summer, snow shovels in the winter. Though Reginald was not the most engaging sort, he was a competent enough salesman, and it's a good thing too because, had it not been for his store, who knows how he might have earned his living. He had graduated high school but he had no special talent, however, he did play the accordion.

Every evening when Reginald got home from work, he hung up his cap and jacket, then took off his shoes and put on his slippers. There was never anyone to greet him, no one to hug him, kiss him or to say, "Did you have a good day?" Other than himself there was no one there. That he was alone made him gloomy but, as mentioned earlier, he had long since come to appreciate life on his own terms. Most importantly, he knew how to avoid making himself vulnerable to great emotional upsurges; in other words, he made a point of staying away from women, at least as much as was humanly possible. Besides exchanging a few words with them here and there, he would let it get no further than that. Though he was a man and like all men had his moments of craving, in the end, intimacy was not for him. Learning to pleasure himself and find gratification, he imagined himself a happy man. And in such a way he stayed contented never having to admit to himself or to anyone what he might be missing.

In his teen years Reginald had developed affections for certain girls but even then he knew to observe them from afar, never to display his painful yearnings. He was well aware it would only make him the subject of laughter and ridicule.

There was one time, however, he got ahead of himself and against his better judgment fell head-over-heels in love with a beautiful young woman. With auburn hair and piercing blue-green eyes, her name was Julia and she worked in the newly opened Polish bakery across the street from his store. She had the perfect face and her lips were plump as cherries. She had wakened something within him. Life at once became full and meaningful and he could hear the birds sing. Julia had the sweetest smile, and though she constantly teased him about his diminutive stature, it never came off as offensive; quite the contrary, it was more like music to his ears. These are the kinds of things she would say:

"Hello my little Napoleon," or "what would my little Napoleon like today?" or "is my little hunchback happy with his life?"

Her tone was always so comforting, so soft, it made his heart quiver away. He was convinced it was the real deal, that she was drawn to him as much as he to her. It made him feel alive. And incredibly it didn't seem to matter to her that in height he was well below the national average, that his roundish skull had hard brown bristles sticking out of it, and that his voice sometimes came out in croaking sounds. At last, he had found someone to love.

But unfortunately, what Reginald failed to see was that Julia's friendliness was fuelled by pity and it was artificial. One day when he came into the bakery and asked for a plum-filled doughnut, his favorite, he leaned over the counter and tried to kiss her. Shocked by this unexpected gesture, without a moment to lose, she reviled him viciously.

"What did you go and do that for? Ugh! Imagine, me with someone like you, no one would believe it!"

She then started to laugh and her laughter filled the bakery and bounced off the walls. And she wouldn't stop.

Reginald was mortified. A feeling of self-contempt surged within him and he wanted to flee but fleeing wasn't enough, he wanted to die. How could he ever have thought this lovely creature might have feelings for him such as he was? Then he caught his own reflection in the window. What could he have been thinking? Squeezing out a little cry, hurrying out the door, he ran down the street and he couldn't run fast enough.

Since that awful day, which was now almost twenty years ago, Reginald had come to accept that the more tender side of life did not exist for him. But the problem was he loved women too much and found them irresistibly beautiful. He had loved many but never had he been loved back. As much as he tried to deny it, hidden in his subconscious, way at the back of his mind, lay dormant the search for love, a search that was capable of being activated at any time and without notice, the way it had been for Julia. But he swore he would never let it happen again and if it did, he would do everything in his power to stop it.

And so, Reginald continued to experience life and love through the windows of his neighbors, where he could pretend and be part of something outside of himself. Though this appeased him and allowed him to carry on, he was no fool. Deep down, he knew it was all just make-believe and that he really had nothing. No woman loved him and never would. All he wanted was to be ordinary, to have a life and a wife. With the years slipping imperceptibly by, though there was still a glimmer of hope, it was quickly fading.

Chapter 2

The Pregnancy

The sun was slowly setting and its dimming rays were making their way through the open window, plunging across the far wall, and then hitting up against the side of the table. Soon it would be dark enough for Reginald to go out and do what he did almost every night – spy on his neighbors. Pouring himself a glass of red wine, sitting down to a dinner of salad and leftover stew, he ate heartily.

Tonight, he was feeling all charged up because over at Number 49, that red brick Victorian by the park, there was some unfinished business for him to tend to. Putting on his cap and jacket and stepping outside, he hastened down the street. The row of houses on either side stood silently against the darkened sky and somewhere in the distance came the barking of a dog.

He was almost there. Last night he had come upon quite the drama between mother and daughter; in fact, it couldn't have been more riveting. Through an open window, he had heard everything and clearly, mother and daughter arguing, crying both at the same time, equally upset. But because the window had been curtained and screened, he couldn't see a thing and neither could he determine who was saying what. In any case, the following is what he heard.

"Pregnant! What do you mean you're pregnant?"

No answer.

Same voice again, "But how could this have happened? Pregnant, of all things. There's something called protection you know."

Then sobbing, sniveling. "Oh, I know, I know. This is all too much, oh, I shouldn't have said anything. You shouldn't have to deal with this."

"Really!"

"And you're only sixteen. I'm such a bad role model."

"Well, we can't worry about that now, we have to be sensible about this. We have to figure out what to do. Abortion's not an option because it's too late for that. Why did it take you this long to say something?"

No response.

"Why?"

Still nothing.

"Tell me! Why?"

"Oh, why, why, you ask? Why this, why that, why's the sky blue? I don't know why. Maybe I was hoping it would all just go away. But what am I supposed to do now? Father will be home tomorrow. He'll do the math. He's going to have a fit! Oh my, I have such a headache!"

"You have a headache? Well, now I've got one too. Just look at you, you're even starting to show! Oh my god, who's the father?"

Silence.

"Who is it?"

More silence.

"Tell me! Who's the father? It's going to come out sooner or later anyway."

"Oh, all right, all right, I'll tell you; it's Pepe, Pepe's the father."

"Pepe? Oh, Mother! Are you kidding me? The plumber from down the street? Have you lost your mind? And isn't he married too?"

Mother was now in a frenzy and she was blowing her nose.

"It was wrong of me, I know; what can I say? It was a moment of weakness. He came over to fix the drain pipe. One thing led to another and before I knew it, we were …"

The daughter cut her mother off sharply, she had no desire to hear the specifics, "Mother, please! What we've got to do now is come up with a plan before Father gets home. He's coming tomorrow night around eight, remember? Does Pepe know about the baby?"

"No."

"Good. Then let's keep it that way, at least for a while. Let me think about what to do."

A few minutes passed. There came no sound only the ticking of a clock. Suddenly the daughter cried out, "I've got it! I've absolutely got it!"

Mother clasped her hands, "Oh my dear little girl, always so well-reasoned. Whatever would I do without you? So, what is it?"

As Daughter was about to explain, right at that moment the two decided they were thirsty. Picking up, heading for the kitchen, their voices trailed and soon disappeared altogether.

"Dammit!" Reginald stomped his foot. "Now I'll never know what they're up to."

He felt like banging on the window and shouting out to them, "Don't leave me in the dark, ladies! Come back, please! I want to hear the details!"

Hurrying over to the kitchen window to see if maybe he could pick up from there, to his dismay, it was sealed shut and the blinds completely drawn. He got into a terrible state of mind. As it stood, he had no way of finding anything more out. Then he remembered hearing Mother and Daughter mentioning Father, after a long absence, was due home around eight tomorrow night. Not all was lost after all! Tomorrow he would return and learn everything, and he would learn it as it would be explained to Father.

That night he hardly slept. All day he was restless.

So now here he was, seven forty-five, hurrying back to Number 49 to pick up where he left off. When he finally reached the house, he got behind a cedar hedge and waited. Not a sound, only the leaves of an old oak rustling softly overhead. The stars high in the sky were bright and calm and a crescent moon hung over the rooftops.

At once a cab pulled up and a man got out. Of average height and with a head of curly yellow hair, he was in full army uniform and carried two duffel bags. Reginald could tell right away it was Father home from an oversees deployment. Looking smart in his khaki pants and a jacket full of decorations, he hurried up the porch stairs. At long last, he would see his two best girls. In his left hand, he carried a bouquet of yellow roses, his wife's favorite, and under his arm a box of chocolates filled with caramel.

He rang the bell. The front door opened wide and Mother and Daughter came rushing at him, embracing him warmly, welcoming him back home. There came shouting, screaming, crying, first Mother, then Daughter, then Father, and one covered the other.

"Jimmy! Angie! Father! Cindy!"

There was quite the brouhaha and it lasted several minutes. The family then went inside to continue their happy reunion.

In the living room, they sat down on the sofa, which, luckily for Reginald, happened to be by an open window and with no curtains. A big lamp with a red shade rested on a table and lit up the room. The walls were all dark with white trim, and over a couple of chairs upholstered in gold chintz was a fake watercolor landscape in a heavy metal frame.

Father addressed Mother in a loving way.

"Angie, let me take a good look at you. It's been so long, too long. But you look fantastic! I see you've put on a few extra pounds but it hasn't hurt you any. And you have a special glow about you too, you're simply beaming. I missed you so much!"

Mother, who was wearing a loose-fitting dress with big patch pockets, strained a smile. She gulped down some water. If she felt guilty of anything, she tried not to show it. Out of the corner of her eye, she kept a sharp lookout for her daughter, worried she might be too quick in letting something slip.

But Daughter sat there quietly, hardly stirring, obviously trying to work up the courage to start in on the little plan they had concocted. Daughter was the spitting image of her mother, though taller and prettier than she had been in her youth. Her hair, like her mother's, was pitch-black with a brilliant shine to it and her eyes were the same black coal. She looked nothing like her father, who was fair-skinned and blue-eyed; as a matter of fact, she didn't even look related to him. And where on earth did she get those high cheekbones, that cleft chin, and not to mention those long lashes?

Getting up, rubbing her hands, Daughter was ready to come out with it. Opening her mouth before anything came out, she chose her words carefully.

"Father, um, there's something I have to tell you. It's really hard, especially since you've been away so long, but please don't get angry with me, and please, don't lose your cool. It's best for me to just come out with it. Okay, here it goes ..." She took a breath and closed her eyes, "What I'm trying to tell you is that I'm, I'm... I'm ..."

Father's set and earnest face suddenly changed and he seized on the spot. There was something bad coming his way, he knew it. He waited for the dreaded words to come at him, and sure enough out they came.

"Father, I'm pregnant."

Even though he half-expected to hear what he'd just heard, the look of shock became etched on his face.

Daughter then let her voice crack and quaver for effect and she bit her lower lip. Before long, she started in on her story.

"Father, I know it's a lot for you to take in. I'm sorry to spring it on you like this; you just barely came home. Mother and I have given this a lot of thought. I'm three months along now and will be showing soon. It's not long before the neighbors will start talking and then the rest of the family will get involved, and you know how Aunt Lorraine can be. Mother and I have decided it would be best for the two of us to go away somewhere till the baby's born. She has some money saved up. We could go to Europe, maybe Spain. I have only one semester left of school and Mother could home-school me, so I wouldn't lose my year. The curriculum's online anyway."

Father for the longest while didn't know what to say or do; he was still letting it all sink in. His daughter, pregnant at sixteen. It certainly wasn't something he ever would have expected of her. A great misfortune had befallen his family and he wasn't quite sure how to deal with it. He glanced at his wife for support, but she was of no help, looking so feeble and frightened as if it were all too much for her. But how could this have happened? His precious little girl, pregnant! He started blaming himself for having been an inadequate father, for having been away so much, but soon all feelings of blame turned to anger. His face swelled.

"Who's the father? Is it Leo? It is, I know it is. I never trusted that kid from the minute I saw him. I'm going over to his place right now and have a word with him, and with his parents too while I'm at it."

Daughter gave a start and began to show signs of panic. She had to find a way to prevent her father from going anywhere, and especially to Leo's. "Think, think, think," she said to herself. She decided she had no choice but to be harsh, "No, Father, don't go to Leo's, you can't! The fact is, about the father, well, I'm not sure. It could be Leo's but there were, um, gulp, others around that same time. Three or four, as a matter of fact."

Father opened his eyes wide and his heart seemed to stop; he could hardly move the emotional impact was too much for him. Three or four others? Is that what she just said? He couldn't believe his ears. His daughter who had always been an A student, who had been in the school chess club, and who had been captain of the debate team was now not only pregnant but had just admitted to sleeping around. He did his best to process it all and remain calm, though he was choked up completely. But the last thing he wanted was to start quarreling with her, especially in her delicate condition. He noticed his wife was upset too and that she was sobbing and her hands were trembling.

He pulled himself together at once. Straightening his back, he took a breath. Good thing he was the sensible one in the family and lucky for them he came home when he did to help deal with this big mess. He totally agreed going to Spain was a good idea but he took it one step further.

"I have it all figured out. This is what we'll do: the two of you will go to Spain and make it look like for a holiday, and you, Cindy, will have your baby there. When you get back, we'll say the baby is ours, mine and Mother's, that is. We can even say the baby was premature. No one will be the wiser for it."

The daughter clasped her hands and then gave Mother a quick glance. She couldn't believe how easy Father was making it for them.

"Brilliant, Father! Absolutely brilliant!"

Father then turned to Mother who was sitting there earnest and distressed. He said to her concernedly, "But Angie, why are you still sobbing and why are you so pale? It'll all work out somehow, I promise. Is there maybe something else on your mind?"

At once, the room became quiet. All conversation ceased and the three sat looking at one another hardly moving. The situation was a sensitive one but they would work it out because they were a family and that's what families did. Then mother offered to make a pot of tea and prepare some sandwiches. Father and Daughter ate with great appetite, Mother, however, only drank tea because she was feeling nauseous.

A few days passed. On the fourth day, Mother and Daughter packed their bags and Father, still oblivious to all that was going on, loaded up the car for the airport. As they pulled out onto the street Reginald happened to be watering his lawn. He waved to the family as they drove by and they waved back. He couldn't have been more thrilled to be in on Mother and Daughter's plan. He wanted to call out to them but in such a way Father couldn't hear:

"Not to worry, ladies, your secret is safe with me!"

So, there they were, the two of them, Mother and Daughter, in the beautiful town of Comillas in the north of Spain, where they rented a small house with a view of the sea. They spent their days ambling along the ancient cobbled streets, looking in on ancestral homes, and strolling along the fine sandy beaches.

The air in Comillas was salty and warm. When January came around, pausing one day to rest on a bench in the Plaza de Corro, Mother suddenly went into labor. Rushed to the hospital, on that very same day she gave birth to an eight-pound baby boy. He had long arms and plump legs, and Mother noticed at once he was the spitting image of Pepe. She let out a cry, "Oh dear, what now?"

Mother called Father on the phone to tell him the wonderful news. Though she felt bad about being unfaithful, there was no other way around it. And it's not like she had an affair on purpose. Like all women, she had her moments of weakness. And in Pepe's case the two had fallen into each other's arms so suddenly and unexpectedly there virtually was no time for protest. With no protection at hand, they simply threw caution to the wind. But that didn't mean she loved her husband any less or never felt drawn to him when he was around.

Mother said to Father, "Cindy has decided to name the baby Oliver, after my father's father."

"A fine solid name," Father agreed.

Mother took some quick photos of Oliver on her cell phone and sent them to Father.

Father could hardly wait to welcome the new baby home. And he took things a step further. Being a man of considerable conviction and integrity, he vowed when Oliver was old enough, he would tell him everything – he would tell him about his birth in Spain, about his very young teenage mother, his very young teenage father, and he wouldn't miss out on a thing.

Mother and Daughter stayed on in Spain another month or so to allow Mother to get her body back into shape – she jogged, exercised, and took salt and mineral baths at the local spa. At the end of March, they were ready to go back home. Dressing little Oliver up in a cute blue jumpsuit and placing him into his carrier, they took a cab to the airport. They got on a plane and off they flew.

High in the sky, Mother rocked Oliver to sleep. She sang him a lullaby, "Hush little baby, don't say a word ..." Then she whispered in his ear, "Of course, Oliver, when you're old enough I'll tell you everything – I'll tell you all about your birth in Spain, about your mother, your biological father, and I won't miss out on a thing."

When spring came round Jimmy happened to be pushing little Oliver along the street in his checkered baby carriage. Birds were chirping all around, lilacs were in full bloom, and it couldn't have been a finer day. Jimmy was a proud father indeed and he kept his head high. Coming upon Reginald on his veranda, he called out to him.

"Hello there, Reginald! How goes it? What a beautiful day it is today. Did you know I have a new son? His name's Oliver. The wife gave birth in Spain. Come and have a look."

Reginald couldn't wait to see the baby. Hurrying onto the sidewalk, he stuck his head inside the carriage. The baby's eyes were wide open and he was making little cooing sounds.

"Oh, how adorable!"

Reginald was truly impressed by the fine-looking baby. But he knew too much. He was itching to look Jimmy in the eye and to tell him everything from beginning to end. This is what he wanted to say to him, "Hah, old boy, if only you knew what I knew!" But he didn't want to make waves, he was too much of a decent person for that.

Yet, at the same time, he couldn't help himself, he just couldn't. Smiling, he said instead and there came a devilish look to his eye.

"Yes, your baby is cute, cute as a button, and if I may say so myself, he does have your nose."

Chapter 3

Noble Knives

It was a dull overcast morning with not much to do. Reginald was sitting on his veranda reading a book. Upon hearing footsteps, looking up, it was then that he caught sight of a tallish man in a gray pin-stripe suit going up the walkway of his next-door neighbors' house. With his hair cropped short, sporting a pencil-thin mustache, in his left hand he carried a black leather case the size of a small suitcase. It looked of some importance. Climbing the porch stairs, pausing briefly to catch his breath, the man rang the bell. This is what happened.

 Two men answered the door, one taller than the other, one blond, the other dark-haired. They were both good-looking, one more good-looking than the other, one black, one white. John and John (they both happened to have the same names, and, incredibly, their last names were the same too). John Jones and John Jones. So, when they got married one bright summer afternoon at city hall it was John Jones marrying John Jones. The ceremony was a tearful, joyful occasion and no one cried more than the parents of both. Though the two were as different as night and day, no one could ever figure out which one was which, but that was mostly because of their names. Eventually, to make things easier for everyone, they came to be called Big John and Little John because one was tall, the other short.

Big John and Little John at once saw the man on their porch. He was funny-looking with thin lips, a hawk-like nose, and thick black brows as if painted on. On his left wrist he wore a big stainless-steel watch with fake diamonds and there was a gold chain around his neck. The leather case was now tucked under his arm and he held it there as if afraid of dropping it. There was a big warm smile upon his face, and if one didn't know any better, one would think he was a long-lost friend. But his voice was phony.

"Hello there, gentlemen. What a beautiful morning it is. What a lovely garden you have, and such an amazing house. A mid-Victorian, I would say?"

Little John was quick to respond, "Yes, you're quite right, a mid-Victorian."

The man continued but now in a very exaggerated way, "And such beautiful geraniums, so many pansies too, and your perennials are so lush. The scent is exquisite if I may say so."

Big John became suspicious immediately, he looked the man over. Narrowing his eyes, he started wondering to himself, "Hmm… What perfect stranger comes around talking like that, and why is he being so overly friendly?" Then it struck him. In an agitated voice he said to Little John but in such a way the man couldn't hear.

"Dammit, he's a salesman!"

But to Little John it didn't matter; rather, he was intrigued, even excited at the prospect. He whispered back, "A door-to-door salesman! Why it's been years since we've had one of those come round! How amusing! What a relic!"

The salesman advanced slightly. Placing one foot forward and his free hand on the brick wall by the door, it was clearly a calculated stance. He was indeed selling something and whatever it was, it was in his leather case. It was obvious he was working himself up for the pitch.

Big John couldn't help show disapproval. He wanted to close the door on the man and have him be gone, but Little John was feeling generous. Truth be told, Little John felt sorry for him; after all, not only did the man have one of the shittiest jobs around, but then there were his sartorial choices – a cheap-looking much too small suit, patent leather shoes, and that oh so tacky tie!

Nudging Big John slightly in the arm and signaling with his head, Little John made it clear to him he had every intention of allowing the salesman to stay.

The salesman, picking up on his good fortune, had not a minute to lose. Extending his hand, he introduced himself in a most pleasant manner, "Clyde O'Malley is my name, nice to meet you, gentlemen."

He got right down to business and he couldn't have been smoother about it, "Today, gentlemen, is your lucky day. Do I have a deal for you; yes, look no further because it's right here in my case. But the offer ends today, so don't even think of putting it off. What's in my case, you ask? It's a beautiful three-piece set of kitchen knives, American made, of course, the best there is. Noble Knives is the brand."

Then with his attention fully on Little John, taking note of his hands, he knew exactly what to say next, "I can tell by your long, lean fingers that you are the chef of the family. Yes? Well, then, you absolutely must try out these Noble Knives because when you do you will never go back to anything else again."

Big John could only but shake his head and roll his eyes. He knew exactly what Clyde was up to and he could almost predict his next move.

And sure enough, Clyde was aiming to somehow get himself into the house. Craning his neck, on his tiptoes, he was already peering over the shoulders of Big John and Little John. Getting into the house would improve his chances of making a sale. He said artfully:

"Please, allow me to display the knives for you and give you a demonstration. On your kitchen table perhaps, if it's not too much of a bother?"

And so, he was invited in, but only by Little John. Big John, trying not to be rude, had absolutely no interest in further hearing Clyde out. He decided instead to leash up their little pug-dog Maxi and go for a walk in the park. On his way out, pulling him aside, he cautioned Little John.

"These salesmen are a sneaky bunch. Just don't let him take you for a ride."

Maxi barked and growled as if in agreement and wagged his tail.

But where Clyde was concerned, he couldn't have felt luckier. With Big John out of the picture, he had Little John all to himself. It would be a piece of cake.

Looking round, he saw the house was immaculate and had been renovated from top to bottom, but in keeping with the Victorian style, of which he knew a bit about. He noticed there were refurbished baseboards, meticulously restored crown moldings, and refinished oak paneling. With his eyes on the doors, he knew exactly what to say.

"Oh my, I see you've even brought the brass keyhole covers back to their natural beauty. I know for a fact you can't get those anywhere anymore. And they've got such a brilliant shine to them!"

When he looked down at the floor, he continued with his flattery, "And your floors have been sanded and polished to perfection! The rich dark oak certainly gives them that original Victorian feel, and not only that but it helps them keep their captivating earthy look."

Little John couldn't help but beam, as it was the floors he was proudest of. He said at length, "I have to admit, it was quite the job getting all the original stain off and replacing some of the damaged boards. I took on the floors as a labor of love. I wanted to bring out the beautiful knots and marks, not to mention the fabulous grain. And just in time for a little event John and I are planning for tomorrow night. It's our second wedding anniversary."

Careful so as not to mark or scratch the floor, Clyde slipped off his shoes, and in his stockinged feet, followed Little John into the kitchen. Along the way he refrained from touching anything as he was afraid of breaking something accidentally.

★

Reginald, still on the veranda and watching with keen interest, got up and hurriedly ran into his kitchen as it was through his kitchen window he could see directly into Big John's and Little John's. And he could hear everything clearly, too.

Clyde was already standing over the kitchen table laying out the knives: one eight-inch chef's knife; a six-inch utility knife; and a three and a half-inch paring knife. Like an actor about to give a performance, he started in on his presentation. He was very good at it and had his lines memorized to perfection.

"These are the three most used knives in the kitchen, and if you consider yourself even half a cook, then you absolutely cannot be caught without them. Noble Knives is a premium brand of authentic American knives, all handcrafted from the finest quality carbon steel alloy. The handles are made of olive wood and are of industrial strength. Allow me to demonstrate by slicing into this orange. Ah, you see! Clean, effortless, pure heaven! The value of these knives far outweighs their cost."

Seeing he had Little John's undivided attention, about to disclose the price, he decided to wait a minute, maybe two. He remained cool and collected. Then he came out with it, "These Noble Knives can be yours for only three hundred and fifty dollars!"

A kind of strained silence followed and it lasted a few seconds.

"Three hundred and fifty dollars!" Little John couldn't believe the price. There was no way he would pay that much, absolutely not!

The problem was, however, no sooner had he thought this thought when he found himself faced with a dilemma. Truth be told, he was taking a liking to the knives, and they certainly were handsome-looking, definitely not your run-of-the-mill hardware store variety. Suddenly he was eager to try them out for himself. Taking hold of the smallest one, he cut into a dinner roll, then a cucumber. The knife couldn't have handled better. He then picked up the largest one. It worked just as impressively. He became conflicted. More than anything he wanted those knives, but three hundred and fifty dollars!

Clyde knew he had to step things up and fast. Just a little more and he would have Little John right where he wanted him. What should he do? He thought a moment. But of course, he would use the oldest trick in the book! He would create a need of urgency, and make him see that buying the knives was the most sensible thing in the world. Careful not to push too hard, he went about it in a roundabout way.

"Um ... I hope I'm not being too personal but you mentioned earlier you were hosting a dinner party tomorrow night, a celebration of your second wedding anniversary, I believe?

And I imagine you'll be doing all the cooking? Yes? Well, then it's a good thing I landed on your doorstep when I did. These knives will do a knock-out job slicing all your fruits and vegetables, not to mention carving up your roasts. At the dinner table, absolutely everybody will be talking about your Noble Knives, that's the kind of effect these knives have on people."

Watching Little John from the corner of his eye, seeing he was still hesitating, Clyde determined now was the right time to hit him up with some kind of deal. He said, trying to sound sincere:

"I'll tell you what, I can see you've taken a fancy to these knives. I'll do something for you I've never done for anyone – I'll sell the knives to you at a reduced price and cut into my commission: for you, the whole set for only three hundred dollars."

Little John raised his brows. He liked the sound of that. Fifty dollars off was considerable. But still the price seemed high and there were the taxes to consider.

It was as if Clyde could see inside Little John's mind. He was quick to further sweeten the deal, "All right then, for you, I'll make it even more attractive – if you give me cash, I'll knock off the taxes."

Little John did some mental math. "No taxes?" he thought, scratching the back of his head. "That's not a bad proposition, not a bad proposition at all, especially with the already fifty dollars off. Hmm, what should I do? I'd be crazy to pass it up." Then seeing Clyde standing there looking so natural and friendly, suddenly he felt assured there was only but one decision for him to make and that was to buy the knives. He said decisively:

"Okay then, you've got yourself a deal! Three hundred dollars it is!"

Disappearing into another room for several minutes, Little John came back with the cash.

Counting the bills once, then twice, Clyde made sure the money was all there. A smile strayed on his face. He was more than pleased how his day was progressing, and it was still only morning. Quickly packing up and hurrying his departure before there could be a change of mind, he called out to Little John from the hallway, "Enjoy your Noble Knives and have fun with them tomorrow night. You just got yourself a deal of a lifetime; yes, a deal of a lifetime. Have a good day!"

Within seconds he was out the door. Already on the street, reaching his car, which happened to be an older model blue sedan, he jumped in and drove off.

When Big John returned from the park with Maxi, the first thing he saw were the knives on the table. He laughed ironically, "Oh, no! Don't tell me you bought the knives. How much?"

Little John was only too ready to boast, "I got an amazing deal, you wouldn't believe. Three hundred dollars, and no tax!"

Big John raised his brows. His suspicions were only redoubled. Making for his laptop which was in the den, he started typing.

"Now let's see, Noble Knives, you say? Made from quality steel alloy? Yes? Handles made of olive wood? Yes? Oh, here it is, the exact same set, and just as I thought — one hundred and ninety-nine dollars, taxes included, *and* free shipping. How much was it you said you paid? Three hundred dollars?" He burst into a fit of laughter. "What a deal you got, what a deal! Hah, hah, hah!"

Little John's face colored. He felt greatly upset and embarrassed and he brooded several minutes. Damn Big John, he wasn't about to let him dampen his spirits. He put on a happy face as though nothing. He said to him:

"Laugh all you want, even if I overpaid by a thousand dollars, I don't care. Tomorrow's meal will be like no other. With those knives I'll chop, slice, carve everything up not like a chef but an artist, a true artist. I'll show you!"

★

Around seven that evening the guests started to arrive. Luckily for Reginald, he could see everything from the edge of his veranda: John and John's living room, their dining room, even a bit into their kitchen. The lights were on low. Reginald loved parties and he was thrilled that one was unfolding right next door. There would be music, singing, dancing, food. He couldn't wait.

The rooms were specially decorated and they gleamed and glistened – the furniture, the walls, the doors. But undeniably it was the floors that really stood out and gave the house that unique ambiance with their natural richness and extraordinary depth of color and texture: little John's labors had paid off indeed. A huge colorful banner ran from one end of the living room to the other reading, "Happy Second Wedding Anniversary, John and John!"

The house could not have been more ready for a party, and sure enough before long things started to happen.

There came full of noise and activity. Guests were already in the dining room and living room and more kept coming. It was a diverse bunch and they were all in a good mood. There was Morris, the accountant, with his hair colored and waved, and two or three business types with hair just like his. An artist in a plaid shirt and blue jeans; a corpulent man with an irritable expression; a very tall woman, slender, who obviously had great confidence in her good looks. There was a young law student; a poet; an architect. Two women were standing whispering in the doorway but did not venture to come in.

A twenty-something woman by the name of Bernadette was sitting on the sofa sipping wine, and she was laughing, gesticulating, talking to a small group about her life as a dancer. She had flaming red hair with a dress to match, and with her ample bosom and bare shoulders, she could not have looked more stunning. When she had first arrived at the party, unlike the other guests, she did not happen to notice the big sign on the front door reading, *"Please take off your shoes due to new floors."* As a result, she was the only one there with shoes on her feet – and not just any shoes but bright red four-inch stilettoes. With the lights turned down low, no one, including Little John or Big John, noticed.

The guests, lingering in all the rooms, sipped wine and made boozy conversation; they went on about politics, work, their likes and dislikes. Bernadette continued about her life as a dancer to her small group.

The food came out and soon the dining room table filled. There were trays of small juicy oysters with caviar, roasts with the scent of rosemary, baked cauliflower with pesto sauce, toasty brown potatoes, foie gras, Norwegian salmon and more. The exquisite aroma spread throughout the house. Then the guests saw something absolutely remarkable. Intermixed with all the food was an amazing display of Thai fruit carvings – cut apples looking like leaves, watermelon like lotus flowers, birds and swans out of cantaloupe, cherry blossoms out of kumquats. Everyone agreed, the entire presentation was of high sophistication, a culinary triumph. Little John was not only a genius but an expert Thai fruit carver, a connoisseur of connoisseurs.

The thin woman with good looks got up and made a toast, "Here, here, to Big John and Little John on their second wedding anniversary!"

Everyone clapped and cheered, a few whistled.

Morris said, "I'm starving. But how can I possibly dig into such a lavish display, especially those Thai carvings? They're veritable masterpieces, works of art, each and every one of them. How extraordinary!"

The poet chimed in, "Yes, I agree, poetry, pure poetry."

Someone else called out, "And those perfect chunks of cheese, oh, my, it's as if they were cut by a Frenchman!"

The corpulent man with the irritable expression wanted to know, "But Little John, back to the carvings. Tell us, how did you do it? You must have spent hours on those tomatoes to make them look like roses."

Little John's chest inflated with pomposity. He listened to what the guests were saying and it made him positively joyful. Giving Big John a sneering look, he began:

"I've been practicing Thai fruit carving for quite some time now. As most of you know, it's a respected art form that's been around for centuries. It requires neatness, precision, and meditation. But now I've got the precision part down pat, thanks to a set of knives I bought just yesterday, and quite by chance, actually – Noble Knives is the brand. It's because of the Noble Knives I was able to accomplish all of this. Why, those Noble Knives are so amazing, they practically cut by themselves!"

The corpulent man dared to take a bite into a peach carving. Detecting a faint creamy spearmint, light and fluffy to the center, he marveled at the flavor, "Oh, how utterly divine! How decadent! And the carving gives it that special punch. You say the knife brand you used is Noble Knives? I definitely must look it up."

The poet sank his teeth into a chunk of pineapple cut to look like a toad. He closed his eyes to relish the taste, "Yum. The cut on this pineapple is the perfect thickness – it makes it even more delicious – it literally lingers on the tongue. Noble Knives, you say? Hmm…"

The guests ate heartily. Everything was so appetizing, so tender. Then Little John, with the help of Big John, brought out the desserts – white chocolate raspberry cheesecake, baklava, French meringues, cappuccino mousse cake, pecan tarts, a big bowl of whipped cream – there was no end to the extravaganza.

The law student patted Big John on the shoulder, "You're one lucky fellow to have a chef for a husband, and those knives of his, what were they called again? Oh, yes, Noble Knives. There's no telling how far they will take him, maybe even to Paris!"

Meanwhile, Bernadette, who had a sweet tooth and a predilection for cheesecake, had not one, not two, but three pieces of the white chocolate raspberry cheesecake. Overhearing the law student, she called out with her mouth full.

"Yes, yes, with those Noble Knives Little John's possibilities are limitless! This cake is so finely cut it's truly astonishing, and there's even no crumbling! I've never seen anything like it!"

It was not long before again she started up on her life as a dancer, but this time she held the attention of the entire company. She went on about her warm-up exercises which she did religiously, about some dance troupe she was with, about her red stilettos that were in reality very expensive dance shoes. By the bored looks on everyone's faces, it was clear they were having trouble taking it all in; and then things went from bad to worse when she started repeating herself.

The artist, in an attempt to shut her up, tried to change the subject.

The poet poured her some wine and started reciting poetry, as if that would be enough to distract her.

The man with the irritable expression kept clearing his throat and emitting small coughs.

Big John, fully aware of what was going on, not wanting to see his guests further taken hostage, in an act of desperation, grabbed a CD from his CD pile and put it on. He cranked up the volume, hoping it would drown out her voice. It happened to be 'The Girl from Ipanema'.

Luckily, it worked like a charm. Bernadette jumped up, "Oh, I love bossa nova!"

She started to snap her fingers and swing her hips, even sing along. She became so completely overwhelmed with the urge to dance, she forgot what she had been talking about. She started sashaying around the room. Her eyes shone and a look of joy passed over her face.

The very much relieved guests all turned to Big John as if to give thanks, and then their eyes fell back on Bernadette, who was now in full dance-mode.

She had made her way into the living room, clapping, making time with her heels. She invested such intensity and brilliance into her every move, each step she took, she took with power and understanding. There were spins, sharp movements, crisp turns, along with some very sultry samba maneuvers. So energized was she there was no stopping her. It was obvious she was indeed a professional dancer and the guests were quite captivated by her every stride.

Little John and Big John had long since disappeared into the kitchen to prepare midnight snacks.

With the music blaring, Bernadette's feet now struck the floor with even greater power, her heels as if hammers pounding the ground beneath her. She moved from the dining room to the living room, and then back again, clapping and laughing – one, two, three, step; one, two, three, step. It was like she was putting on a performance in some dance theater with all eyes on her. It was as if Little John's floors were made for dancing and the floors were taking dancing to new heights.

She called out to everyone, "What better way to burn all those nasty cheesecake calories! Come on everyone, join in!"

A man by the name of Cooper, a dancer himself, got up. Taking her by the hand, they started to swing. Cooper in his bare feet and Bernadette still in her four-inch stilettos, they moved from room to room doing the cha-cha.

Half an hour had passed since Bernadette had taken to the floor, and now she seemed to be slowing down, and Cooper too. The two paused to quench their thirst.

"Ah," Bernadette declared finally, "I'm pooped!"

Plopping herself down on the sofa she fanned her face. Loosening up her shoes, she kicked one then the other off her feet and sent them flying across the room. And who should they fly by but Little John, who at that very moment happened to be coming out of the kitchen with a tray of small sandwiches. One of them practically hit him in the head.

"What the hell!" he proclaimed when he saw the shoes. He turned a lobster red. "Shoes! In my house? I specifically left a sign on the front door saying, NO SHOES ALLOWED!"

And when he saw they were not just any shoes but four-inch stilettos sharp as knives, he started to breathe very heavily. Bernadette had just been dancing and in those very shoes! Immediately he thought of his floors. He was afraid to look down and he couldn't look down. When he finally dared a peek, he went as if into an anaphylactic shock. His beautiful restored hardwood floors were now punctured everywhere as if with a million bullet holes – in the living room, in the dining room, the hall, everywhere. What a shock! What a horror! Sweat built on his brow. Looking round with flashing eyes and a fierce expression, he was searching for the guilty party. And there she was sprawled out on the sofa, laughing, chatting away with the poet as if nothing. With an impulse to pounce on her right then and there, to choke her, even kill her, any consequences were the furthest from his mind. But instead of going at her for some reason he swung around and started for the kitchen. He could only think of his Noble Knives. Barely a minute passed when he returned with the biggest one, brandishing it in the air. He looked completely unhinged.

The guests jumped back in fear. The knife looked dangerous. Never before had Little John assumed such a violent form. The unfortunate situation at hand completely changed his character and he was no longer the self-composed, mild-mannered individual they had all known him to be. Rather, he was now a raving lunatic, waving that Noble Knife around as if a Samurai sword swinger.

Everyone sat unmoving.

Little John drilled his eyes into Bernadette with a frenzied malice. He couldn't stop growling and cursing through his teeth, "You bitch! You bitch! My floors! Look what you did to my floors!"

Bernadette became pale and there came an expression of such dread on her distorted face, she couldn't help but scream. She started to shake. At once, she became fully aware of the great damage she had done.

"Shit," she exclaimed, looking down, "did I really do that? I'm sorry."

Little John started toward her in full force, he was in such a state of excitement he could hardly breathe. With his Noble Knife still in hand, half way across the floor suddenly he tripped over something and fell. It was her stilettos. Down on his knees, like a maniac, he began to laugh and he laughed so hard he cried. Taking hold of one of her shoes then the other, with his Noble Knife he started hacking away at them, gashing them, slicing them, chopping off the heels.

The guests watched pinned to their seats; it was impossible for them to guess to what point the hacking would go on. Little John kept at it until both shoes were destroyed, and then with what was left of them, he hurled them straight at Bernadette.

"Take that and that, you bitch!" he shouted.

Bernadette gasped and choked, "My dance shoes! You didn't have to go and ruin my expensive dance shoes! I said I was sorry. Oh, my poor dance shoes!"

When it looked as if Little John was about to lunge at her together with his Noble Knife, not taking any chances, Bernadette picked up as fast as she could and ran out the front door. The poet, the corpulent man, and several others, fearing for their safety, followed close behind.

Soon Little John calmed down, or so it seemed. He stood there crying, rocking back and forth, clutching at his head, "My floors. My poor floors."

Big John moved toward him; he couldn't have been more sympathetic. Rubbing his partner's back, he said quietly, trying to calm him down.

"Hey, Little John, how about an espresso? Looks like you can use one about now."

Carefully taking the Noble Knife out of Little John's hand, pulling him over to the sofa, Big John laid him down and covered him up with a blanket. He tried to get him to eat a biscotti.

A few minutes passed.

Big John, being the attentive host that he was, then turned to the few remaining guests and said, "Snacks, anyone?"

Reginald, still on the veranda, himself getting a bit peckish, decided to call it a night.

Chapter 4

Carlito and His Three Sisters

When Reginald was about fourteen years old a Portuguese family, the Ribeiros, moved into Number 49 Bank Street. He remembered specifically because it was pouring rain that day and a big moving truck rolled in the size of a house. It was a family with three girls Maria, Nella and Lurdes, all roughly a year apart, and there was a young boy also of about eight or nine by the name of Carlito. There had never been a Portuguese family on the street before and they were from the Azores that small group of volcanic islands right in the middle of the Atlantic Ocean. Reginald found it fascinating they had come from an archipelago and he even went so far as to look it up on the map – there were two, three … nine islands in total and the terrain was steep and rugged. Almost at once Reginald formed a big crush on Lurdes, who seemed about his age and he wondered if she spoke English. Her eyes were big and round like saucers and her dark straight hair was well-brushed and parted down the middle. She was soft and gentle and she had the sweetest smile. So attracted was he to her he was hoping in school they might be in the same class, if they both ended up going to the same school that is, as there were several in the neighborhood.

The father's name was Miguel and in the Azores he had been a deep sea fisherman, having fished for cod in the Grand Banks off Newfoundland or Terra Nova as he liked to call it. Fishing was in his blood, even though he now worked in construction and hadn't been out to sea in five years. But he could still hear the sound of the ocean, the waves beating and foaming against the sides of the boat, and the voices of the fishermen blending into a single tone. His trawler was the Santa Herondina and he had labored round the clock six to eight months of the year. The heat burnt his body by day and when night came around, he spent hours slitting, gutting, and salting the day's catch. His people, the Portuguese, had fished the Grand Banks for four hundred years and it had driven their economy. Though Miguel only had a grade four education it was more than enough to be a fisherman. Terra Nova brought steady work and kept food on the table for his growing family. He was a proud man.

Theresa, Miguel's wife, was a good woman and they had been married at the age of eighteen. She was strong physically and mentally and though petite she had broad shoulders and hands in the shape of shovels. She had worked on the beach, unloading the boats, sorting out the various fish, and later selling them to the vendors in the marketplace. In the black sand, along with other women from the village, she also made and mended the trawling nets. She was a hard worker and never not even once stopped to complain.

The three daughters like their mother were fine-looking and energetic and they all had her pure, noble face, though it was Lurdes who resembled her most. Back in their village, before and after school, the girls worked around the house washing and cleaning, and the oldest, Nella, twice a week was sent out to Señiora Olivieri's, wife of the local magistrate up on the hill, to dust, scrub floors, and polish furniture. Señiora Olivieri for the most part was pleased with Nella's work and paid her a fair rate, which Nella, in turn, gave to her father to help run the family household. Now that Nella was almost thirteen, she would soon be finished school and would undertake other such jobs and be frequently employed. The Ribeiros had a strong work ethic because work brought in money and hence stability. Nella, being the sweet and gentle creature she was, wanted only to please her parents, especially her father.

But her father was a stoic and aloof man and paid little attention to her; in fact, he not only paid little attention to her but to her sisters as well. The three girls rarely got comfort from him when they needed it and he remained emotionally absent. There was something authoritative in his bearing and they were never able to form a close, loving relationship with him. But the girls needed so much: they needed for him to tell them that they were funny and beautiful and talented and that he loved them. They needed more than just shelter and food on the table.

But the problem was, Miguel didn't care for girls; all he cared about was having a boy, and unfortunately for him, he didn't have one. The girls could only feel the pain. The mother, too busy with work and with demands of family life was unable to adequately fill in the void.

Miguel could not help but feel hard-done-by not having a son. It was not untypical for him to brood over it for days on end. Not only did he feel distressed but it made him resentful of his own flesh and blood. Though in his way he did love his daughters, at the same time he felt himself a failure. With a man's primal desire for a boy dating back thousands of years, deep down in his heart of hearts, that's all he wanted. But here he was stuck with not one, not two, but three girls. Sometimes it awakened within him brutal instincts and all he wanted was to take it out on them, to grab them and hit them, but he never did. Sometimes he blamed his wife, that it was her fault, that she was incapable of giving him a son.

Often he would ask himself: "What is the meaning of life if I can't have a son? A boy would take care of the family, a boy would continue the family name, a boy would fish the high seas."

Each of the three times his wife got pregnant, Miguel prayed for a son, and each time he prayed more fervently than the time before. When the day approached, for example, that Lurdes, the youngest, was to be born, out at sea, he even went up on deck, and looking to the heavens, cried out to God for his blessings:

"Please, God, give me a boy."

But God didn't listen. He gave Miguel Lurdes.

Whenever the Santa Herondina would come to dock in the port of St. John's off the coast of Newfoundland, in a tavern there, Miguel would drown in his sorrows. His fishermen buddies who were always sympathetic to him, even the ones who themselves had no sons, would pat him on the back and offer words of condolence. They were mostly encouraging.

"Cheer up, Miguel," this was Martim.

"It's not the end of the world after all," put in Francisco.

Celestino added, "You never know what the future will bring."

Then something exciting happened and, as luck would have it, it happened the day Miguel was getting a three-month break from the sea. A fellow-fisherman, Marcelo Matos, came to him with some vital information about having a boy, and the information was very specific. Miguel had never heard anything like it; he couldn't wait to tell his wife.

"Theresa, Theresa, I have great news! Do you remember Marcelo Matos? You know that young fisherman from Santo

Espirito? Well, I had a talk with him a couple of hours ago and he had something very interesting to tell me. Actually, *incredible* would be a better word for it. It turns out he knows all about boys, and not just *about* boys but about *having* boys. He said if we listened to him there was no reason why even at your age you shouldn't get pregnant and with a boy. He said there were special things we could do and these 'special things' were as easy as one, two, three."

But Theresa was skeptical and her eyes narrowed.

Miguel became irritated, "Why are you looking at me like that? What, you don't believe me? Well, let me tell you, this Marcelo Matos is one smart guy because he even went to high school, and if anyone knows anything about anything, it's Marcelo Matos. And he especially knows about having boys because guess how many he has. Four! Yes, he has four sons – Angelo, Diogo, Gaspar, and Nicolau! And his wife is pregnant again!"

As per Marcelo Matos' instructions, this is what Miguel and his wife were to do: they were both to drink special Chinese teas; Theresa would eat foods high in potassium and sodium; Miguel would wear loose underwear (tightness was known to damage male sperm more than female); Theresa would avoid dairy products, shellfish, and spicy food; and they would use special love-making positions that enabled deeper penetration, allowing for male sperm to be placed nearer to the ovaries.

The pair wasted no time in getting down to business. The whole village knew about it. When Theresa became pregnant no one questioned what she might be having. When she finally went into labor, no surprise to anyone, lo and behold, she gave birth to a boy!

Miguel was in seventh heaven; he felt king of the world. His fishing buddies at the tavern congratulated him and brought out the *aguardente*. Hooting, cheering and banging the table with their fists, they then started in on some Portuguese ballads. Miguel stood up and made a toast. It so happened, he had just come to a major decision and he wanted all to hear. He shouted boastfully, "I've chosen a name for my son. Carlito! Carlito means strong and masculine and that's what he will be."

The buddies clapped and cheered and stomped their feet, "To Carlito! What a name! May he live to be a hundred!"

For the next couple of years Miguel continued to go out to sea, and each time upon his return he was pleased to see Carlito growing into the man he would become. Miguel doted over him and consistently put him first. He indulged him with *pudim* and chocolates and was blind to any faults he might have. He now had a son, a son that would follow in his footsteps. So excessively fond was he of the boy, he neglected his daughters even more. If Nella, Maria or Lurdes would try to get his attention, he was always busy with Carlito. As a result, he did not notice the girls were flowering into lovely young women, that Maria loved the sciences, that Nella had dreams of moving to Lisbon and going to beauty school, that Lurdes drew beautiful pictures of horses.

Then one day the unimaginable happened. Life for the Ribeiro family came crashing down on them, and not only on them but on their entire village. It all happened when the Canadian government, becoming more conscious of protecting its waters, reduced foreign fishing in the Grand Banks. As if overnight Miguel, along with the other fishermen, lost his livelihood, and as for Theresa it meant no more work on the beach.

With no means of making a living, Miguel packed up his family and went in search of a new and better life. So, they traveled across the Atlantic leaving the Azores behind them forever. And that's how they came to live in one of the largest cities in North America. Miguel was lucky enough to secure a job almost immediately in road construction as there was a boom in the city, and Theresa found work by night cleaning office units in a high-rise building downtown. The family took readily to their new way of life, miles away from the sea, and prospects for the future looked good.

Scraping together a small down payment, they managed to buy a two-story brick house on Bank Street, and they were pleased to find many of their soon-to-be neighbors would also be new arrivals from the Azores. The first thing the Ribeiros did was paint their house a lime green, and then in the front yard put up a little statue of the Virgin Mary. Later they renovated the basement and rented it to help pay the mortgage.

Now that Carlito was nine, Miguel was happy to see that not only was his son healthier and more robust-looking than other boys his age but taller and with already developing muscles, especially on his forearms. Miguel poured all his time into him, taking him to soccer games, boxing matches, and signing him up for judo and karate lessons. He even took him out on the job site to teach him about road construction. Miguel was proud of Carlito and he was even more proud that he was much like himself at that age.

Meanwhile, the girls, as they had done in the Azores, continued to do everything around the house, the cooking, the cleaning, and on alternate days one of them went with their mother to clean offices downtown, always the midnight shift. Often the girls skipped school the next day because they were too tired from staying up all night working. As far as Nella was concerned, according to her parents, she would soon come to clean offices full-time; she was in her last year of high school and that was already more than enough for a girl. She would eventually marry anyway.

But the girls had dreams, big dreams and they would share these dreams with each other in private. They all three of them had ardent natures and cleaning offices was not for them – it was boring work and offered no fulfillment. They wanted freedom but felt caged. Nella hadn't told her parents yet but she had already enrolled into a beauty program at a local school and classes were to start in a few days. Maria and Lurdes had plans to attend university and art college respectively. The girls felt their parents were too old-fashioned, too caught up in old-world ways.

Another responsibility given the three sisters was taking care of Carlito. They fed him, clothed him, took him to school, and put him to bed. Carlito loved his sisters very much and was happy to have them around; they were fun and gave him lots of attention.

Then one day something completely unexpected happened and it was cause for alarm. Carlito came home from school and he bore traces of a recent fight: his face was red and swollen, his neck all scratched up, and his eyes were full of tears. It was Theresa who heard everything and came rushing from the kitchen.

"Dear God, what on earth happened to you? Why your shirt is all ripped!"

Taking him by the hand, she pulled him into the bathroom and with a damp cloth proceeded to wipe the blood off his face. "I don't know what kind of trouble you got yourself into, young man, but we'll talk about that later. First, we have to clean you up."

Miguel who was in an adjoining room couldn't help but hear the noise. As he did every evening, he was sitting in his easy chair, and like a true Portuguese, enjoying his *vinho verde*, drinking as many as three glasses. He didn't know what all the commotion was about out there but his wife's voice was grating his nerves, and he didn't appreciate how she was fussing over Carlito, talking to him as if he were a baby. He decided to get up and find out for himself what was going on. Opening the bathroom door, upon seeing Carlito, he was completely taken aback.

"What on earth happened to you?"

Carlito lowered his eyes, he was embarrassed and ashamed. He couldn't look at his father. He said faintly, "Manuel and his gang did it; they came after me."

"What do you mean they came after you."

"They chased me into the laneway, knocked me down, and then started to punch me."

"Did you at least fight back?" Miguel put his hands on his hips.

No answer.

"Well, did you?"

Carlito was trembling, his father now stood over him, and he was breathing heavily. Finally, he said, "No, I couldn't."

"What do you mean, you couldn't."

"They held me down, there were six of them, and then Manuel kicked me."

"But why? I don't understand … "

Carlito struggled with his words, "Well, they said that I …"

"They said that you what?"

"They said that I… They said I … That I …"

"Yes? Yes? What?"

"They said that I … looked like … a girl."

Miguel froze instantly; he couldn't believe what he had just heard.

"A girl?" he finally exclaimed. "They said you looked like a girl?"

As much as he tried, he couldn't understand his son's words; it wasn't possible. There was not a feminine thing about him with his thick brows, square shoulders, and strong build. But it didn't make sense.

Carlito wanted to say something to his father but he didn't know where to begin. It was all so confusing to him. His head went round. He wasn't even sure himself what was going on though something was, and it was all so complicated. He felt afraid.

Miguel was starting to have an uneasy feeling. He could think of nothing better than to send his son to his room as punishment.

The next day Carlito again came home crying and all beaten up. This time he had a bloody nose and a black eye.

Miguel watched him come in. There were words of scorn and outrage on the tip of his tongue, and his temperature rose.

"And what happened today, young man?"

Carlito couldn't stop the tears. "They were at it again; they said I looked like a girl. They hate me. They hate me because I'm not like them."

Miguel looked at his son askance not knowing what to say, and then there came a nervous tremor. What on earth was he talking about? It was almost as if something new was taking place within Carlito, something that was taking him away from himself, his family, his friends. Could it be maybe his son was … ? He couldn't bring himself to say the word, he couldn't even think it.

Truth be told, for a while now Carlito was starting to think Manuel and his gang might be on to something, that maybe they were right, that he was a girl, at least in his head. But he really didn't understand any of it, this girl thing, or why it was happening to him. He was not like other boys and he knew that for sure. But to get beat up for it? It's not like he ever did anything wrong.

With one day passing into the next, Carlito continued to get bullied.

Of all people it was Reginald who at last came to find out what was going on.

As Reginald was bicycling down the street one day on his way to the park, passing the Ribeiro household, he heard voices from the backyard. Was that Lurdes he had just heard? He decided to stop and see what was going on. Sneaking up the walkway, jumping behind a shrub, there she was sitting with her sisters, Nella and Maria, in the shade of a grape arbor hanging with heavy clusters of fruit. The garden was cool and dark and there were shadows falling across the ground.

The sisters were talking, giggling, and kidding each other. Lurdes looked especially pretty with her sparkling gray-green eyes and she had a healthy look about her. A smallish table stood before the girls and it was filled with all kinds of little bottles, compacts of various shapes and sizes, and tubes about as big as a finger; as it turned out, the items were beauty products such as eye shadow, lipstick, face foundation, perfumes and so on. Without her parents' knowledge, Nella was already into her third week of beauty school and for homework she had to practice applying the various makeup. Her sisters were only too happy to be her guinea pigs: Lurdes had a thick coating of mascara on her lashes and above her eyes was a blue-green eye shadow; Maria had a soft blush on her cheeks and her lips were painted a deep red. Then Nella decided to test a bright pink nail polish because she wanted to see what it looked like against the bright green of her dress. But unfortunately, her nails were already painted, so she turned to Lurdes and asked for her hand, but Lurdes' nails were also already done, and so were Maria's. Nella thought of getting nail polish remover for her nails or maybe removing Maria's but that would take too long. Then she caught Carlito sitting up against the fence playing with his toy trucks. She called out to him cheerfully.

"Oh, Carlito! I need you. Can you come here for a minute? Give me your hands; yes, like that. Try not to move."

She proceeded to paint his every nail. When done, placing his both hands against her dress, she exclaimed to her sisters, "Why, the pink is perfect! I'll definitely use this color combination in my class presentation tomorrow."

Carlito was pleased to be of help to his sister and it made him feel as if one with them.

Completely ignoring Carlito, the sisters now turned their attention to the various eyeliners piled at the end of the table. Nella applied a dusty blue kohl to her own eyes, then put a cream liner on Lurdes, and a black liquid on Maria. So busy were they with all their applications, they didn't notice Carlito had wandered to the front of the house. But Reginald behind the shrub saw everything. Carlito was going straight for his bicycle that was leaning up against the veranda. That's when Manuel happened by. Manuel was twelve going on thirteen and the biggest bully on the street. He had his gang with him too. He noticed Carlito at once.

"Nail polish today? Hey, guys, look, he's gotten even more girly!" Then he began to chant, "Carlito's a girly-girl; Carlito's a girly-girl."

The gang joined in. One of them gave Carlito a shove, Manuel kicked him in the stomach, and then another boy punched him between the eyes. Carlito was in great pain. As he was about to undergo another round, making a quick twist, somehow, he managed to get up and run away. The catcalls followed: "Carlito's a girly-girl! Carlito's a girly-girl!"

The next day the three sisters were at it again but this time they were experimenting with lipstick. Nella applied a soft pink matte on Lurdes and on Maria she put on a plum rose. On herself, she favored a long-lasting nude rouge. But she wanted to see what the glossy peach looked like. She applied some to her hand, but it really didn't give her a sense of color. Then she noticed Carlito with his Lego blocks.

"Hey, Carlito," she called, "Come here, I need you again. Yes, stand like that and don't move. Good boy."

Putting the lipstick on him, she was delighted at how it looked – it made his lips softer and more tender. Then she decided a hairdo would compliment the lipstick, so she put his hair up in braids.

"Perfect," she declared. "Couldn't be better."

Carlito looked into a small mirror and was quite impressed with what he saw. He didn't look like a boy at all. He looked just like his sisters, a girl. Then his mind started to run afield, and he imagined he had girl body parts. He didn't know quite why he was identifying with the opposite sex, but that's when he decided the only thing that would make him happy was to be like his sisters, a girl.

The sisters then turned their attention to a rather large box filled with various hair accessories. As Nella put some bows in Maria's hair and clips in Lurdes', Carlito again somehow wandered into the front yard. The same as the day before Reginald was hiding behind the shrub, watching. He saw Carlito mount the porch stairs, grab a big red ball from under one of the chairs, and proceed to kick it around on the lawn. As the ball rolled onto the street, who should come by again but Manuel and his gang. They noticed Carlito at once. They could hardly believe it – this time, he was wearing lipstick! And if that wasn't enough, he even had his hair up in braids! They began to jab and jeer at him.

"Hey guys, look what the little girly-girl's wearing today, lipstick! And look at that hair-do! Doesn't she look pretty? I do believe our Carlito is really a Carlita! Hah, hah, hah!"

"Carlita! Carlita!" they all repeated.

Grabbing Carlito by the hair, they threw him down and pinned him to the ground. Manuel then began to wipe off his lipstick with his fist and another gang member undid his braids.

"There," Manuel proclaimed, "now he's a boy again!"

Roughing him up several minutes, laughing, they took off.

Carlito was left crying and he lay there holding his belly. The beatings were getting more severe. Picking himself up, he made for his house.

His father happened to be in the living room drinking *aguardente*. When he saw Carlito pass by, he gave him a stern look. What on earth was going on with his son, and why these daily beatings? And why didn't he fight back? That's what boys do they fight back! He couldn't stop thinking about it, he just couldn't wrap his head around it. He became angry, so angry all he wanted was to cause his son further pain, to teach him a lesson. Then a strange sort of panic set in and he couldn't calm himself.

Carlito was sent to his room without supper. He was sore all over and his head ached. Everything around him seemed crowded, dull, and scary. It was still light outside so he didn't have to turn on the lights. Everywhere was quiet and he could hear nothing. After a while chairs started to be shuffled around in the kitchen and dishes clattered. Soon there came the smell of frying cod, and then the sound of voices. His mother and father were arguing about something and he wasn't sure but he thought it might be about him. He caught his name now and then.

He heard his mother say, "Miguel, don't upset yourself like that. How can you even think such a thing! He's just going through a phase, I'm sure."

Then his father's voice, "Can't you see what's going on, Theresa? Carlito's different. He likes to play with dolls. Dolls! And there's only one kind of boy who likes to play with dolls!"

Theresa began to cry.

Miguel went on, "And he's so big and strong but he doesn't fight! He never cared for soccer or judo like the other boys.

What will people say? They'll call him a misfit, a deviant. Our son the deviant they'll say."

His mother was now all choked up, "Miguel, what are you saying? Miguel, answer me! *Meu Deus!* Oh no, no, please, Miguel, no!"

Carlito heard every last word his parents were saying. He didn't know why any of this was happening to him but it was. He knew one thing for sure: from deep down there came muffled whispers and they were telling him about his gender, that he was a boy but acted the part of a girl. What he wanted was to be seen as the gender he felt he was, which was a girl. He worried his parents would try to stop him, change him, and ruin his life. He could hear them talking, and they were now talking louder than before, about looking for cures, going to the priest, getting him therapy. But he vowed never to keep his femme side hidden because there was nothing shameful about it.

Making for his closet, humming quietly, he brought out a dress he had taken from Maria when she wasn't looking. He put it on. It was bright red with frills around the neck and it had a thick yellow belt. Though it was a bit big on him, still he thought it fit quite nicely. Standing before the full-length mirror it made him feel good, confident. He would wear the dress to school tomorrow he decided and maybe even put on a pair of Lurdes' shoes, the black ones with the open toes. But then he decided against it as it would only further upset his father, and he certainly didn't want to upset his father more than he already was. Things were bad enough.

★

Twenty years passed. Nella, Lurdes, and Maria were all married with children. Nella had her own beauty salon over on Ossington Avenue, Lurdes worked as a graphic artist for a design company downtown, and Maria, though she had graduated university, was a stay-at-home mom. No one knew about Carlito, as he had left the neighborhood a few years back and had never returned. But there were rumors.

One day a youngish-looking woman walked into Reginald's hardware store. She was very tall and pretty and came in to buy some painter's tape as she had just purchased a house over on Florence Street and was painting her kitchen. There was something familiar about her but Reginald couldn't quite pin it. He noticed her body was very malleable and sturdy.

"Are you from around here?" he asked her finally. "I know I've seen you someplace but I don't know where."

The woman gave a wry smile, "Yes, you've seen me before but I can easily understand why you don't recognize me. It was quite a while ago. I'm Carlita, one of Miguel Ribiero's daughters. I've been gone for some time and now I'm back. I haven't seen my father in ages, we lost touch. I'm going home now to surprise him. He's retired from what I understand."

Reginald watched Carlita walk out the door and start along the pavement. Her hips swayed in an exaggerated way and there was a certain fluidity in her movements. He, or, rather, she, looked stunning and Reginald was curious to know how many surgeries and hormone therapies she had gone through to look like that: her nose was smaller and more delicate, her eyebrows were thinned and raised, and her chin was much rounder, softer. Her hair was done-up in a pompadour style and looked very stylish. To Reginald she seemed so fully whole.

Then he got to wondering. What will Carlita's parents say when they see her, and will Miguel especially be able to navigate through it? Somehow, he didn't think so.

Closing up shop early, starting down the street, he hurried to Miguel's house. He would find an open window and look inside. He wouldn't miss this for the world.

Chapter 5

I Killed Him!

"I killed him!" Antonia could be heard screaming from an open window. It was from Number 31. "He's dead; he's stone cold dead!"

"What are you talking about? Who's stone cold dead?" there came another voice.

"Fabio, that fellow I'd been seeing, you know, that young guy; he's in my bed and he's dead!"

"Dead in your bed? You say you killed him? But how?" Then after a moment's pause, "Antonia, what have you concocted now? What did you do?"

Silence.

"Antonia?"

More silence.

"Antonia, answer me!"

Antonia was on the phone with her sister Matilde and she was having trouble articulating. The phone was on speaker-phone.

The two sisters were very close and had worked side by side for many years on an assembly line in a chocolate factory near

Lansdowne Avenue. Having taken early retirement, they often went out to the movies together or to the Gladstone Hotel to get a little drunk and do some socializing. They were both in their fifties, Antonia the younger, a widow for just over a year, her husband, Duarte, having drowned in a freak boating accident his body never found, and Matilde, married to a furniture salesman, newly divorced with two grown children. Since the window was wide open, their conversation drifted out onto the street.

And who should come walking by at that very moment but Reginald. Stopping dead in his tracks, he pricked up his ears. The words coming out of Antonia's house were unbelievable to him, shocking. It was about a crime that had just been committed and not just any crime but a murder! He needed to hear more. Creeping onto the veranda and crouching beneath the window, he peered straight into Antonia's living room. This is what he saw going on in there:

Antonia was pacing the room, looking fatigued as if she could hardly stand. She was pale and her voice was breaking.

"All right, Matilde, I'll tell you what I did. You know that special powder I have, well, I gave Fabio a bit in his coffee this morning, but I think I gave him too much. He didn't look very well. I just wanted to scare him, really I did, I ..."

Matilde cut her sister off sharply. "Did you say powder? You mean you still have some? I thought I told you to get rid of it. It's a noxious substance, remember?"

No answer.

"Antonia, did you get rid of it?"

Nothing.

"Tell me, yes or no?"

Still nothing.

"Antonia!"

Then finally, "Well, um, it's like this. Oh, I'm such a bundle of nerves right now. I don't know where to even begin."

Matilde lost patience, "What do you mean you don't know where to begin. I should have known I couldn't trust you. Now you've gone and got yourself into another mess — just more headaches for me." After a brief pause, "Are you absolutely sure he's dead? Was he breathing? Maybe he's still alive."

"No, he's dead all right," Antonia took a tissue from her pocket and wiped her nose. "I checked for a heart beat and there wasn't one, and he wasn't breathing either. Matilde, you've got to help me get rid of the body. Think of something."

There was a prolonged pause and the pause only made Antonia more anxious. As it turned out, Matilde was mulling something over. At last, she said but in serious tone, "Antonia, listen to me, I want you to forget about Fabio for a minute. I'm more concerned about you right now and your state of mind. We have to deal with this rationally. I'm worried you'll get another one of your panic attacks. I want you to go and take that special pill of yours and right away. I'll be there in about fifteen minutes. Don't do anything till I get there."

Obeying her sister's orders, Antonia took the pill and downed it with a glass of water. Sinking into an armchair, laying back her head, she dozed off.

In the meantime, Reginald continued to look on. He had known Antonia on a casual basis for many years but only to greet her in the street or to exchange a few casual words. Secretly he had a crush on her and had had one for the longest time, though she never gave him a second look. She always seemed so soft-spoken, and he loved her well-groomed tightly-packed body and the abundance of her bosom. And now to find out of all things she was a murderer, he simply couldn't believe it. Considering what to do until Matilde arrived, Reginald thought of maybe running home and grabbing a sandwich but he quickly reconsidered as he didn't want to take a chance on missing out on anything. He settled into a clump of bushes.

Everything was quiet and when the wind picked up there came the rustling of leaves. Clouds moved slowly as ever across the sky. A dog barked in the not-so-far distance and later a car honked. Matilde was half an hour late. As it turned out, she couldn't get her car started and instead had to borrow her son's Vespa but had trouble finding the keys. When she finally came through the door of her sister's house, pulling a white shawl off her head, she called out:

"Oh, yoo-hoo, Antonia, I'm here!"

Finding her sister in the armchair, giving her a bit of a nudge as if to wake her up, she got right down to business. "Antonia, now tell me exactly what happened."

Antonia opened her eyes then closed them again, "Oh, it's all so horrible, just horrible. I didn't mean to kill him. Really, I didn't."

Matilde put her purse down and took off her gloves. Her manner was matter-of-fact. "If he's dead, then he's dead, there's not much we can do about it. Not to worry, we'll figure something out. Don't we always?"

Matilde and Antonia were good-looking women with bodies that were curved and full, and breasts that were big, high, and round. They were voluptuous as they were sexy. With their dyed blonde hair, painted lips, and rosy complexions, they could easily have been mistaken for twins. Often, they would get on each other's nerves and argue. Antonia was on the capricious side, but Matilde had a no-nonsense sensibility and she presented herself as extremely efficient and someone with extraordinary assurance.

Matilde was accustomed to helping her sister out of jams and she had done so since childhood. Though she never minded and even demonstrated a certain enthusiasm, truth be told, as of late, she was growing tired of it. Barely a year ago it was a dead husband, a dead boyfriend before that, and now a dead boyfriend again.

Matilde looked at her sister decisively, "Before we do anything, I'm going to go and look in on Fabio. I want to double-check, to make sure he's really dead. You stay here."

When Matilde entered the bedroom, she quickly scanned everything. And there on the bed under the covers lay Fabio, dead, just as her sister had said. He was a ghastly sight as dead people typically are – his face was contorted and very pale, his lips like chalk, and his neck stiff and blotchy. But for some reason, his eyes weren't bulging out of their sockets like a dead person's, and in a strange sort of way he looked more buried in a deep sleep than dead. Maybe he wasn't dead after all. When Matilde checked his pulse and couldn't find one, she came to the conclusion that, yes, indeed, he was dead.

As she was about to leave, out of the corner of her eye, she caught something else about him, something completely out of the ordinary, no, extraordinary would have been a better word for it. It was literally inspiring. Beneath that dead exterior, what a strapping, good-looking fellow he was. He had a broad forehead, a slightly narrow aquiline nose, thick black hair. Everything about that face of his was so Romanesque – powerful, majestic, noble. In fact, he couldn't have looked more magnificent under the early evening light coming in through the open window.

Then Matilde became giddy and before long there came a rush through her body. She was having trouble containing herself. She had to see what else he had going for him. Picking up the covers, she snuck a peek. When she saw his chest, she let out a gasp, when she looked further down, she said to herself "Oh my," and when at last she came to his junk-parts she couldn't help but scream – he was sensational down there, unlike anything she'd ever seen. She had to fan her face she was getting so hot.

Barely recovering herself, Matilde had trouble accepting that this gorgeous piece-of-a-manhood was no longer among the living. She said half under her breath, "What a waste, what a waste."

It was not long before her mood changed and anger took over. Storming back into the living room, she flew at her sister, "Antonia, have you lost your mind? Such a looker and so young, why did you have to go and kill him? Are you crazy?"

When Antonia gave no answer, Matilda looked hard at her, "All right, if you don't want to answer me then fine. Let's go at it from a different angle, let's start from the beginning. Where did you find him?"

Antonia sat motionless, withdrawn into herself. She stared blankly at the floor. After several minutes, she started as if awakened from some deep sleep. "Actually, it was the other way around, I didn't find him he found me. It was up at the Lula Lounge."

Matilde blinked in bewilderment, "The Lula Lounge? Whatever possessed you to go up there? I didn't know you cared for Salsa music."

"Oh, I don't know; I needed some kind of diversion, especially after Duarte. I had to get my mind off things. They give Salsa lessons and I thought it would be fun. Fabio was there also taking lessons. He asked me to have a drink. I felt flattered that a younger man was interested in an older woman."

As she went on, suddenly she drifted off with her words. She half-closed her eyes, "He was the perfect lover, funny, kind, romantic, an elegant dresser. And he had that bit of chin growth that drives women wild, and, oh, not to forget those smoldering green-gray eyes. When he moved his shoulders, I could see his muscle definition not to mention his six-pack. I loved giving him massages. There was such an enormous amount of sexual energy between us it was unbelievable."

Matilde listened attentively to her sister but at the same time she was confused. "I don't get it, if he was so irresistable and if you enjoyed him so much why did you kill him?"

"I already told you, it was an accident."

Matilde showed irritation, "This is so typical of you, Antonia. Ever since you were small, I had to clean up your messes. Remember when little Johnny's cat from next door went missing? Was that an accident too? You have all these 'accidents'. Well, I've had enough; this is the last one for me."

"Why are you being so unreasonable?"

"Unreasonable, is that what you call it? I'm finished, that's all."

"Come on, admit it, you don't mind it one bit. It gives you a kind of thrill, always did."

"Not anymore, I'm getting too old for this; after this one, I'm done."

"That's what you say but what you say and do are two different things."

"Well, this time I mean it."

"Oh, just shut up!"

"No. You shut up!"

"Shut up yourself!"

The women continued in this way for the next several minutes; Antonia raised her voice and then Matilde raised hers even more. Before long they fell into a straight-out shouting match and it became so loud, Reginald, still under the window, had to cover his ears.

Then, completely out of the blue, to add to all the cacophony, somewhere from the back of the house there came a loud, overdrawn wail, more like the roar of a lion. Reginald caught it at once, but the sisters, still going at each other, didn't hear a thing due to their own noise-making. As it happened, there was something going on in Antonia's bedroom, where the dead man was. But how could that be? It didn't make any sense.

Reginald hurried over there to see what he could see. Careful not to damage the flowerbed, reaching the window, he got up on a garbage can to get a better look. It did not take long for him to come upon the gruesome sight: there on the bed lay poor Fabio, unmoving, stiff as a board. But what about that loud wail? Where did it come from? Certainly, it didn't come from the dead man.

What happened next was shocking to Reginald, so shocking he almost lost balance and fell over. The bed covers started to move. At first, he thought he was seeing things, but, no, they really *were* moving. Suddenly he saw an arm come out, then a foot.

"Fabio? Alive?"

Reginald then saw Fabio open his mouth wide and let out a long, overdraw yawn. It sounded like the roar of a lion. It was the same sound he had heard just moments ago. Fabio got out of bed and he couldn't have looked sicklier. He was rubbing his stomach as if in great pain and his legs were wobbly. Reginald followed him with his eyes as he made across the room. He could hear him muttering something but it was barely audible. This is what was going on with Fabio.

"Ugh, I feel like shit, almost like vomiting. But I never get sick. Weird. Maybe I caught a bug or something."

Then with his voice louder, "Food poisoning! That's it! I must have got food poisoning! Come to think of it, those scrambled eggs this morning tasted kind of bitter."

Fabio looked round for Antonia, he wondered where she might be. He was used to her fussing over him, coddling him, and now she wasn't there. His mouth felt dry and what he wanted more than anything was a drink of water.

About to call out her name, at once he heard voices from behind the door and they completely filled the room. It was that of two women and they were arguing over something. Listening closer, he was startled to learn they weren't arguing about just anything but it appeared to be about him. His name kept coming up again and again. One of the voices he recognized as Antonia's, the other, he wasn't quite sure. It was not long before he realized the other voice belonged to Matilde, Antonia's older sister. This is what he heard Matilde saying.

"I can't believe you killed him! Such a specimen of a man, and those junk parts of his – to die for! And he was partial to older women, you say?"

Then vexedly, "The problem with you, Antonia, is you're selfish, you just always think of yourself. You could have at least waited till I had a turn."

Antonia sighed, "Trust me, Matilde, I did you a favor. Fabio was partial to older women, it's true, but not in the way you might think. I'm glad he's dead after what he did to me and I would do it again if I had to. Accident or no accident."

"But murder? Oh, Antonia, come on, please. Duarte barely a year ago, and now another one? You've really got to give it up."

Antonia acted as if she didn't hear her sister. She went on at length, "At first, Fabio was filled with love, romance, and passion, and he even said he loved me. Our age difference didn't matter; oh, no, it was all fine with him, he said. I never had so much fun in ages. He helped me feel young again. Last week he asked me to marry him and I said yes."

"Marry him?"

"Yes, but that's when things took a turn. I found out he was cheating on me, playing me for a fool. Something made me check his cell phone and laptop when he was in the shower this morning. It turns out he has an accomplice, another woman, and their aim is for him to wine and dine women, gain their trust, and then milk them dry. I'd already given him thousands of dollars in gifts. He and his girlfriend had a scam going, they went from bar to bar, he preyed on vulnerable older women, she on vulnerable men. Turns out he was working three of us at the same time, she four."

Antonia paused to catch her breath before continuing, "And the most horrible thing about it was in all his messages to his girlfriend he never once referred to me by name. Of course, to my face, it was always Tonia or Tony, or sweetheart but behind my back, it was 'old hag' or 'old biddy' or even 'old witch'. Can you imagine being called those awful names? Oh, I feel so stupid, not to mention humiliated."

"Oh, you poor dear! What he put you through! He sounds absolutely horrible. No wonder you lost it."

"At first, I thought of going to the police but in the end I decided to take matters into my own hands, to give him some of my special medicine. He was trying to bamboozle me and he cheated on me. But he chose to tangle with the wrong woman. No man ever pisses me off like that and gets away with it!"

Fabio, with his ear still to the door, gasped at the women's every word. Their conversation sent such shock waves through his system he froze completely for an entire minute. Antonia had tried to kill him and he had had no idea. What disturbed him most was finding out she was not just a killer but possibly a serial killer and he was her latest victim. Clearly, she was smarter, craftier than she had let on, and she was computer savvy too. Who would have thought, a woman her age? Thank God he had lived to find this all out.

Suddenly he remembered what had happened that morning, and he could have kicked himself for not picking up on it. His feeling sick had nothing to do with the eggs, it had come from the coffee. Antonia had poisoned his coffee. She added sugar to his cup, and then he remembered she added more but it was a slightly different color, and she had stirred it longer than usual. And he recalled lapping it up so passively, like a lamb while she watched and smiled away. Good thing he was super fit and able to fight off the toxins. Had it not been for all those trips to the gym and all those body-building exercises, he never would have made it. Yes, he was already feeling much better, in fact, he was almost as good as new.

Stretching his ears to hear more, for some reason, only silence followed. As it happened the sisters had become thirsty and had retreated into the kitchen. There came the sound of boiling water, then the clinking of teacups.

With the women gone, Fabio took pause a moment to consider everything going on. It was all so much to take in, so unreal. Suddenly it occurred to him he was in quite the pickle. If he didn't watch his step, things could end badly for him.

"Let's see now," he said to himself. "I'm supposed to be dead but I'm not dead, rather, I'm very much alive. Antonia and her sister, however, still think I'm dead. And now this being alive part gives me a whole set of problems, problems I would never have had to deal with had I been dead. When Antonia finds out I'm alive, she could either try and kill me again or go to the police with my cell phone and laptop and get me arrested, even thrown in jail. All the incriminating evidence is there – the embezzlement, the fraud, the complicit girlfriend. The police would only have to take a look and it would be game over for me. And all the other women would be revealed – Helena, Mildred, Sophia."

Then another scenario came to mind, "Of course, I could also point the finger at Antonia and explain to the police how she tried to kill me, and that she had possibly killed another man by the name of Duarte. But no, that would be a bad idea, they would never believe it."

Trying to decide how to best go about handling the situation, at once it came to him. Above all, he needed to get rid of any evidence. Tiptoeing to the small bedside table, where his laptop and cell phone were, he started deleting all the messages.

Barely having finished, there came footsteps from the living room. The women had returned and from the sound of it had brought their tea with them. Fabio, quickly putting on his underwear, hurried back to the door to hear what more they had to say. Matilde spoke first and her words were so insidious, so beyond imagination, he got goosebumps.

"Now let's be sensible about this, Antonia. What are we going to do about Fabio? It's not like we have a car that we could just dump him somewhere."

Then laughing as if it was all too much, "Good thing the police took my tip and went looking for Duarte in the lake when he was in your backyard all along. I have to say, your petunias couldn't look lovelier. Oh, but your poor dear husband. They sure fell for that one! Hah, hah, hah!"

Fabio jumped back in horror, "What? So, Duarte was Antonia's husband and his murdered body is in the backyard beneath the petunias?" To find out there was a murdered man only a few feet away sent shivers down his spine.

Suddenly Matilde clapped her hands, "Sister, I've got it! I've absolutely got it! This is what we'll do. We'll bury Fabio next to Duarte. No one will ever think of looking for him there – not in a million years. We'll roll him up in that rug over there and carry him out after we dig the hole. Let's get started the minute it gets dark. Do you still have the shovels?"

The women drank up the rest of their tea and then ate custard tarts, which Matilde had brought with her from the Lisbon Bakery over on College Street. Chatting about this and that and chuckling over a few jokes, they completely forgot about Fabio.

Antonia, thanks to her special pill, which had now fully taken effect, had not a trace of panic or fear left in her, and Matilde was able to relax completely knowing her sister would not disrupt their plan with a sudden hysteria.

In the meantime, Fabio couldn't calm himself down.

"These sisters are psychopaths, they're diabolical! They think I'm dead and now they're getting ready to bury me as if it's no big deal. What I need is to get the hell out of here and fast before they find me out."

Buttoning up his shirt and zipping up his pants, with his electronic devices in hand, he jumped out the window and landed bottom-first on the little brick walkway that led out onto the street. He thought of what to do next. Suddenly it struck him and he was pleased with himself. He let out a chuckle.

"Hah, hah, hah! I hold the trump card now; I can get back at them but in such a way they'd never know what hit them. I'll call the police. I'll show them!"

Quickly he dialed 911 and asked to speak to the homicide detective on duty.

"Hello, detective. I'm calling to report a murder. It's at 31 Bank Street, south of the Dundas-Dufferin intersection. In the backyard, beneath a bed of petunias, a man is buried there by the name of Duarte. The murderer, or, rather, the murderess, whose name is Antonia, is at this very moment in the house sipping tea and eating custard tarts with her sister, Matilde, who is an accomplice. Duarte is Antonia's deceased husband, falsely believed to have drowned about a year ago. There may be other victims."

Putting his cell into his shirt pocket, whistling, Fabio made for the street. He was entirely absorbed in a new overwhelming sensation of life and strength. The day might have got off to a bad start, but now everything was coming up roses. He stood patiently on the sidewalk and waited for the sound of sirens.

Within minutes a police cruiser showed up and broke in front of Antonia's house. Neighbors rushed to see what was going on, including Reginald, who had long since wandered out onto the street. Two police officers emerged with guns drawn and went inside. A forensic team soon arrived and started for the backyard. And who should they dig up but Duarte. Before long Antonia and her sister came out in handcuffs. They both appeared confused, dazed as though not understanding how it was the police had come to find them out.

By chance, Antonia glanced across the street. She noticed a man standing there, and not just any man but one that was familiar to her. Straining her eyes, she tried to get a better look. Her face turned white from shock when she saw who it was. She let out a scream, "Fabio? Is that really Fabio? Impossible! But how could that be when he's dead in my bed?"

When Matilde saw him, she just about fainted.

Fabio stood there waving, smiling broadly. He called out to them, "Good evening, ladies. Going somewhere? As you can see, I'm not dead after all; look, I'm even breathing and my heart is ticking. But poor Duarte, not so lucky. And now they've dug him up and you have me to thank for it. But not to worry, soon you'll be off to your own private luxury resort somewhere, maybe even for life! Hah, hah, hah!"

The women started swearing at him, calling him every name in the book. Once in the cruiser they waved their fists and made faces. Within minutes they drove off and disappeared down the street.

It was now well into the evening; the full moon was shining brightly and across the sky was a profusion of stars. Fabio was in a good mood, he felt up to having some fun. He would head over to the Lula Lounge and do a bit of dancing, maybe even get a bite to eat – yes, he could certainly sink his teeth into one of those delicious Cubano sandwiches about now. What a crazy day he'd had! But lucky for him everything had worked out in his favor: "I sure outsmarted those two old hens!"

Then he started in on a conversation with himself and for some reason he spoke loudly. He didn't realize Reginald was close by and within easy hearing range:

"Hah! They didn't count on me being the clever guy that I am. If they try and send the police after me out of spite (and spiteful they are), nothing will ever happen because all my devices have been erased, it's all gone. But clever me, I backed up my information on a memory stick. Yes, it's there in a little box beneath my bed – telephone numbers, addresses, names, Sarah, Bridgette, Eloise. Yes, for me, it's still business as usual."

As he went on talking to himself, accidentally he bumped into a small strange-looking man who happened to be standing idly by. He had no idea it was Reginald the street busybody, and what's more, he had no idea that this same street busybody had been peeping through the windows of Antonia's house the entire time and had seen and heard everything. Not only did he know about the complicity of the two sisters, but also about his, Fabio's, shady operations. And now, thanks to Fabio's own admission, he even knew about the memory stick.

Unknown to Fabio, Reginald, so full of information, at that very moment was on his way to the police station to spill the beans, so to speak; if anything, Reginald, had a great sense of community. He would tell the police there was more to the Antonia/Matilde story than met the eye. He would tell them everything he knew, and he would end with Fabio's illicit activities, including the memory stick that was in a box beneath his bed.

But how was it he, Reginald, had come to be witness to all of this, the police would ask.

"Purely by accident," is how Reginald would explain himself. "I was just passing by when I heard it all; yes, I was just passing by."

Chapter 6

The Cabbagetown Jazz Band

There was 33 Bank Street and 33A Bank Street, and it was 33A that had a 'For Rent' sign on it. 33A wasn't really a house, moreover, it was a coach house, and it stood directly behind the main house, which was a tall, sturdy red-brick Victorian now painted a pinkish-purple. It was accessed by a stone walkway starting from the street, running along the west side of the house, and ending in a rather spacious courtyard made of concrete. The coach house was over a hundred years old, rectangular in shape, made of wood with a tiled red roof. Its walls were overgrown with vine and the vine was now starting to cover some of the windows. It was crumbling here and there and the foundation was cracked and in need of repair. From the street in wintertime one could see it vaguely through the ice and sleet but in summertime when everything became lush and dense with foliage it was almost invisible.

One hot summer day the 'For Rent' sign came down.

The neighbors wondered who had rented it: Silvio from Number 15 said, "Probably a young family, maybe with a couple of kids"; Beka from around the corner and whose backyard hit up against the coach house, disagreed, "I saw a couple with teenagers and a dog come by, and they looked really interested"; a chesty woman with thick lips and a blotchy face, living next door, shook her head worriedly, "Well, whoever it is I hope they're not going to be rowdy like the last bunch."

A few days passed. Then one bright sunny afternoon an old school bus rolled onto the street and stopped in front of the walkway that led to the coach house. The bus was painted a bright blue and on both sides in bold black letters it read: The Cabbagetown Jazz Band – HotJazz-Bebop-GypsyJazz-JamBand. One by one, about six people got out in loose-fitting colorful clothing of the vintage variety. They were as if in costume. Some wore Fedora hats, others broad fluttering skirts, and still others wildly sequined robes. There was a great uproar of shouting and laughing among them as they opened up the side door of the bus and started to unload. An additional ten people soon showed up in a van to help and they were dressed in the same colorful attire but with faces partially concealed by masquerade masks.

"What on earth is going on?" The neighbors were curious to know. "The Cabbagetown Jazz Band? Who are these people?"

Boxes big and small were pulled out followed by various bits of furniture such as a red and yellow upholstered sofa, a kitchen table, some chairs. What came next completely caught them by surprise. There was every instrument imaginable: trumpet, bassoon, violin, drums, banjo, trombone, stand-up bass and more.

The chesty woman with the thick lips was first to cry out, "Oh, good Lord, no! Please, tell us it isn't so! Is the whole band moving in? The noise!"

Then a young man in high-waisted pants and with his black hair parted down the middle called from the bus, "Hey, someone, give me a hand with this tuba!"

The neighbors chattered amongst themselves and they were gravely concerned, "A jazz band here on our quiet street?"

A woman broke off, "Hey, The Cabbagetown Jazz Band, aren't they from Cabbagetown? If they're from Cabbagetown, why don't they stay in Cabbagetown? Why come all the way over to our part of the city?"

At once and without warning right there on the spot several musicians took hold of their instruments and music broke out – a trumpet, a sax, shakers, a banjo, even a concertina. It was so loud the ground shook as if from an earthquake. The tune was a heartfelt one, full of joy and festivity and very danceable.

"Hey!" an onlooker shouted, who happened to be an aficionado of popular jazz, "That's 'Body and Soul'! A great standard! And just listen to the chords, they have such an unusual nature." He soon began snapping his fingers and clicking his heels.

The crowd started feeling it too.

But the chesty woman was up in arms. The music was giving her a headache already. Waving her fists and with a grumpy expression, she demanded the noise-making to stop at once. But she was drowned out by all the racket. Then, suddenly, as if out of nowhere, something strange took hold of her and she was as if cast by a spell. Her face changed completely and she appeared transformed. Perfectly calmed, she was beginning to feel the music. Smiling, whistling through her teeth, she began clapping and putting rhythm into her hips.

Before long everyone was singing and dancing, young and old alike, spilling out onto the street.

When the music stopped, the musicians went back to unloading the bus. When done, in single file, along the stone path that led to their newly rented coach house, The Cabbagetown Jazz Band, smiling, waving, called out to their neighbors in a friendly way:

"See you all later!"

★

Reginald, stuck in his hardware store the whole time, had missed out on the spectacle. Luckily, a neighbor who had come by to pick up some fertilizer for her garden explained to him in detail what had happened. She told him about the strange new renters, their even stranger music, their odd clothing, and, not to forget, their unusual theatrics.

To Reginald, it all sounded so exciting, bizarre even. He couldn't wait to see for himself. It's a good thing he would be closing up shop soon. The minute it got dark, he would head over to the coach house and have a look.

The night sky was beautiful and filled with stars. The moon passed behind a cloud. Reginald was on his way and he couldn't get there soon enough. Passing his own house with no time to stop, finally he reached the coach house. The courtyard was empty except for flower boxes filled with geraniums running along the edges. Careful not to knock one over, he noticed almost immediately several windows were wide open, and better still, without curtains. The new neighbors couldn't have accommodated him better.

He found a window where he could see everything. There were about twenty musicians scattered about a rather spacious room, drinking, toking, and tuning instruments – a trumpet, a guitar, a violin to mention a few. Reginald quickly decided this was no ordinary band. And their clothes were impulsive and unusual, strange-looking, just as his neighbor had said, and they all looked as if from the 1920s. There was one man wearing gangster garb, another in a double-breasted three-piece Gatsby suit, and another in a rainbow-colored straw Boater hat. Nothing like this had ever happened on Bank Street before.

Then unexpectedly, a woman appeared from behind one of the doors. She was tall, lean and very pretty, and her skin was like satin ebony. Sparkles of every color were scattered about her face and her lips were painted a bright red. She was dressed like a 'flapper' girl in a Deco gold-beaded dress and around her neck was a long string of pearls. Her hair was bobbed and from her ears dangled gemstone drop earrings. She was very brash-looking, dazzling, and sultry. And she was hitting a tambourine first lightly, then harder, then lightly again. She moved across the room and her movements were so graceful and elegant Reginald couldn't stop staring at her. When she picked up speed, he could almost hear her bare feet hitting the ground, whizzing the air around her. Everything about her fit together perfectly. He loved the tilt of her nose, the fullness of her mouth, her strong chin. She couldn't have been more exotic-looking. Feelings of desire surged within him and he could not stop his imagination from running afield.

The woman then came by his window to take pause. Resting on the sill with her back to him, she fanned her face. She was so close to Reginald he could literally touch her if he wanted to. He felt a longing to say something sincere and lovely to her, as lovely as she herself was, but he wouldn't dare. She would become alarmed seeing him there lurking in the dark, and worse yet, she would see how unattractive he was, how he stood small and bent and full of abnormalities. She would see what a physical freak he was. No, he couldn't risk it. He would continue to admire her from afar.

At once there came the pinging of a phone. It was coming from the 'flapper' girl's pocket. There was a text message for her, and by the way she held it, Reginald could easily read the text. He saw her name was Elisa.

"Elisa," he thought to himself warmly. "What a beautiful name for a 'flapper' girl."

He started to read the message. It was from a Darnell Jackson. Wasn't that the same Darnell Jackson who played the trombone and was the lead vocalist in the band?

And there he was sitting at the far end of the room with the dreamiest look on his face, and that look was aimed directly at Elisa. Elisa was right back at him with that same dreamy look. Suddenly their eyes locked as if there was no one else in the room with them.

Reginald's heart throbbed and sank as he continued to read the texts.

Darnell: "Elisa, I love you today more than I did yesterday."

Elisa: "I love you too, Darnell, and I'll love you more tomorrow than I do today."

Darnell: "Elisa, will you marry me?"

Eliza: "Yes, Darnell, if you'll marry me, I'll marry you."

Then Darnell waved to Elisa and pressed his hand to his breast. Elisa waved back, her face flushing and her expression showing deep affection. At once they both got up and came together in the middle of the room, embracing each other tenderly. They called for quiet and made their happy announcement:

"We have great news! We're getting married!"

There was a burst of excitement and everyone took to clapping, cheering, and stomping their feet. It was cause for celebration, and if there was one thing The Cabbagetown Jazz Band knew how to do it was celebrate. First the fiddle started up, then the piano, and once the trumpets got going all the other instruments followed. There came a dizzying explosion of music. The atmosphere was so uplifting even Reginald, tapping his foot, couldn't help but feel the joy. The band then started in on 'Ain't Misbehavin'' and Darnell wasted no time in coming in with the vocals.

Reginald loved music and to him music of The Cabbagetown Jazz Band was more than just that – it was jubilant noisemaking, it was a cultural revival, it was the ultimate of jam bands. He clapped and whistled along. At once, his accordion came to mind, which he had stashed in his closet and which he hadn't touched in months. As a child, he had had many accordion lessons and till this day, though somewhat out of practice, when he played, he played beautifully. Playing had always taken him to another world and offered him great enjoyment, and he even remembered some jazz tunes his teacher had taught him like Barrel House Stomp; however, as of late he had become too wrapped up in peeping through the windows of his neighbors to give it much attention. He never realized how much he missed playing it till now.

Then it struck him. But of course! With his accordion, he could play with The Cabbagetown Jazz Band! He could stop being a window peeper and become a musician. He made a decision: he would run home, get his accordion, come back, and then ever so quietly crawl through the window and start playing as if nothing. Who would even notice him, there were so many musicians there anyway. He looked down at his clothes and became disheartened. His pants, his shirt, his tie, they were all so wrong, so drab, so ordinary he would give himself away in a minute. He would have to find something more suitable to wear, something on the exaggerated side, maybe with a bit of flare. Then his pirate costume from Halloween came to mind, yes, it would be perfect! Though it wasn't vintage, still, it was better than nothing. He not only had the shirt, the bandana, and the sash stashed away in a wooden box in his closet but also the eyepatch and a pretend sword. Yes, in his pirate costume he would fit right in.

When Reginald returned to the coach house all decked up, he looked like the smartest little pirate there ever was. And strapped to his chest was his accordion, a small, light-weight one specially made to accommodate his limited size.

To his surprise, the band had moved outside and was now playing in the courtyard. The clarinet was doing a solo.

Suddenly the alto-sax player, a tall robust looking fellow, yelled out, "Better out here than in there. Party on! One, two, three!"

The music roared and it only got louder and bolder. Forming a circle, with Elisa and Darnell in the middle, the band then started up on 'Scrapple from the Apple'. Later they fell into improvisation. Elisa and Darnell laughed, kissed, and jumped up and down.

Reginald weighed the situation carefully, trying to determine how to best get in with them. Looking round, being discreet as possible, he slipped into the circle between the bass guitar and the vibraphone. Everyone, busy with their own instruments, didn't notice him, or at least that's what he thought.

Making sure his accordion was properly balanced, he took his participation very seriously: he didn't slouch and he was careful to keep his head high. His fingers knew exactly where they needed to go. Hitting the keys first softly, gradually he got louder and louder, and before long he started playing his little heart out. His melodies were not only magnified and illuminated but there came a very rich, reedy, organ-like sound. He could feel his musicianship was top-notch; he was playing like a virtuoso. He couldn't believe it but it was true, he was now playing with The Cabbagetown Jazz Band! Lost in the music, without realizing, he made himself heard above the rest.

That's when the vibraphone player suddenly noticed him standing there. He shouted to his fellow musicians:

"Hey, everybody, look over here! We have a pirate in our midst!"

The band stopped playing at once and there came a dead silence. All eyes fell on Reginald. Who was this uninvited, strange-looking little man with an accordion, dressed in, of all things, a pirate costume? Obviously, he was someone with an eccentric condition. But where on earth did he come from? Being new to the neighborhood, no one in the band could say for sure. Yet he played exquisitely, whimsically, and he had real musical talent. There came a hubbub of talk and exclamations among the musicians. In a matter of minutes, it was decided – the strange man in the pirate costume was welcome to join The Cabbagetown Jazz Band, if he so desired.

Reginald was in seventh heaven. Being invited into the band wasn't real as much as it was surreal. He was even invited to go on tour with them, to fly around the world, and to play beautiful festivals in Germany, France, Italy, Greece and Norway, and not to forget the Montreal International Jazz Festival. Was this really happening to him? *Yes, it was!* Closing his eyes, it was as if he was flowing in rhythmic waves.

At once, someone shouted, "And now, to Elisa and to Darnell! To their engagement! Let's take our celebration out into the streets!"

Another threw in, "May our elfin Blackbeard lead the way!"

Like a Mariachi band the musicians made down the stone walkway and out onto the sidewalk. The night was quite dark but the sky was calm. Big dark shadows fell strikingly from one end of the street to the other. Reginald, at the helm, assumed an air of importance. First delving into merriment and playfulness, he then started up on melodic variations. With his chest out and shoulders back, he marched like a true soldier. Directly behind him hand-in-hand was the happy, newly engaged couple, Elisa and Darnell, and behind them, the rest of The Cabbagetown Jazz Band.

Heading toward the park, the musicians turned left on Sheridan, then right along Florence, then to Brock, and then straight up to Dundas. As their music gained force, people came out of their houses, cheering, clapping, dancing, some on their verandas, others on their lawns. A few women shouted out their congratulations to the young in-love couple, while others threw rice their way.

The band started in on 'Cheek to Cheek'. It filled the air.

Before long neighbors began joining up with their own instruments. Silvio brought out his Bombo, Pierre his spoons, and the chesty woman, pots and pans. As they passed the Lula Lounge, Salsa dancers, upon hearing the music from the open windows, abandoning the dance floor, rushed to join in, only to continue their dancing in the street.

The sound of The Cabbagetown Jazz Band was everywhere. It was a mix of exhilaration and chaos, traditional and abstract, it was music in the street. The crowd only grew, and as it grew it was lifted to a higher place of existence. Never were there so many people out in the neighborhood. Before long fireworks started up. There would be a wedding and everyone was invited.

His head in a whirl, still at the helm, Reginald started playing robust 'Oom-Pah-Pah' chords. With his fingers racing up and down the keys, he then fell to making sounds full of movement and passion, blending it with ragtime and folk. He was on fire. He was in The Cabbagetown Jazz Band now, and not only that but he would soon be going to a wedding and later traveling the world.

Yes, he, Reginald Rutley would be doing all this. It was all so out of this world. And it wasn't just an absurd happy dream he was having, it was real, it really was. He pinched himself to make sure, and then he pinched himself again to make double sure.

Chapter 7

The Writer Sholomitsky

Reginald had just turned twelve and for his birthday his parents bought him a bicycle. It was bright green with high handlebars and had a white leather banana seat. It was all the rage back then and no one on the street had anything like it. Most of the kids had beat-up old bikes from the junk store or ones passed down from older siblings, usually with missing fenders, loose pedals, and sometimes bald tires. But Reginald's bike was brand-new. There was a baseball game on at the park and he thought he would go and show it off. All the kids would be there. He had it all figured out. He would circle the field several times, not too fast, not too slow, and he would make sure everyone saw him. He couldn't wait to see the looks on their faces. They'd all want to be friends with him now.

As he sped off his mother called after him, "Don't stay out too late, Reggie, you have school tomorrow! And watch out for cars!"

Cycling down the street, the early evening sun was peeking out from behind the drifting clouds, and the air was moist with the fresh fragrance of lilac. There came the sound of a lawn mower and from one of the verandas lingered the trail of cigarette smoke. Finally, the park. The game was already well underway full of spectators rooting for their respective teams. Reginald cycled boldly right up to the field.

Ralphy, who happened to be in Reginald's class at school, was on the home plate batting. Strike one, strike two, and just as the third pitch came at him, looking as if it would be another miss, Ralphy ended up whacking the ball so hard it flew all the way to the far end of the field. Running as fast as he could, touching all bases, in no time he made a home run. His teammates rooted and cheered.

Then one of the players noticed Reginald on his brand-new bike. He shouted out but in a sneering way, "Hey, look, everyone, look at shorty over there, is that a cool new bike he's got or what!"

Someone else called out, "A bike like that for a shrimp like him? A tricycle would have been a better idea!"

Then Ralphy, "Hah, hah, hah, frog-face should leave the bike with us and go back to the pond where he belongs!"

The catcalls kept coming. Reginald became disheartened. The bike was supposed to make him get noticed and be popular but instead it was doing the opposite. Couldn't they see how much they were hurting his feelings? They were nothing but bullies, all of them. He wished there was a way he could make them stop being so mean. If only he could stand up to them. And then he decided right then and there that's exactly what he would do, he would take them all on and single-handedly. But it was not long before second thoughts set in. There was only one of him and many of them, he would get pulverized in a minute. They started coming after him. Falling into a panic, jumping on his bike, never in his life did he peddle so fast. He got away seconds before they could nab him.

To calm his nerves before going home he thought he'd go for a ride around the neighborhood. When he finally came back to Bank Street, he chose to walk his bike rather than ride it. To his great relief, the baseball game was over and the park had emptied. The sun had long since set. It was quiet everywhere, and in the quiet a sudden strength and self-confidence was born inside him. He was proud of his new bike after all and he vowed no amount of bullying was ever going to take that away from him. He made up his mind to say nothing of the incident to his parents, as it would only upset them.

Passing by several houses, at once he heard a strange noise. He stopped to listen. It was some kind of tapping sound but ever so soft, and it had a kind of rhythm to it, though there was no harmony.

"What could that be?" he wondered.

The sound came again, "Tap, tap" then, "tap, tap, tap," then once more but now the tapping went on for several minutes. He couldn't figure it out but one thing he knew for sure, it was coming from Number 9.

"That's Emma's house," he said to himself.

Emma was in his grade at school but in a different class, and all he knew about her was that she was very pretty, good at math, and even better at writing. He also knew her family was from Eastern Europe, possibly Russia or Poland, and that they had lived on Bank Street for about a year. He'd secretly had a crush on her from the moment he saw her.

He decided to peek through one of the windows to find out what was going on. Resting his bike up against the fire hydrant which was in the middle of the lawn, he crept onto the veranda. Looking through one of the lower panes, he saw a fairly large room with a wood floor, a high ceiling, and a big brown door, probably leading to the hallway. A couple of paintings hung on the wall, one a portrait of a woman with a dark face, another a summer landscape. But there was something unusual about the room. Though it was a living room, it didn't look like a living room, rather, it looked more like an office, and it was a big mess. There were stacks of papers all over the place, piles of books on the floor, and a wastepaper basket overflowing with scrunched up paper. Then he saw a man sitting at a desk bent over a typewriter.

"So that's what was making those sounds, a typewriter!"

Reginald could vaguely see the man's face but by the way he was sitting, he seemed to be concentrating on something, as if overwhelmed, overburdened even.

The man went on typing, stopping briefly, then starting up again. He was obviously going through some kind of ordeal as though everything was too much for him. Pulling the paper out of the typewriter, crumpling it up into a ball, he threw it on the floor. He cussed out loud, "Dammit, it's all wrong, all wrong!"

Reginald wondered what was going through the man's mind to make him act like that. Who was he anyway? At first, he couldn't see clearly, then straining his eyes, he realized it was Emma's father. In the evenings sometimes he would run into him walking home from the print shop where he worked a few blocks away. Unlike other grown-ups, Emma's father always stooped to his level and looked him in the eye when he talked to him. He would say in his heavily accented English, "Hello, young man, and how are you today?"

Reginald's eyes wandered about the room. The typewriter caught his attention. It was made of heavy cast iron, gray in color, and looked at least thirty pounds. As Reginald was to learn later, the typewriter was one of the few things Emma's father brought with him from England, where he had lived briefly after the Second World War. Reginald could see the keys were not English keys but keys from another language. A friend of his mother's, who was Russian, had a typewriter something like that, and he remembered her explaining to him about the letters:

"The letter 'P' is really an 'R', the letter 'H' is an 'N', and the letter 'B' a 'V'."

He noticed at the time the typewriter also had a lot of other letters, funny-looking, and he remembered trying to imagine what they might sound like. All he knew was the letters were called Cyrillic.

At once a woman walked into the room. It was Emma's mother, Klara. She had big, round, clever-looking eyes, a fine nose, and an angular and irregular face. Dressed in a fitted blue-green frock she had patterned and sewed herself, it was obvious she was the type who was very efficient in her work. On her left hand she wore a little gold-plated watch and in her ears were imitation clip-on earrings. She took a seat opposite her husband as if he was expecting her.

Emma's father began to read from his manuscript. Words like *gulag*, *NKVD*, and *Stalin* kept coming up. When finished, he said to her seriously, "I want to make sure my writing lays bare the truths of Soviet state terror. I want it to be comprehensive, powerful and lyrical. Tell me, am I doing all that?"

Klara assured him with her eyes that, yes, in her opinion he was doing just that.

At once Reginald realized it was late, at least nine o'clock, maybe later. His mother would be angry. Jumping on his bike, he made for home as fast as he could. He had missed dinner and soon it would be time for bed. His parents were in the living room watching TV. His mother called out, "Reggie, is that you?"

Grabbing a quick bite, taking a shower and changing into his pajamas, he got under the covers. Turning out the light he couldn't get Emma's father out of his mind. He wanted to learn more about him and about his writing.

The next night was clear and light and a stand of trees at the end of the street stood vividly on the edge of the horizon. Riding around on his bike, Reginald felt free and easy. The best thing, there was no one around to bully him. The kids had gone off somewhere or were in their houses. Listening to his transistor radio, which he kept in his shirt pocket, at once he saw a crowd of people in front of Emma's house. They were smoking, talking, laughing. All were dressed up, the men in suits, the women in flowing cotton dresses. Cars kept pulling up one after the other and small groups were arriving on foot. They were carrying trays of food, bottles of booze, and musical instruments.

"Who are these people?" wondered Reginald. "And why are they coming together like this?"

Soon they disappeared inside.

Putting down his bike, Reginald felt he needed to have a look. He snuck up onto the veranda.

The room was no longer the office of the previous night but was now completely transformed – the desk, the stacks of paper, the filing cabinet, all were pushed to the side. The doors leading to the dining room were opened wide and you could see straight into the kitchen. There were rows of chairs lined up, maybe twenty-five, and in front was a raised platform, sort of like a small stage. It was as if the whole downstairs had become a makeshift theater of some kind. Everyone was seated in the chairs but the children had a place in the corner on a blanket on the floor. Against the side wall there was a table with plates, napkins, and salt and pepper shakers. There would be a food buffet but that would not come till later.

A stout man with bushy brows and a smiling face appeared on the stage. Taking hold of a microphone that didn't seem to be working properly, he spoke in a foreign language. Though Reginald didn't understand, somehow, he managed to pick up on the gist of things.

"Welcome, ladies and gentlemen! Tonight, we have a superb line-up. Music, dance, and the highlight of the evening, our very talented, one and only mezzo-soprano, Eleanor Berbenetz. She will be performing from Mozart's *Don Giovanni*. And to end the evening, for those of you that have been following his work, Theodore Sholomitsky will read from his manuscript."

The crowd applauded politely.

A young man came out and started to play the violin. The audience was completely enthralled. When he finished his performance, these were the comments the people made: "So much passion", "such emotion", "so inspirational."

Next came the poet, Komarenko. He had an uplifting, flamboyant style but with a humorous twist. His rhythmic enunciation delighted everyone.

At intermission the guests remarked on the performances thus far and they couldn't find enough good things to say. They were looking forward to the second part of the program. After about fifteen minutes a little bell sounded and they returned to their seats.

Reginald, still at the window, was more intrigued than ever by what he was seeing. But he needed to get closer. Then he came up with an idea. What if he crawled inside and sat with the children on the floor – from there he would be able to see and hear everything so much better. And with such a big crowd, who would even notice, he would be as if one of them. With one foot over the sill, then the other, with little effort he slipped into the room. He sat down next to a little girl with pigtails.

The time had come for the much-anticipated Eleanor Berbenetz. With her perfect pitch and compelling artistry, her big voice dazzled the crowd. She had been a rising star with the Lviv National Opera but when war broke out, she was forced to flee. Now, here she was on Bank Street, on the other side of the world, on a makeshift stage in someone's living room, giving the performance of her life.

And finally, the last act of the night, Theodore Sholomitsky. A stand was brought in from a side room. Theodore laid out his papers. He began to read. His voice was solemn but well-paced, "Scientists, writers, artists, educators, all were being branded bourgeois nationalists … conspirators against the Soviet government …"

Reginald sat there listening intently. Though he didn't understand a word, he was picking up on sensations, modulations, intonations, trying to put it all together. Theodore caught him sitting there and wondered how it was the boy had come to be there. The two exchanged glances and then they smiled at one another.

When the reading was over, there came a round of applause.

The buffet table was filling up. Vodka, rum, and a few varieties of beer stood at one end, and at the other, trays with cabbage rolls, pierogis, chicken Kiev, baked fish, poppy-seed cake, compote and more.

Reginald was famished. Coming up to the table, he was quite shy about it. He didn't know where to begin. So much food! Some kindly old woman with wide hips and a huge bosom took it upon herself to help him. Bending forward, practically touching his nose with that huge bosom of hers, she said in a singsong, "Ach, what a *holubchik* you are, and so cute!" She loaded his plate with perogies, and then threw on some caramelized onions and a big glob of sour cream. Reginald had never tasted anything so delicious. He thought to himself, "These people sure know how to eat!"

When the clock struck midnight, the guests started to pack up. It was announced next month the event would be held at

Eleanor's house, which was on Beaconsfield, several blocks away. Everyone agreed to be there.

Reginald set off for home. He took his time riding his bike. Slipping quietly through the front door, passing his mother asleep on the sofa, he tiptoed up the stairs and got into bed.

★

A few days passed. One evening as Reginald was out cycling up and down the street, gray clouds rolled across the sky and it started to drizzle. A woman with exceptionally skinny legs holding a big umbrella hurried along, and later a young man in black galoshes. There came lightening and then a clap of thunder. Reginald thought of going home before there was a downpour, and as he was about to do just that, in the distance he caught sight of a man coming round the corner. Tall and lean, in a darkish trench coat, the man was walking slowly, as if unsure of his next step. It was Emma's father. He was obviously on his way home from work but for some reason he was early by at least an hour.

"They probably let him off work to beat the storm," Reginald figured.

But there was something not right. There seemed an uncertainty in his movements and he appeared to be staggering. He almost looked drunk. Coming closer, Reginald noticed he was very pale and he even looked a little feverish. Yet he was smiling but his smile was strained.

"Hello, Reginald; a fine bike you have there. A bike like that you can ride to the ends of the earth if you wanted to. Did you know a bike is a symbol of progress, freedom and promising times? I wish I had a bike like that when I was your age. Yes, if only I had had a bike like that." Then looking up at the sky, "There's a storm brewing – any minute now it'll be here."

Turning onto his walkway, opening the door to his house, he disappeared inside.

Barely a minute passed when as if out of nowhere there came a loud crash, so loud it sounded like an explosion. Reginald didn't know what to think. It had come from Emma's house, from the front room. Something was wrong, terribly wrong. Dropping his bike, running to the veranda, he put his face to the window. He was horrified at what he saw. There on the floor lay Emma's father face down, and he wasn't moving.

Klara came running in and when she saw her husband on the floor she started screaming and flailing her arms as if not knowing what to do. Then, with an enormous burst of strength, she seized him in her arms and within seconds had him on the sofa. Was he alive? Was he dead? Was he even breathing? Rushing to the telephone, she called 911. Within minutes an ambulance arrived. The paramedics tried to revive him but it was too late.

All the while, Emma was standing in the doorway shaking. Going up to her mother, hugging her, she tried to calm her down but she was inconsolable. Emma then said softly in her ear, "Hush, Mother, don't cry, everything will be all right. None of this is real. It's just a dream, we're both only dreaming."

★

Many years passed and it was now the new century – 2000-something. A book shop opened up on Dundas Street a few doors down from Reginald's hardware store. Surprisingly, given the influx of e-books on the market, not to mention online shopping, it was a very popular place. There was even a little café in the back with several tables where people could drink lattes, browse, and chat amongst themselves. In the window was a display of books and one of them caught Reginald's attention. It had a hammer and sickle on the front cover and superimposed was a face in the likeness of Joseph Stalin. The title read: Wave of Terror. It looked familiar to Reginald but he couldn't quite place it. He thought for several minutes. And then there was the author's name in bold black letters – Theodore Sholomitsky.

"That's it!" he felt a rush of emotion, "That's the book from so long ago!"

And right beneath it, it read, translated by Emma Sholomitsky.

"After all these years, and Emma did it for him!"

Going inside, taking a copy off the shelf, Reginald then went to the little café in the back and ordered a cappuccino. He scanned the blurb on the back cover: " … through Sholomitsky's eyes, we witness the tragedies of Stalinist domination… where people are randomly deported to labor camps or tortured … Hidden from the English-speaking world … this novel is truly remarkable."

Chapter 8

Mamma Mia

A beautiful August sun was shining warmly over Bank Street and it couldn't have been a finer day. As Reginald made his way to the variety store to pick up a carton of milk, he saw Mamma Mia sitting on her veranda peeling garlic. Bent over a bucket, she was covered in it, her hands, her face, her hair, and the pungent smell permeated the air. In a light cotton blouse half-open, she showed an ample bosom, and on her skirt the zipper was undone as if to give her extra breathing space. She appeared to be sweating and she looked exhausted. Something was going on with Mamma Mia and it wasn't the garlic doing it. Could it be she was pregnant – again?

Mamma Mia was a very fat woman, the fattest on the street, and it seemed she just got fatter all the time. She got pregnant a lot too but when she was pregnant no one could tell if she was really pregnant or just getting fatter again. When a baby appeared then everyone, of course, knew that she'd been pregnant. But pregnancies made her hungry and after each one (so far there were six of them) she gained more weight. She would eat everything in sight – chicken, spaghetti, scaloppini, tortellini, and she went for desserts too such as tiramisu, biscotti, and ricotta cheesecake. Her last pregnancy, for some reason, was an anomaly because she only craved canned snails, and, oddly, toothpaste. This strange combination, being low in fat, at least for those nine months, put her on a weight-gaining hiatus.

Mamma Mia had lived on Bank Street for ten years in one of the smaller detached houses by the park, having immigrated from Sicily with her husband, Franco. The house was brick, two stories high, with a peaked roof, and blue shuttered windows all around. The lawn was well maintained, and in the middle stood a fairly large statue of the Blessed Virgin Mary constructed of heavy, hard plastic made to look like marble.

Money within the Mamma Mia household was tight. Franco worked when he could, usually earning only minimum wage. Like Mamma Mia, he had little education, grade three if that, and as an unskilled laborer, his prospects did not look good. He often stressed over being unable to support his forever growing family.

Luckily for Franco, Mamma Mia had a natural bent for business and a talent for making something out of nothing. When she needed diapers, for example, rather than running to the store, she'd cut up great swaths of flannelette, sometimes from discarded pajamas, only to later wrap up her babies in such a way she didn't even need pins; she sewed all her children's underwear and this was no secret because on laundry day she hung them on the line to dry; and when her children outgrew their shoes she would take a pair of scissors and cut an opening for the toes to give them more wiggle room. Where food was concerned, Mamma Mia also proved resourceful. She would clip coupons, prepare meals from scratch, and in the summertime from her vegetable garden she would cook up great batches of sauces for winter use. If ever something needed to get done Mamma Mia found a way.

Having such an inventive, dollar-stretching wife certainly helped ease things for Franco, and he had no qualms about letting her run the whole show – the kids, the bills, the groceries. He would boast to his neighbors, "What a lucky man I am to have such a wife!"

When Mamma Mia and Franco first moved to Bank Street, they had only one child, a girl, Anna-Maria. Mamma Mia was quite slender back then with curly black hair, a lovely smile, and wonderful charcoal eyes. Her olive-colored skin was soft and glistening, just a gentle reminder of her distant Arabic ancestors who ruled Sicily a thousand years ago.

Having first laid eyes on her, Reginald thought her exotically and blissfully beautiful and he felt immediately drawn to her. He couldn't help but fall in love. However, she being married and he with his obvious shortcomings, it was impossible for the two of them to ever get together. Her real name was Rosa, actually, Roswitha, but when she became grossly overweight everyone started calling her Mamma Mia, even her husband got into the habit. Reginald too called her Mamma Mia, but when she entered his imagination, which, as of late was often, to him she was nothing but Roswitha.

It took the ten years Mamma Mia lived on Bank Street for her face to show signs of wear and tear. In those ten years she became flabby, red-faced, with a big nose, and not much of a neck. She must have gained at least a hundred pounds. No one thought her attractive anymore, and when men passed her by, mostly they looked the other way. If anyone was pleased with this metamorphosis it was her husband, as he no longer had to worry about men hitting on her. What he never realized, however, there was a certain percentage of men fond of full-figured women, and Reginald, of all people, happened to be one of them.

Reginald was even more in love with Mamma Mia now that she was fat. He loved the rolls on her stomach, her big, round behind, her bubbly breasts, but what he loved most was how her love handles wiggled when she walked. She was like something out of a Rubens painting. There was no one like her anywhere and he couldn't help but long after her.

And if that wasn't enough, as of late crazy ideas were entering his head, they were absolutely consuming him, and he wasn't able to repress them. They were all about one thing – about him and Mamma Mia getting intimate, and not just intimate per se but getting intimate all the way. As shocking as it may sound, even though she was a married woman, what he wanted more than anything was to impregnate her. It's true – Reginald wanted a baby and he wanted one with Mamma Mia.

Back to Mama Mia's veranda. Finishing up with her garlic, that's when she caught sight of Reginald walking by. As it turned out, he happened to be the very man she was looking for. She knew he had a thing for her, and though she found everything about him repulsive, today she made sure there was a certain tone of flirtation in her voice. She needed something from his hardware store and was looking for a bargain. Her toaster was broken. Already the whole street knew about it, even Reginald had heard. Getting up, leaning over the bannister, she called out to him in a rather exaggerated voice.

"Yoo hoo! *Buongiorno*, Reginaldo!"

Reginald couldn't help notice her thin blouse had slipped off her left shoulder and exposed the top of her lumpy arm. Her heavy, ball-shaped breasts and the dimples on her rosy-red cheeks were all too much. He knew it was because of her toaster she was throwing herself at him today. Last week it was her coffee pot.

"Oh, Rrrreginaldo, Rrrreginaldo," Mamma Mia rolled her Rs for effect and batted her lashes, "you wouldn't believe what happened to me today. My toaster broke and my kids won't eat bread unless it's toasted. And poor Franco's out of work again. What's a poor woman to do?"

Reginald pretended not to know of her troubles but of course he knew everything. In fact, he had already that morning prepared what he wanted to say to her.

"Not to worry, Mamma Mia. Come to my store first thing tomorrow and I'll show you what I've got. I'm sure we can set up some kind of arrangement."

Mamma Mia's eyes lit up at once and she clasped her chest. She couldn't have been more pleased; she had struck up a deal and so fast!

With her mind on her toaster, little did Mamma Mia know Reginald, like herself, was up to something. As it happened, he had already set up a sort of trap for her, one she was guaranteed to fall into it. Yes, something was brewing inside that head of his, something so unimaginable, so unexpected, it bordered on the insane. Mamma Mia would come to learn she was essential to him, even more so than he to her, and the toaster, crazy as it may sound, would be at the center of it all.

It was all about having a baby. Reginald had had baby fever for quite some time now; it was inexplicable to him, really, but seeing Mamma Mia pregnant and so often awakened in him a craving such as he had never known. He wanted to feel the pride and importance of having fathered a child, and more than anything, being single and with no prospects of a married life, he wanted an heir. He wasn't fussy either, a boy, a girl, it was all the same to him. One way or the other, he would impregnate Mamma Mia, he decided.

He convinced himself: "As long as my approach remains a practical one, I'm confident I'll be able to win her over."

This is the way he figured it: Mamma Mia was forever short of cash and he, being well-positioned and proprietor of a local business, could easily establish a kind of control over her poverty. Should she have a baby with him, he would offer her a free line of credit at his store, he would make generous monthly child-support payments, and, in the end, the child would inherit his entire fortune, which was considerable – his house, his store, his savings. Mamma Mia would get more than she ever dreamed of. That she was the type to be tempted by money only gave him hope.

But what about Franco, Mamma Mia's husband? Reginald had that one figured out too. Right from the start Mamma Mia could simply let him assume the baby was his, or, if she preferred, she could easily conceal her pregnancy with her obesity and then give the baby to him to raise. He would leave that up to her.

Next morning bright and early Mamma Mia, grabbing her purse and hat, hurried up Dufferin Street to Reginald's store. Moving with a heavy tread upon the pavement, she had forgotten to powder between her hefty thighs and now there came a burning sensation from all the rubbing. She paused briefly to catch her breath. The street was heavy with rush-hour traffic – cars, buses, people going every which way. Her thoughts were on the toaster and she was worried Reginald might have forgotten or changed his mind. When she finally reached the store, she was excited to see it placed by the cash register as if waiting for her. It was magnificent – stainless steel, with five toast settings, and good for four slices at a time. Mamma Mia had never seen anything like it. But it looked expensive and she worried she wouldn't be able to afford it, even at a reduced price.

Reginald, behind the counter, was smiling but it was a crafty smile. That morning he had practiced everything he wanted to say to her.

"Hello, Mamma Mia. I see you've already seen the toaster; well, it's yours, and not only is it yours but today is your lucky day because it's yours for free. I hope you don't mind that it's last year's model."

Mamma Mia clasped her chest, "Last year's model? No, no, I don't mind, no, not at all. And you say it's free! I've never heard of such a thing! But how?"

Reginald watched Mamma Mia closely. Her frock had a hole in it which she tried to hide with patchwork, the soles on her shoes were worn and thin, and her brown leather purse had seen better days. Yet at the same time he noticed she was trying to maintain an air of dignity with her hair washed and combed, mascara on her lashes, and lipstick on her mouth. It was all quite amusing to him and gave him a kind of vanity and conceit. Everything about her was wonderful, she was so womanly, so finished, so complete. If anyone could give him a baby it was Mamma Mia. With her his dream would be realized.

As he was about to come out with what was on his mind, suddenly he grew nervous as if having a change of mind – his legs started to wobble and a perspiration built on his brow. Her poverty and obesity, unlike a few moments ago, now made him jittery, and everything about her intimidated him. He became convinced beneath that flirty façade of hers she felt him an object of repulsion, a man to be disdained. But he had to be brave. It was now or never. He began his approach in a roundabout way.

"About the toaster, um, yes, it's free ... and there's more where that came from, plenty more ... but ... but there's a catch."

Mamma Mia stood back and gazed at him in perplexity. "A 'catch'? What do you mean? What kind of 'catch' can there possibly be?"

Reginald mustered up his willpower. He decided to keep his tone formal. "Mamma Mia, as you probably know, I do quite well financially and I have a lot to offer in terms of benefits and advantages. I'm looking to write my last will and testament but the problem is I have no one to leave my money or my store to, no family, no friends, no surviving relatives. I thought if only I had a child that would solve everything. However, my prospects of finding a partner are pretty slim, given my physical deficiencies. So, I'm looking for a sort of partnership, not in the conventional sense, but one that could possibly give me a child."

A second passed, then another. Reginald swallowed hard. Finally, he came out with it, "What I want is to go into partnership with you, Mamma Mia. I want to have a baby with you."

Mamma Mia's mouth dropped; she could hardly believe her ears. She looked at him in disbelief.

Reginald stood still in hesitation and his voice gave a croaking sound. He said at last, "Please, don't be offended, just hear me out. Human relations can be complicated. It may sound callous to you, even business-like but it makes perfect sense. Of course, if you go along with it, you can keep the child if you like and I'll just watch him or her grow from afar, or I can keep the child for myself and raise him or her if that's better; whatever would be best for the child. If you agree to it, you'll have many financial advantages, and the baby will inherit everything I have. I've led a frugal lifestyle and I have money in the bank."

Mamma Mia tried to say something but couldn't. Her chin wouldn't stop jiggling. Finally, she flew at him, "A baby? You say you want a baby, with me? You, a misfit, of all people! And I'm a married woman, what would my Franco say?" Then clutching at her head, looking up to the Heavens, "Oh, Mamma Maria! Help me! *Follia! Pura follia!*"

She had to get out of there and fast. This was nothing short of insanity. As she made for the door, not forgetting the toaster, she fled outside. Hastening down the street, her head was in a whirl. "The nerve of him! He wants a baby, of all things! And with me!" Within ten minutes, she was back home. She managed to calm down. Going into the kitchen, setting the toaster on the counter, she made herself an espresso. Her children were playing in the backyard and she could hear them through the open window. Franco was napping upstairs. Looking round, the signs of poverty were undeniable: the wallpaper was faded and torn; the cupboards were in dire need of repair; and up against the wall the small sofa that acted as a bed for two of her children was lopsided and tattered on the edges. The money Franco brought in would never be enough.

Then her eyes rested on the brand-new, shiny toaster. It certainly gave her kitchen a new kind of respectability. She thought of Reginald's proposition. Somehow, she was no longer struck by the outrageousness of it all and instead started to see it in a more positive light: he was well-off; his financial offering was quite a generous one; he ran a thriving business.

"That's a damn good deal," she muttered to herself. "Why only a fool would pass something like that up. And I'm no fool. But what should I do, what should I do?"

She started to imagine the changes she could make. She could put up new wallpaper over the stove, she could hire a worker to lay down a more durable floor, she could get a new washing machine. Her future would be brighter indeed. But why did Reginald have to be so ugly, so detestable in every way? And then there were those frog eyes of his and that greenish skin tone. Just thinking about him made her cringe. How could she possibly have sex with such a thing? But then again, she reasoned, it would be dark when they would 'do it' and she could keep her eyes closed the entire time – five, ten minutes tops she figured and it would be over. Unorthodox as it was, this was definitely a favorable circumstance she was presented with, one that wasn't about to come her way again anytime soon. She seriously contemplated accepting his offer.

But what about Franco? She thought a minute and quickly came to her own conclusion. *Never mind about him, nothing to worry about there. I've always taken on various business ventures without him knowing, and this would just be another one of those ventures.*

She decided to go see Reginald at once and take him up on his offer.

When she arrived at his store, he was rearranging one of his display shelves. It was almost as if he was expecting her. They glanced at one another, but did not exchange words. Then Mamma Mia held out her hand to him and pressed it tightly. Reginald felt a twinge. She said calmly and quietly:

"In back of my house, under the big maple tree I will be waiting for you, ten o'clock, tomorrow night."

And that's where they met the next night on the dot. A soft breeze wafted from the sky and from a neighboring house there came the sound of a television. The full moon dipped behind a clump of clouds and the stars came out in full profusion. They decided to get down to business right away.

When they lay down it was cool, then it became hot. Reginald was amazed by Mamma Mia's gentleness and softness and her skin was moist like a spring rain. He was aroused beyond end and he inhaled the fragrance of her well-padded body, a mixture of cheap perfume and chicken parmesan, a meal she had prepared for her family before setting out. Her big form moved slowly beneath him full of energy, and she didn't in the least seem burdened by the weight of her flesh. Sexually she awakened him and he couldn't help but show great emotion. She was so wild and untamed. When he undressed her, he whispered in her ear, "What lovely thighs you have." Never had he seen thighs so ample.

But the question remained, how did Mamma Mia feel about Reginald? She found the whole act offensive, like a bad dream, his little feet, his little arms, his little legs on top of her, digging into her flesh. How could she ever have permitted this to happen? The entire time, in the dark, with her eyes closed, she was pretending, pretending not to be with him but with someone else. But with who? Randomly, she chose a hunk out of one of her favorite Italian soap operas. Yes, that would do the trick! She was with Enrico, and with images of Enrico it was all so splendid, so magnificent. It was because of Enrico she was getting hotter and more fired up. She even went so far as to let out shrieks of ecstasy. She called out his name, *Enrico! Enrico!* which, sadly, Reginald mistook for *Eureka! Eureka!*

Reginald, for his part, was in a world of his own. He took Mamma Mia with great intensity, kissing her mouth, her breasts, all the while gasping for breath. The heat of his body increased. He pounded her and pounded her, yes, he did, and then there came the explosion. What a man he was! What a man!

When it was all over Mamma Mia lay there a moment hardly able to breathe. Enrico was gone and suddenly the vague dreadful reality set in: she had just done it with Reginald the street weirdo! Making the sign of the cross, looking up, she cried out, "Please, mother of God, forgive me!"

But mostly she couldn't get over the size of Reginald's penis. Why she barely felt a thing, just a little prick is all. She repeated to herself in Italian, shaking her head, *"Piccolo, piccolo!"*

Then suddenly she started to think and she became distressed, "How on earth am I ever supposed to get pregnant from such a *piccolo* thing? The deal will fall through for sure. I'll end up with nothing." It was not long before another thought set in, and she became distressed even more, "Dear Lord, what if he asks me to do it again?"

Getting up, putting on her dress, Mamma Mia hurried away. Looking down, she ran into her house as fast as she could.

Reginald called after her, "Hey Mamma Mia, where are you going? Oh my, what's going to happen now?"

★

Next morning by a miracle of miracles Mamma Mia woke up nauseous and vomiting. Yes, she was pregnant. She couldn't believe it but it was true.

Franco already knew the signs. Laughing and joking, pounding his chest, he couldn't help but parade around the house, "What a macho man I am! What a macho man! All I have to do is look at my wife and she gets pregnant!"

In exactly nine months to the day Mamma Mia gave birth. But something remarkable happened: she pushed out not one but two babies. She and Reginald had twins, a boy and a girl. They were born quietly one Sunday morning at St. Joseph's Hospital.

Mamma Mia couldn't believe it, "Two babies and from such a *piccolo* thing! Who would have thought?"

Though the babies were on the smallish side and had Reginald's greenish complexion, for the most part, they were the spitting image of Mamma Mia.

Franco, still unaware to everything going on, was thrilled. Twins! He couldn't get over it. He hurried over to the pool hall to brag to his buddies, "My wife just had twins. Now I'm knocking off not one but two babies, next it'll be triplets!"

He ordered a round of drinks.

The twins were named Rocco and Susana. Mamma Mia raised them with Franco, while Reginald watched from afar. Both Mamma Mia and Reginald decided this was for the best. Over the years the arrangement worked well, and most importantly the children were raised in a happy, healthy environment. Franco loved them dearly and couldn't have been a better father. For Reginald, it was enough just to have fathered two children. It overwhelmed him with a new sensation of life, it was more than he could ever have asked for. Now he had not one but two heirs.

But on the street, there was gossip. Everyone wondered how it was Mamma Mia came to afford all those top-of-the-line items for her house, not to mention the brand-new appliances. Her children had more toys than they knew what to do with and their clothes were all of fine quality and brand-names. And Mamma Mia was never strapped for cash anymore either, though her husband hardly worked. The whole thing made no sense.

★

Years passed, sixteen to be exact. Business at Reginald's hardware store thrived. Needing help to keep up with the store's fast pace, Reginald put a help wanted sign in his storefront window. It read as follows: "Two part-time jobs available, stock room and sales. Please apply within."

That same day two young people appeared in the doorway, they looked very much alike, though one was a boy, the other a girl. Reginald recognized them at once, it was Rocco and Susana.

Rocco spoke first. He looked a little anxious, "Hello. We've come to apply for the two jobs. We don't have much experience, especially in hardware, but we're really hard workers and willing to learn."

Susana was the more confident of the two, "In case you don't know who we are, we live down the street from you, on Bank Street. We're Mamma Mia's kids. If you hire us, you won't regret it. We're fast learners and reliable, too."

Reginald stood overwhelmed. Tears came to his eyes but he held them back. His two children were standing before him, Rocco and Susana, and it was all so incredible. Their hair was a light brown, much lighter than his, and their eyes were like their mother's, black and round. And Susana was Mamma Mia over again, the way Mamma Mia had been in her younger days. Reginald saw a glowing light in both their faces. He would have loved to talk freely to them, and as much as he wanted to, he quickly checked himself. It was a secret after all, a promise he had made to Mamma Mia, and he would not break that promise. Their mere presence gave him such pleasure as he had not known in a lifetime. He was transfigured by his love for them and it made him feel extraordinary.

Trying to stay composed, he said at last, "Yes, I'll give both of you a try. Can you start tomorrow after school?"

Reginald couldn't help but lick his lips (his most irritating habit when he was nervous), and then Rocco licked his lips in the same manner. Then Susana croaked by accident, and Reginald croaked too, and suddenly so did Rocco. They all three of them stopped for a moment and glanced at one another as if to ask why they were all there, then they looked away.

As Rocco and Susana made for the door, Reginald called out after them.

"Tomorrow I'll show you the tricks of the trade. I'll teach you everything. Who knows, you might even own a hardware store some day!"

Chapter 9

Christy Throws a Housewarming Party

A block up from Bank Street was a business street, Dundas. The shops there were two stories high and they stood all in a row pressed together as if holding onto one another for support. Some were larger than others but each with a broad wooden door, a generous display window, and a flat tarred roof. Not much had changed on the street in a good twenty years and many of the shops were beginning to show their wear. Most were drab-looking with crumbling plaster sometimes revealing bare lath and almost all had faded and unpleasant paint jobs. There was an Italian bakery, a fish store, a florist, and Maciuk's Smoke Shop, where locals often came to socialize and gossip.

It was rush hour and everywhere was crowded with people, some making a run for the bus, others the streetcar. There was no quiet or peaceful place on Dundas and there always came the clamor of voices. Not a tree or a low-standing bush on which to rest one's eyes could be found anywhere – only concrete and more concrete. Few outsiders ever ventured this way, either they lived there or worked there, or used it as a means of getting from one part of the city to the other. It most certainly wasn't a place to go out of one's way to do shopping or to take a leisurely stroll. But that's not to say it didn't have a certain inner charm, though to appreciate it, one really had to look at it from the inside out.

Having just closed up shop, Reginald hastened down the street. He was feeling rather stiff today. He had restocked too many shelves and had strained his back. It was hard for him to admit but age was catching up to him, and it was only this afternoon he started contemplating hiring a part-time worker, maybe a student, to help with the heavy lifting. He really didn't care to have a stranger around, as he was accustomed to working alone, but he acknowledged the fact it would be difficult to manage otherwise.

Turning down Dufferin, Reginald could hear his footsteps resound on the pavement. With his head bent his mood was somehow more melancholy than usual. There was so little change in his life and it was quite tedious living alone, doing the same thing day in and day out; truth was, it was all getting to him. He was a solitary man going home to a solitary house, where there was nothing but emptiness. If only he had a friend to talk to, like one of those people in the street, maybe that old man he saw going into the bank or that young woman in the flower shop. There were moments he just couldn't bear his loneliness such as now; it was so completely crushing. Though he generally thought he had a grip on things, the truth of the matter was, he really didn't.

When at last he came to Bank Street, he brightened. In about an hour's time, it would be dark enough for him to go out and do what he loved most – spy on people. Spying gave him pleasure and strength to carry on. He was looking forward to seeing what his neighbors might have in store for him tonight.

But there was still that pesky little problem regarding his back. How could he possibly go out with it so sore? Why, even when he tried to straighten himself out, he could hardly manage it. He decided on a long, hot shower. If that didn't do the trick, he didn't know what would. When he got home, going straight upstairs, taking off his clothes, he got into the tub. Turning on the water, it splashed down upon him for five, maybe ten minutes. Slowly but surely his muscles started to feel soothed and the aching left his joints. Before he knew it, he was good as new.

After a quick dinner and a shot of scotch, he stepped out into the street. It was quieter than usual and everything lay in full moonlight. For some reason most of the lights in the houses were off, though he could see televisions and computer screens flickering here and there. A man he didn't recognize passed him by, followed by a woman in a blue dress, then a boy on a skateboard. There came not a sound otherwise. He was disappointed there didn't appear to be much going on.

But then wait a minute, there was some kind of commotion at the end of the street. He craned his neck to get a better look. There seemed to be something going on at Number 3, at that new woman's house, what was her name again, oh, yes, Christy. Christy had moved in a couple of weeks ago with two young children, Jessica and Dawn, but there was no husband, at least not one Reginald had seen. Christy had come into the hardware store the other day looking to buy light bulbs, that's how he came to know her name. She was vey pretty with arched brows, dark absorbing eyes, and a long, slender neck. And there was something captivating about her, which he couldn't explain. He decided on the spot it would be easy for anyone to fall in love with someone like her.

Now in full view of her house, Reginald watched curiously. Several cars pulled up with people emerging, carrying bottles of booze and gift-wrapped parcels of various sizes. The outdoor lights were on and thin colorful paper lanterns with Japanese characters dangled from the veranda.

"It must be a housewarming party," thought Reginald. He loved parties, all kinds, and they always put him in a good mood.

Sneaking round back to where the living room was, through one of the open windows, he could hear noise and animated conversation. Several guests were sitting on a rather large clumsy sofa nibbling on bite-sized sandwiches, while others stood sipping wine from crystal glasses. The lights were turned down low and the air was filled with high-end perfumes. Afro-Cuban jazz played in the background.

"But Christy, where was Christy?" Reginald ventured to look through an upper pane.

And finally, there she was standing by the door with some youngish-looking man in a well-fitted suit and black cowboy boots. Reginald noticed the man had a bright red handkerchief stuck in his upper left jacket pocket. Given the grin on his face, clearly, he was out to impress.

"What a dandy!" thought Reginald. "And so conceited-looking!"

By the look on Christy's face it was obvious she was having a good time, and she was even being a little flirtatious, and the man was being flirtatious back. They were being much too close for comfort Reginald decided and he couldn't help but disapprove. What about Christy's husband? He listened to what they were saying. They were both a little tipsy.

"Come on, tell me," this was the dandy. "It's about your husband, isn't it? Something's up and I think it's important."

"No, I don't want to spoil it."

"What are you saying?"

"Oh, my, what am I saying? I'm saying all I want is another drink. It makes me happy, so very happy."

Christy was a remarkably attractive woman. With her flowing black hair, high, almost Slavic-looking cheekbones, and full red mouth, she was unlike anyone at the party. Though her complexion was pale it was a healthy pale and made her look younger than her thirty-odd years. She was wearing a black dress that fit like a glove, a lot of jewelry, and makeup. Downing more booze, it was apparent she was being greatly affected by it.

Exchanging a few more words with the dandy, with bottle in hand, she stumbled to the middle of the room. She stood there several minutes, teetering, scanning her guests. With her eyes contracting and her features broadening, she looked as if about to speak. Everyone wanted to hear what she had to say, and they suspected it had something to do with her so-far absent husband. She stamped her foot for attention. Her voice was slurred.

"Welcome friends, welcome to my new home, but let me tell you something first. The more I drink the more sober I become. I bet none of you can make a claim like that. The drink doesn't make me angry; no, it makes me happy, it makes me so happy all I want to do is sing. La, la, la … Come on everybody sing along with me."

A few sang but most were puzzled and had no idea what was going on with her; some were embarrassed. Christy was not known to be a drinker.

She continued, "You're all probably wondering about my housewarming party. I hope you're having a good time. Do you like my new house? Please, don't be afraid to speak up. Yes? No? No need to pretend. Well, I know what you're all thinking – it's a real shithole. You're probably asking yourselves, what sort of place did poor old Christy come to? The ceilings are low, the rooms are small and narrow, the wallpaper is tacky, and yes, the floor is, oh, gasp, linoleum. But you know what? I don't care because I like it here; actually, no, I *love* it here. And my neighbors are wonderful people, just wonderful. For example, I love that Maria sings to her plants in the evenings; that Augusto's rooster wakes me up every morning; that Elivra brings me leftover cod with boiled potatoes because she thinks I'm too skinny. I wouldn't give up my new place for anything in the entire world."

Stopping a moment, dropping her head, she buried her face in her hands. She started to cry, "Oh, boo hoo, poor me, what on earth am I saying! What? What? What, I ask. Oh, the truth is, I'm lying to you; it's all just a big act. I hate it here; I absolutely hate it. Anyway, there's no going back for me now – never, ever."

The guests looked puzzled.

"What's going on with you, Christy?" a friend from work wanted to know; the two often ate lunch together and sometimes caught a movie in the evening. "What do you mean, *never, ever?*"

Christy seemed to be having a hard time articulating. The drink was making her head spin. "My physical and mental states are in complete ruin, and the problem is I can't seem to find a way to move forward."

"Move forward?" another guest asked. "Tell us what's going on, maybe we can help."

"Help? Hah, hah, hah! And yes, something is going on but I can't tell you because it's really private; it's so private that I've kept it a secret. Even my kids don't know, at least not yet. They're with their grandparents now. But they'll know soon enough, maybe even in the morning."

"What on earth are you talking about?"

Christy downed more booze and stared at the floor, "Okay, I'll tell you but you have to listen carefully. I guess you've all noticed my husband Jeremy's not here tonight. Well, he's not here because I despise him, I despise him more than words can say; no, I detest him, I abhor him! I used to love him, at least I thought I did, and now I hate him. It's all because of him that my life's been turned upside down. He's ruined everything."

"Oh!" a forty-something woman clasped her chest, obviously deeply affected by the news. Then looking round, her voice in a singsong, "This smells like an affair coming to me."

But the friend from work wanted solid answers: "Is there someone else, Christy? Did Jeremy cheat on you? Is that it? But he never seemed the type."

Christy broke into a paroxysm. The dandy rushed to her side with a box of tissues.

"But I loved and trusted him. I even married for love and he said he loved me. And now what does he go and do? Yes, that's right, he betrayed me."

"You poor dear!" the friend from work was full of sympathy.

"Yes, it's true. He admitted to me he loved someone else."

The guests, now on the edge of their seats, tried to take it all in.

A former schoolmate of Christy's, who herself had been cheated on, couldn't help but jump in, "Men! So typical – it doesn't surprise me one bit. Your Jeremy's no better than my Leonard. I bet just like my Leonard Jeremy found a twenty-something bimbo and lost his head over her. And I bet she's a blonde too." Then looking round, raising her brows, "Aren't they always?"

Christy was in distress. "Oh, why did I tell you my secret? I should have kept quiet; it's all too much! Now you all know, but you don't know everything; you only know the half of it."

"Only the half of it?" the guests were now in full suspense.

But the friend from work ignored the fact that there was still another half to consider. She was quick to voice her own conclusion: "I know who the other woman is; it's Chantelle, that woman Jeremy works with. I've seen them around together going for lunch, laughing, chatting away. I thought it was kind of strange. Is it Chantelle?" Then answering her own question, "Of course it's Chantelle, who else can it be?"

The others felt sorry for Christy and then they all fessed up, "Yes, it's Chantelle. We've seen them together too and more than once. We've stayed mum about it because we didn't want to stir things up."

Christy was now crying vehemently, she was almost hysterical, "Oh shut up! Shut up, all of you, just shut up! You're all wrong! It's not Chantelle, okay; it's not Chantelle! It never was Chantelle and it never will be Chantelle because it's … it's … it's Bernard. He left me for Bernard! Now you know all of it."

There came a collective gasp. No one said a word because no one saw it coming.

The schoolmate got up but her face was red and she was looking very vexed. With her hands were on her hips she said aloud. "Bernard, do you mean the same Bernard I recommended to you, the artist who's painting your daughters' portraits? Dear God, you mean Jeremy's having an affair with Bernard?" Then unable to hide her disgust, "But Bernard's barely twenty! You'd think Jeremy would have at least had the decency to find someone his own age. Men! Didn't I tell you?"

Silence fell over the room, not even a whisper.

Christy started again, but this time quietly, barely audibly, "What can I say, I've been had; I had no clue. My life for the last twelve years has been a lie, a big fat lie. Nothing was real. Even the children were conceived from a lie. Oh, how I don't deserve this!"

One of the guests, a rather corpulent woman in a bright yellow dress and hoop earrings listened with keen interest. Her face looked as if made of butter. She didn't appear very sympathetic to Christy's story, instead, she seemed to be deriving a kind of guilty pleasure from it all. As it turned out, she had always been jealous of Christy who had everything – the perfect life, the perfect body, the perfect husband, kids, job, a beautiful home. For fear of betraying her secret feelings, feigning a smile, she cried out as if she meant it, "But Christy, you poor dear, this is all so impossible!"

Christy heaved a sigh, "He duped me, what more can I say? Yes, I've been duped. But he duped himself too because deep down he knew the truth."

"Well, at least he wasn't a womanizer!" someone shouted, as if that would help.

"But I would have felt the same way if he had left me for a woman. Betrayal is betrayal. He may just as well have been a womanizer. Now because of him, I've lost my trust in men, all men, and not just the gay ones."

"However are you coping?" a man asked.

"How am I coping? Not very well! But I'm trying to look at it from his perspective. I now know he'd been struggling with his sexuality since boyhood. And then in high school, he came up with this notion that marriage would 'fix' him. That's where I came in. Honestly, he never appeared gay to me and I had a few gay friends – maybe I just didn't want to see it. But he was just too good-looking for me to pass him up and we looked so good together. Then we got married.

"Anyway, a few months ago he started acting strange. He was becoming more and more detached and more withdrawn into himself. Even the girls noticed it. I guess it's because he denied it to himself for so long, he was having trouble facing the truth. I never really knew him because he was always someone else. And now he's happy. He looks different, he dresses differently, and he even colored his hair and added highlights. He looks good; actually, he never looked better. One thing's for sure, he never looked that good for me."

Christy was now pacing the room. She lit a cigarette. "That's why I had to move out of our big house. I found this little property because that's all I could afford. Believe it or not, I don't even have a garage; I have to park out on the street, if I can even find a spot. This neighborhood's so crowded, the houses are close together and a lot of them are connected. And the people are all from someplace else like Italy or Eastern Europe, but mostly Portugal. 'Little Portugal' is what they call it. When they go to work the men wear drab-looking clothes and carry these strange tin lunch pails and the women are forever in coarse cotton dresses with kerchiefs on their heads. And the air smells like cod-fish all the time and this cod-fish has a name, it's called *bac... bacal ... bacalhau*. But I hate the taste; I absolutely hate it even though I've tried liking it. I'm here in this godforsaken place because I have no choice.

"But the good news is there appear to be changes coming: a couple of cafes opened up on Dundas, the Lula Lounge has been up and running a few years now, and there's an old hotel over on Gladstone that's been refitted for studios. They say the neighborhood is on the up and up. Change is always good and for me that's more than good, especially if it means no more *bacalhau*!"

The guests sat listening with keen interest.

It was not long before Christy went back to her troubles, "I'll never forgive him, never! I'm in so much pain! He's ruined everything! We put our house up for sale; it's completely emptied. Jeremy moved in with Bernard to a condo downtown overlooking the lake. It's a pretty big place, apparently, and Bernard's taken one of the rooms and designed it for when the girls are over. It's supposed to be beautiful, absolutely beautiful."

Pausing briefly, when she started up again it was as if to herself. A dreamy look came to her eyes and she was smiling slightly, "Oh, but that Bernard, what a good-looking fellow he is, and so sweet. Just looking at him sends shivers up my spine. And the body on him, you wouldn't believe. So big, so strong, nothing but solid muscle. Hot, hot, hot! Jeremy's one lucky man. I'm so jealous. Oh, dear god, what am I saying? Really!"

Studying her glass, several minutes, finally she added, "To be honest, I don't know what I would do without all this booze."

The friend from work tried to help ease things, "This is all so fresh for you right now, Christy. Time will heal. You'll see. Maybe you and Jeremy will even become friends again."

"Friends?" Christy laughed. "Wouldn't that be lovely! Because that's all we ever were to each other anyhow, except I didn't know it."

The clock struck midnight. The guests called it a night. Gathering their belongings and giving Christy hugs of reassurance, they made for the door. As the co-worker friend passed the food table, she popped a couple of pastries puffs into her mouth, and the corpulent woman grabbed a handful of spring rolls and stuffed them into her bag. After everyone was gone, only the dandy remained.

"Good grief," Christy lifted her arms and swept back her shoulder-length hair. "Letting it all out didn't help the way I thought it would. Oh, I was wrong, so wrong to go on about my problems tonight. It just made things worse. Now I have this horrible sick feeling inside of me."

The dandy rubbed her back and stroked her head. He said softly, "Sh ... now don't start up again. You have to be strong. You'll get through this."

Sitting her on the sofa, he settled next to her. He reached out and touched her hand and she touched him touching her with her other hand.

The dandy moved closer. Running his fingers along her cheeks, the bridge of her nose, her mouth, it was obvious he wanted to make love to her. And he knew she wanted to make love to him too. They were both so drunk that when their limbs suddenly touched, they both stifled a cry.

Reginald, still looking on could feel his heart throb. He wanted to bang on the pane, to warn Christy, "No, don't fall for it, Christy! You're vulnerable right now; he's just a dandy! You'll only regret it. He's not like me!"

Then there came whispering followed by smothered laughter. The dandy was touching Christy all over and she was touching him back. They were up, moving toward the staircase, they were already on the first step, then the second, and now they were half way. There was no stopping them now. Through a window upstairs Reginald could see a light flicker. He could hear Christy screaming with laughter and delight.

If only he could make Christy see that the drink was giving her a lapse in judgement, that the Dandy was taking advantage of the situation. Looking round he noticed a trellis up against the wall, and as luck would have it, it led straight up to the window in question. Good thing it didn't look too rickety; he could easily climb it. He would go up there and try and stop whatever it was going on. But after only a few steps up, at once there came a sharp pain in his back and it shot straight up to his neck.

"Damn, what a time for that to start up again!"

Heading back down, when he hit the ground he did so with a bit of a thud.

He had no choice but to call it quits. With the night gloomy under a blackened sky, he headed for home. He couldn't stop thinking of Christy. He'd give anything to have a woman like that. If only he could be with her, touch her, caress her. But it was the dandy who was there with her and not him. It wasn't fair, life wasn't fair.

Already in his house, Reginald made himself a cup of tea. He was in love with Christy, he decided, and he would let her know it. He was not about to give up so easily. That he didn't stand a chance with her was the farthest thing from his mind. He loved everything about her, the movement of her mouth, the tilt to her head, the way she pointed her litter finger in the air. Thinking what to do, suddenly a plan came to mind and it came in such detail, he even knew what Christy would say and do and how she would respond. This is how it would all play out.

In the morning, once the dandy was long gone, he would return to Christy's house and properly introduce himself. He would say to her and in the friendliest way, "Hello, my name is Reginald Rutley. We met briefly the other day at my hardware store, and I live a few doors down at number 25. Welcome to Bank Street."

Then he would present her with flowers from his garden, which she would graciously accept. After a bit of small talk, she would invite him in and over drinks she would tell him all her troubles. She would begin with Jeremy, her husband, who left her for a man, and she would go on to say it was because of him she had come to live on Bank Street. (Of course, he, Reginald would hem and haw and pretend he didn't know a thing when in reality he already knew everything.) She would then start to cry and her chest would heave with emotion, and he would feel compelled to hug her, console her. She would see that he was sincere and caring, that he was the better man. Even though he did not have the dandy's good looks or swagger, he had heart and it was heart that would win her over. And in such a way, she would come to love him the way he loved her.

Reginald saw this as the perfect plan, a plan he would execute first thing in the morning. He hadn't experienced this kind of strength of will in a long time and he was beyond excited. He was about to let loose and let his passions reign.

Chapter 10

The Wet Dream

Reginald tossed and turned all night; he got almost no sleep. Warm, tingly spasms ran throughout his body non-stop and it couldn't have been a more pleasant feeling. It created within him a kind of frenzied ecstasy, something he wasn't used to experiencing. A big smile was on his face and it stretched from ear to ear.

As it happened, it was all because of Christy. He could hardly believe it but it was true, she was in his room with him, and not only with him in his room but with him in his bed, and she was naked. So excited was he by her presence, every moment felt a thrill. She was everything that was beautiful, and as unthinkable as it sounded, he was in the position of taking her at any time. Sliding his fingers down the back of her white flesh, kissing her mouth, her neck, he then fondled her perfectly rounded breasts. She was an intimate being to him and he loved her more than anything. He became lost to himself in looking at her.

Christy in turn lavished seductive smiles his way and nibbled away at his ears. She didn't seem to mind that his hair was thinning or that he had ugly features or that he was a person of diminutive stature. Surprisingly, she didn't consider him objectionable at all. On the contrary, she saw him as someone with a unique kind of allure, an allure that came from the inside out. She drew him to her and buried her face against his chest.

Reginald could feel himself throbbing and pulsating. His penis was growing big and hard. He climbed on top of her and suddenly it was as if all the blood in his body was rushing down to his man-parts. There came a gentle aching sensation followed by a great build-up of pressure. He thrust his penis inside her and then he thrust into her again and again. After several minutes, there came the profound beating in his genitals followed by a dull twinge in his neck and head. It was like something out of this world! What a performance he was putting on! He was on fire! Finally, it came: the explosion. And he could feel Christy's vagina going into spasm and orgasm as she kicked and screamed with rapture beneath him.

And then it was all over. Reginald lay for several minutes, gasping, sweating, trying to catch his breath. He couldn't believe this had happened to him of all people. Sex with Christy. But it didn't make sense. He gave himself a shake. Looking round he became confused. Christy, where was Christy?

"Christy!" he called out.

There came no answer.

"Christy! Christy!"

And suddenly it struck him. Christy was not there and neither had she been there. He was alone. It was then that a stickiness came on his pajama bottoms against his skin. A disagreeable sensation passed over him. It had all been just a dream, a wet dream. But the colors and shapes had been so vivid, her arms, her legs, her breasts, it had all impressed so heavily on his system.

Reginald became feverish and his body trembled. He hid his face in his hands. Only blackness remained, it was everywhere, and it led to more blackness. His existence was not a joyous one, it was all just pretend. He could never be happy just pretending. Never ever. Would he ever find a way? Taking off his bottoms, rolling over onto his side, he tried to get some sleep.

Chapter 11

Elevator Shoes

In spite of Reginald's rough night, he chose to go ahead with his rather daring plan of going to see Christy that morning. He would tell her how he felt, how much he loved her even though he hardly knew her. From his heart there came such a burning intensity, and he would be damned if he would continue to deny himself his sensual needs. He would not stifle any passionate reaction anymore; he had done so for too long and now he was ready to go all out. His world would be his own. Living with fear and no hope was now a thing of the past, he decided.

As he set out along the sidewalk, the air was fine and fresh, and there was a slight breeze coming in from the north. Birds chirruped monotonously somewhere nearby and pigeons cooed in the trees. There was a scent of damp earth and freshly mowed grass and then there came a whiff of roses. He took it all in. Thinking he heard a sound he paused to take a look. Around the edge of a fence a chained dog's head peered out, shorn to look like a lion. Then the sound of church bells started up from St. Helen's, as they did every Sunday morning. He kept on. Under his arm he carried a small bouquet of lavender from his garden. Though his nerves were on edge, somehow the early morning sun calmed and invigorated him. He was feeling cavalier.

But at the same time there were fights going on inside his head and he was as if on a battlefield: "This is crazy, what am I doing going to Christy's? I can't go there. She'll never accept me such as I am. And what if the dandy is still with her? No, it's almost ten o'clock, he's probably gone. Still, if I had any sense I'd turn round right now and go back home."

No sooner had he thought this thought there came another to counter it: "If there's ever a time I should be going to Christy's it's now. I'm feeling up to form, and all things considered, I'm looking as good as I'll ever look."

And indeed, he was looking quite dapper. He had on his best shirt, the one made from Egyptian cotton, his good-luck tie, and, not to forget, his custom-made elevator shoes that gave him a three-inch lift. For a brief moment he actually saw his wild and passionate dreams being realized, so caught up was he in his thinking.

He would stick to his plan he decided. He would knock on Christy's door and he would say to her what he had practiced all morning.

"Good morning, Christy. You look lovely. We met briefly at my hardware store the other day when you came in to buy light bulbs; I'd like to welcome you into the neighborhood with this bouquet of lavender. It's not so bad once you get to know it, the neighborhood, that is, though it's forever changing. And the changes I've seen, you wouldn't believe. Firstly ..."

Then realizing what he was saying, slapping his forehead, he rebuked himself, "Stop it, you fool! You're just babbling on. The neighborhood? Forever changing? Are you kidding? You sound like an idiot. She's going to slam the door right in your face."

As he walked, he continued having a full-out conversation with himself, nodding, gesticulating, making faces. A young couple coming down the street gave him a strange look. Who was this funny-looking little man? They took him for either a drunk or a patient from the mental health facility down on Queen Street.

Nearing Christy's house Reginald slowed his pace. He watched the shadows fall from the lacy green of the trees in her garden and hit upon her rooftop. Her windows were all shaded, though some were half open. The sun was already well up the horizon and he could feel its increasing warmth as it shone on him from behind.

This was the moment he'd been waiting for. All he needed was to stay calm and make a good impression. He would knock on her door and if she wouldn't answer he would knock again. But what if she didn't answer at all, then what? No, of course she would answer, she had to because she was clearly at home. Her green sedan was parked right there in front of her house.

He quickly went over his plan for the last time. This is how it would pan out.

She would see him standing at the door with the lavender bouquet and she would be thrilled; lavender was her favorite she would say, and then she would tell him how it reminded her of the south of France, where she once went on holiday. She would invite him in and make tea, maybe offer him a bite to eat. She would chatter on about this and that, and then she would break down and confess to him that her life was in ruins, that her husband had left her for a man. Being the needy type, she would throw herself into his arms and thank him for listening and understanding. She was alone and he was alone and they could be alone together. And it wouldn't bother her that his hair was thinning or that he was a little person or that he sometimes wore elevator shoes. Then he'd make his move and kiss her on the mouth to which, of course, she'd make no objection. In return she would kiss his cheeks, his neck, his ears, then tickle him, and throw her arms around him. She would sway with him to all sides and take him to places he'd never been.

At once there came the sound of a door slamming. Reginald wakened as if from a dream. His eyes landed on Christy's veranda, still with the hanging Japanese paper lanterns from the night before. She emerged from her house in a great hurry and was making for the sidewalk.

But where was she going? It wasn't supposed to happen like this. That's not how he had planned it. She was supposed to stay in the house and wait for him to call, she was not supposed to pop out like that. He felt frazzled.

Wearing a loose-fitting dress and big round sunglasses, Christy looked like a movie star. Reginald took a step back. He felt awkward standing there in front of her house, all dressed up with a bouquet of lavender, and in elevator shoes. But where could she possibly be going? Then he realized she must be on her way to pick up her children – he could have kicked himself for not having factored that possibility into the equation. He worried about what to do next. He did his best to keep up his nerve.

Christy started for her car; keys jingled in her hand. Seeing Reginald standing there she stared at him inquisitively and wondered who he might be. Such an unhandsome little man and with such an unpleasant countenance. Where did he even come from? She examined his attire with very little tact and soon her face expressed a kind of disapproval. Though she didn't recognize him, at the same time she felt she'd seen him someplace before. But where? She had forgotten about her visit to the hardware store the other day, about buying light bulbs. Then her face softened and suddenly she remembered. She said aloud, "Oh, yes, you're that little fellow from down the street, and if I'm not mistaken, you run the hardware store up on Dundas. I remember you now, your name is, um, um ... "

Reginald's heart fluttered. He stood there emitting funny little noises that were short, raspy, and sounded frog-like. He cleared his throat.

"Reginald, my name is Reginald."

"Oh, yes, Reginald."

Reginald didn't know what to do next. He couldn't have been more uncomfortable. He had to find a way to get out of there and fast before she put two and two together. "She'll figure out that I came here to see her, that the lavender was meant for her, and that what I really had in mind extended far beyond a simple welcome to the neighborhood. She'll see my true intentions in no time."

Deciding to make a run for it, quite unexpectedly there came a loud noise from the side of her house. What on earth was that? Reginald looked over his shoulder. *Oh, no, not the dandy, he's still here!* Reginald stood in helpless expectation of something terrible and inevitable – things had just gone from bad to worse. The dandy would see him and read into him right away, he would notice his Egyptian cotton shirt, the bouquet, the cologne, and then he would look down at his elevator shoes. It was the shoes that would give him away! Panic set in. Nothing was turning out the way it was supposed to.

When the dandy came to the sidewalk and saw Reginald standing there frightened, quivering, and gasping for breath, sure enough, it did not take long for him to figure everything out. Looking him over, he thought he'd have himself a bit of fun. Embracing Christy vigorously, running his hands down her backside and giving her a long, passionate kiss on the mouth, from the corner of his eye he watched Reginald, who was clearly in pain. He then whispered something into Christy's ear, as though the two had secrets, and together they laughed and they went on laughing.

Then the dandy said to Christy but really meant for Reginald to hear, "How peculiar that little man is. I think he likes you. Imagine him having the hots for someone like you. And get a load of his shoes! Hah, hah, hah!"

Getting into Christy's car, rolling down the windows, they turned the radio on full blast. They drove off. With the wind in their hair, it took them all but a minute to forget about the peculiar little man standing there in elevator shoes.

Reginald was unable to move and the color had long since gone from his face. A wall of darkness had pressed in from all sides and now it was crushing him. He was a phantom man, nothing more.

And he blamed it all on those idiotic shoes. Why did he have to go and put them on anyway? He thought Christy would have needed him for support, for friendship but she was so cruel, so abusive, mocking him together with the dandy. He was angry with himself; he had acted like a clown. Her snub was too hard to endure. Did she even know about the degree of anguish she was capable of? Did she understand the power of her beauty? A bitter hatred for her suddenly passed through him and for the dandy too, and it wouldn't go away.

As Reginald started for home, he tried to regain himself, but he simply couldn't. He fell into an even deeper slump. Not noticing anything along the way, not the trees, not the houses, not the gardens, he felt humiliated and he couldn't shake himself free of the feeling. Several people passed him by, a man, a couple of women, some teenagers. He wanted but one thing: to get inside his house as quickly as possible and to hide himself.

He would never be able to look Christy in the face again. And what if she happened by his hardware store? This only further added to his anxiety. Dropping the bouquet of lavender on his front lawn, rushing into his house, without even taking off his elevator shoes, he ran upstairs to his room and threw himself on the bed. He felt a nervous attack coming on. Everything started flashing before his eyes and so vividly, and it played itself out again and again. He hated himself more than ever.

When several minutes passed, at once the sun hit his window and his room became flooded with sunshine. Sitting up, with a warmth upon his face, somehow, he started to feel revived, invigorated even. True, the morning had been a disaster but now early afternoon he was starting to feel an unexpected triumph. He broke into a sudden laugh but it was an ironic laugh.

"The joke's on Christy. I'm not the big loser here – no, not by a long shot. Her husband dumps her for a man, and now all she's got going for her is that arrogant self-serving dandy. They deserve each other! Hah, hah, hah!"

Chapter 12

Lily's Antiques

Near the corner of Dundas and Dufferin Streets not far from Reginald's hardware store there was a small, dumpy looking shop called Lily's Antiques. It wasn't really an antique shop but a shop selling junk and miscellaneous ware. Lily's Antiques was called that because Lily, the owner, thought it would do a better job in pulling in more high-end crowds than would say, Lily's Junk Shop. In the display window were mismatched cups and saucers, large, awkward ceramic vases, and a lot of fake jewelry, including bracelets, pins, rings, and earrings. When one walked through the door, to the left was a pile of worn-out shoes and next to it a couple of empty boxes. There was nothing of value in the shop but that's not to say from time to time Lily didn't luck out on something precious like a piece of bone china or even crystal. Then she would proudly showcase the item either on the counter by the cash register or in the window. But whatever Lily had for sale, junk or not, she was always honest and fixed a fair price.

Well into her sixties, Lily was a diminutive woman with sharp eyes and chin and a nose that was long and firm. As a rule she spoke little, even to her customers, though she was friendly enough. Her English was heavily accented and she sounded as if from Eastern Europe, maybe Poland or Russia. Normally, she wore some loose-fitting shirt of one color and a plain skirt. Her hair was gray with still a bit of brown here and there and her dark brows were arched. On the left side of her chin was a small mole she had had since birth though now it had little hairs growing out of it, which she sometimes plucked. She was an attractive woman in a strange sort of way however her face was pale and mournful. Usually she sat behind the counter, looking as if trying to forget the past.

Her husband's name was Larry, but instead of being called Larry in the way that Lily was called Lily, Larry preferred to be called Mr. Himmel. Though Mr. Himmel had big round eyes, a head full of hair, and a face that was broad and pleasant, often he looked bewildered, as if barely conscious of the things around him. He was more talkative than his wife but not by much, and when he talked it was mostly small talk – about the weather, about business, or about his granddaughter, Claire, who was away at an art and design college. He especially liked to talk about his nephew, Aaron, and this is what he would say about him.

"My nephew Aaron is a big movie producer. He lives in Hollywood now, changed his name from Himmel to Hamilton and married a famous movie star."

Though it was all true, most who heard the story didn't believe him, they even laughed in his face. But that didn't stop Mr. Himmel from telling it again.

Generally, Mr. Himmel left the running of the shop to his wife; however, once or twice a week he drove around town in his black Buick looking for inventory. One day he came back with an unbelievably good find – a vintage accordion and in excellent condition. The keys were a bone white and the body a pearl-black. He was excited as he met his wife.

"Lily, look what I found, and it was just sitting there on someone's front lawn! It even had a sign on it that said 'Hohner, free to good home'. So, I took it."

Lily clasped her chest, "Oh my, an accordion! It looks hardly used, too. I'm going to put it in the window right away. I'm sure I can get a good price for it."

As Lily just barely started clearing an area, that's when Reginald happened along the sidewalk. Due to slow traffic in his hardware store that day, he decided to close up early. When he saw Lily with the accordion, at first, he didn't think anything of it but when she shoved it closer to the pane, he couldn't help but take notice.

"Well, I'll be!" he fumbled in his pocket for his glasses. "A vintage Hohner, and it looks like it's from the 1940s! And in such good shape!"

Reginald was more than familiar with the instrument because back in high school his music teacher had had one just like it, and he remembered its smooth, rich tone and perfect pitch. He even recalled playing it.

Lily turned to her husband eagerly, "Larry! Larry! I think we have a buyer already! It's Reginald. He's looking straight into the window; it seems like he's really interested. Oh, my, now he's coming into the store!"

"Reginald?" Mr. Himmel, who was eating gefilte fish from a jar, raised his brows, "Do I know Reginald?"

"You know Reginald, of course, you know Reginald, that little hunchback from the hardware store a few doors down. His parents, poor souls, were killed a while back in that horrible car crash, it was in all the papers."

"Oh, yes, Reginald. Now I know who you mean. And you say he plays the accordion?"

"Yes, he plays the accordion. Why else would he be interested in it? He used to be in that funny-sounding band, what was it called again? Cabbage something or other. The band played jazz, and one time over on Bank Street I even heard them play klezmer music but with a jazz variant."

"Klezmer music? Jazz and klezmer together? Interesting. So, Reginald's Jewish?"

"No, he's not Jewish, he's Irish, but he plays klezmer music."

"An Irishman playing klezmer music?" Mr. Himmel couldn't wrap his head around it.

Reginald was already in the store and looking round inquisitively. Though he and Lily had both been business owners on Dundas Street for years, Reginald had rarely entered Lily's shop, as the items she carried did not much interest him. The same went for Lily unless she was in need of a flashlight or maybe a water kettle or a hammer. The two did, however, readily greet each other on the street, though it hardly ever went beyond a polite "hello" or "how do you do."

"Good day, Lily," Reginald said as he came up to the counter. "I noticed you have an accordion in the window. It's kind of big and looks almost too heavy for me, but I couldn't resist. May I have a look at it?"

It took Lily barely a minute to retrieve the box-shaped instrument. Hoping to make a sale, she slid her fingers softly along the bellows, "If I may say so myself, this is a fine accordion indeed."

"Yes," Reginald agreed, "it certainly is. Mind if I try it out?"

Carefully strapping it to his chest, with his short stubby fingers he hit a few random keys. He then started up on a melody that was joyous and full of emotion. It happened to be a klezmer tune, one which he had played many times when he'd been with the Cabbagetown Jazz Band. 'Kona Hora', he knew it by heart but this time for some reason when he played it, he played it without the jazz element. With his left foot tapping away, closing his eyes, the tune filled the little shop. He played it like it was meant to be played, like a human voice, laughing and crying all at once. The sound couldn't have been more uplifting but he played it like an Irishman.

Lily was impressed with his musicianship. She listened quietly. Leaning heavily with her elbows on the counter, she fell as if to reminiscing. She half closed her eyes. She seemed miles away and drew a deep sigh. It had been years since she'd heard 'Kona Hora'. Looking over at her husband, she saw the music too was weighing heavily on him. Somehow, he appeared to have disappeared in the faint light.

Reginald's playing only grew in intensity and before long it poured out into the street. It caught the attention of a few passersby who couldn't help but venture inside. So moved were they by the music they started tapping their feet, clapping, and humming along.

Reginald continued as if passing from one world into another. So immersed was he in the music, he forgot completely where he was.

But then he caught Lily's face and he saw she was looking frightened. Something was up with her; she was quivering and her chest was heaving as if from suffocation. The music, it seemed, was leaving some kind of strange impression on her mind. He stopped playing at once. He said to her with concern, "I'm sorry, Lily, but is it my playing that's upsetting you?"

A certain constraint fell over the shop. Lily sat down, got up, then sat down again on her stool. She tried to raise her eyes but then turned pale and grave. She opened her mouth but did not speak.

Feeling awkward, Reginald thought it best for him to leave. He would pay for the accordion and be on his way. Digging into his pocket for his wallet, at once, from the corner of his eye, he noticed Lily's lips move in an unusual way, as if there was something she wanted to say. She began quietly.

"Yes, 'Kona Hora'... I must admit you play it beautifully. It was very popular where I come from – Warsaw, in Poland. I haven't heard it in years. It was played at all the joyful celebrations, at weddings, birthdays, bar mitzvahs. But then one day everything stopped."

Reginald was quite taken aback at Lily's sudden willingness to talk, especially to him. But at the same time, as she went on, it was as if she wasn't really talking to him but to herself.

"That's when war broke out and Germany invaded Poland. Mr. Himmel and I had just got married. It was not long after that the Warsaw ghetto was formed. Along with other Jews, over four hundred thousand of us, we were forced to live in a tiny area of the city because we were Jews. A walled fence with barbed wire went up and anyone who tried to escape got shot. We were put on near-starvation diets. I scoured the streets for potato peels. We were all given yellow Stars of David to wear on the left side of our chests.

Lily wrung her hands and she looked as if afraid to say more. But a minute later her face suddenly changed and her eyes lit up slightly as though she had just thought of something quite different.

"About the ghetto, there was also a thriving underground movement of culture – there was poetry, art, and theater. That kept us going. There was even a symphony orchestra and the orchestra played 'Kona Hora'. Only by then it had become a different kind of 'Kona Hora', not the happy, festive 'Kona Hora' of my younger days."

Reginald listened to Lily and glanced at her often while she talked. He could see there was a misery tearing at her heart and he braced himself to face something terrible and unknown. He wasn't used to people opening themselves up to him in this manner, and clearly opening up was something new for Lily as well. He waited patiently for her to continue.

"Things just got worse, much worse. And when I think back on that awful time it is simply unreal, I can't believe it really happened. And how it plays on the psyche long afterward! There was a guard by the name of Hans Schreiber and I remember he had a wad of yellow hair and the coldest darkest eyes. He was all smiles but his smiles were full of malevolence and mockery. One day he had a big announcement to make.

"'Attention everybody! Attention!' he shouted. 'I have wonderful news! There is a special truck leaving in an hour for the countryside, where there is a newly-built rehabilitation camp. It was made especially with Jews in mind. The first fifty to sign up will have the honor of going. First come first serve. There you will be well-fed, have decent living quarters, and your children will have lots of toys to play with. But as I said, there are only fifty spots, so hurry!'

"People came rushing from all around to sign up, they were so excited, it was too good to be true. Mr. Himmel and I too were eager to get our names on the list and we got in line but we were too far back. We didn't make it. A big truck came round and the lucky fifty boarded. A few women still managed to run back home to get a few personal items such as blankets, extra pairs of shoes, family keepsakes. I remember an elderly man went to fetch a pair of old trousers because he said a man couldn't be caught with only one pair of trousers."

As Lily talked, Reginald suddenly understood the small-built woman before him had secrets, secrets she had kept for years. And now she was letting it all out, and to him no less. He braced himself for what would come next.

"Hans Schreiber was as cold-blooded as he was monsterous. As the truck drove off, he stood there waving. We could hear him laughing, but it was a hard, sinister laugh, and he had to hold onto his belly he was laughing so hard. He shouted after the people, "Yes, you are the lucky fifty! You will be given hearty meals, and you'll have comfortable quarters, too, it'll be a paradise, a regular paradise! *Auf Wiedersehen!* Hah! Hah! Hah!"

Lily paused briefly and when she started up again it was with an anguish that now seemed unbearable. Tears came up.

"A few days later we learned the 'lucky fifty' weren't so lucky after all. They were not taken to any rehabilitation camp as promised but into the woods and shot. First, they were made to dig their own graves."

Dropping her eyes, she fell silent. When she tarted up again, her voice was barely audible, "This is the sort of thing that breaks down the human soul."

The shop became still for maybe a minute. The soft overhead light had obscured Lily's face and she was now only partially visible. She went on.

"And then the day came, it was our turn, mine and Mr. Himmel's. A group of German soldiers stormed into our quarters (we were eight people to a room) and forced me and Mr. Himmel along with others into cattle cars. This time they told us outright we were headed to Treblinka extermination camp. Treblinka II is what it was known as. We were packed like sardines in a can, no room to move, no air to breathe, and buckets for sanitation. In a couple of hours we would all be dead."

Lily slowly got up and walked to look out the window. She was unsteady on her feet.

"This happened at the end of 1942, and I have not really talked to anybody about it but now I want to talk. It's the klezmer music that brought it out, the klezmer music.

"And I want to tell you about Treblinka II and how it was a fake train station with fake train schedules and fake ticket windows. But everyone knew what Treblinka really was. No regular trains ever stopped there only those Treblinka-bound. At Treblinka II were gas chambers and hundreds upon thousands were gassed there. This is how it worked: new arrivals were immediately sent to an undressing area, and then naked, pushed straight to the gas chambers. Men, women, children. My mother, my father, my siblings, nieces, and nephews all died for no reason. They ought to have lived … and the children, they were so young."

Lily's voice suddenly started to change, it was becoming louder, more distinct, but her face remained painfully self-conscious. She raised her head and looked straight at Reginald. It was as if she couldn't herself believe what she was about to say.

"By the will of God, I never made it to Treblinka and neither did Mr. Himmel. Sometimes you discover light in the darkest of places. It was late afternoon; we were all sitting in the dark. The train was traveling full speed. Mr. Himmel noticed something about the wagon door. Someone had left it unlatched and it was open by a crack. Could this be possible? Jiggling it, Mr. Himmel opened it more and incredibly we could see the countryside passing by – houses, fields of wheat, grazing cows. It was like a miracle! He quickly grabbed me by the arm and told me to be brave. We had to jump. He pushed me out and I went flying into the air. He came out after me.

"We were alive, we found each other in the ditch, and we were in one piece. An old Polish farmer, bless his soul, took us in. He was a widower and we lived in his barn till the war's end. I have no idea how or why we managed to survive that horrible day or how we were never found out in that barn. Was someone looking out for us up there? And now I can only be grateful for our blessings, for our everyday life. Mr. Himmel and I have a tranquil and peaceful existence now, that's what we have."

Reginald's face worked with emotion. About to say something, he could not bring out the first word. He understood everything Lily had said, about the cruelty, about the brutal slaughter. He knew Lily and her husband had been through the war but he didn't know this. He was stirred to the very depths.

It was time to go, it was getting late. Bidding Lily goodbye, already at the door, suddenly he stopped as if forgetting something. He said aloud.

"The accordion, how could I possibly leave without the accordion? How much would you like for it?"

Lily shook her head. She gazed at him, "No. No money today. Take it, it's yours. It's yours for free."

"Free?" Reginald stood bewildered.

Thanking her, carefully placing the instrument under his arm, he turned away and walked out the door.

As he started along the pavement, it was still light outside but starting to get dark. The klezmer tune played in his mind all the way home.

★

A few weeks passed. When Reginald happened by Lily's shop one day, he found her sweeping the sidewalk.

"Good morning, Lily," he gave a tip to his hat.

"Good morning, Reginald," she said back, pausing to lean on her broom handle. She was curious to know, "And how are things with the accordion? Have you learned any new klezmer tunes lately?"

"Klezmer tunes? Yes, as a matter of fact, I have. I'll come by and play them for you sometime if you like. And how's the antique business?"

Lily's face brightened, "Changes are coming but good changes. My granddaughter, Claire, is visiting from college. She's a student of art and design. She wants to remake my store, make it more modern-looking. A fresh new look will drive more customers, she says. She's already got the plans made up. Maybe we'll start a new trend on Dundas Street, maybe we'll even get fancy."

"Fancy?" Reginald smiled and shook his head. "Fancy, imagine that."

With his hands in his pockets he hurried on his way.

Chapter 13

The Bootlegger

Thirteen is an unlucky number, so when 13 Bank Street was built back in the late 1800s, to give homeowners piece of mind, rather than calling it Number 13, the city planning department of the time instead decided to call it 11A. So, 11A it's been all these years.

And it just so happened today 11A was up for sale.

Rogerio Sousa, newly arrived from the Azores, was looking to buy a house. The minute he saw 11A Bank Street he fell in love with it as did his wife and children. Managing to scrape up enough money for a down payment, he purchased the house one cool spring afternoon. Truth be told, had it been Number 13, he never would have purchased it. Not only was he a very superstitious man, but to make matters worse, he suffered from triskaidekaphobia, an affliction he'd had since early childhood. Pleased to say, he felt perfectly happy it being 11A. That 11A might really be 13 was something that never crossed his mind.

The "evil eye" was another thing that scared Rogerio, maybe even more so than the number 13. But at least when he got the "evil eye" he knew exactly what to do to keep himself from getting hexed. He would say three times out loud: "May God bless you, may God bless you, may God bless you," then he would make the sign of the cross, and later run out onto the street and pour salt in the shape of a crucifix. But it was well-known among the superstitious there was no such quick fix for the number 13.

Rogerio's wife, Noela, was not superstitious at all. The number 13 was no big deal to her, and she had no fear of getting the evil eye either. Superstition, as far as she was concerned, was just that, a superstition, and no matter how hard she tried to get her husband to see things her way, he just wouldn't. She was only grateful he had no fear of 11A, which allowed them to purchase their new home without reservation.

Both Rogerio and Noela had come from the sparsely populated Azorean island of Pico, known as the mountain island because it had the highest mountain in all of Portugal. With its rainy winter days and subtropical climate, the island was very lush and fertile with a long tradition of wine-making. It was also known for its whale-hunting. Rogerio's father had been a whaler, spending much time at sea, while the family lived in the island's capital of Madalena. During the summer months as a young boy, Rogerio was sent to stay with his grandfather on a farm nearby overlooking the sea.

Little Rogerio always looked forward to his time with his grandfather, who was an easy-going, friendly man with white hair, white whiskers, and whose face was bronzed by the sun. Bent by time, Grandfather loved the land as much as he loved the sea. On his farm he kept cows, chickens, and goats, and along the shoreline there was a line of fig trees and a vineyard with grapes sweeter than honey. In the early morning hours Rogerio with his grandfather would hitch up the donkey, load it up with produce, and head out to Madalena, to the fruit boat, where it would then sail across the channel to market in Horta. Rogerio was always a great help to his grandfather, especially when it came to loading and unloading boxes.

Though most of the inhabitants on Pico Island were impoverished, Grandfather, by comparison, was well-to-do; however, he was not well-to-do from growing figs or grapes or tending to his farm animals, rather, he was well-to-do from bootlegging. In a wooded area in back of his house, he had his *destilaria* which he had built from sheets of old wood and recycled glass. His still, or rather, *alambique,* was make-shift and set up to produce *aguardente,* a kind of brandy. Strong, smooth and delicious, is how he described it. People from as far as Cachorro came to fill up their jugs. Grandfather's *destilaria* was surrounded by a stone fence and guarded by his old dog, Fausto, who growled and barked at anyone who tried to come near it unaccompanied.

If there was one thing young Rogerio learned from his grandfather, it was the art of bootlegging.

His grandfather would lecture him often, "Distilling alcohol is the easiest thing in the world; it is nothing more than heating fermented liquid and collecting the vapors."

But Grandfather was also full of warning, "Always remember, young man, alcohol and fire are a very dangerous combination. The most important thing is to never, not even for a split second, leave a working still unattended. It can catch fire and blow up."

Then he would end with a wink and a smile, "And don't ever get caught doing it."

Life in the Azores was harsh and it became harsher still when in 1983 an international moratorium on whaling was passed. Not only did whale hunters lose their livelihood, but factories processing whale carcasses for oil and meat were shut down. Every type of business, whether related directly or indirectly to whaling suffered devastating losses, even Grandfather's little bootlegging operation went bust. Being one of Europe's poorest and most isolated regions, the Azoreans were forced to flee the islands in droves. Rogerio, now an adult with a wife and children, packed up, and with promise of a better life, sailed for North America.

They landed in a big city and soon after settled in their new home at 11A Bank Street. Before long more families arrived just like them, all from the Azores – the Oliveiras, the De Sousas, the Barreiras. Rogerio got a job almost immediately in a lumber yard not far from his house but he was not happy there because the pay was meager. He considered other employment, maybe construction but for an unskilled worker that didn't pay much either.

Then it stuck him; why, it was staring him right in the face! But of course! He would start his own business, a business he knew all too well – bootlegging. And his customer base was right there before his very eyes, in his own neighborhood, his fellow Azoreans. If there was one thing his fellow-Azoreans could not live without it was their *aguardente*. With a void in the market such as it was, he was more than confident business would boom. That it was illegal was not a major concern to him. In a city of this size, he figured, the police would be so busy chasing after criminals and issuing parking tickets, they wouldn't have time for a small-fry like himself.

Noela, gentle and timid soul that she was, respected her husband and adored him completely. She had been fond of him and had loved him all her life but this bootlegging business troubled her. And to make matters worse, she herself could be found culpable.

"Rogerio," she said to him one morning, "it's illegal after all; you can get yourself in a lot of trouble. What if you get caught? What will our lives be like then?"

Rogerio could only but laugh, "Not to worry, dear wife. Me, get caught? Never! We live in the big city now and our little street is so out-of-the-way nobody will ever notice. I've already got the basement ready to go, ventilation and all. Trust me; I know what I'm doing. It would make Grandfather proud."

So, one sunny summer afternoon, with his wife's bundle buggy, Rogerio, as invincible as he felt, walked up to Dundas and went shopping for bootlegging supplies. First, he stopped off at Reginald's hardware store. Reginald, who was sitting behind the counter flipping through some catalogues, when he heard someone come in, looked up.

"May I help you?"

Rogerio took out his list: "I'll need some buckets, demijohns, plastic tubing, bottles, caps, several oak barrels, cheese cloth, and a propane tank."

Reginald raised his brows. The items were most unusual. He said as a joke, "What are you planning to do, make your own moonshine?"

Rogerio shifted a little but did not respond. Looking round, he pretended he did not hear.

Having made his purchases, he hurried to his next stop. It was Feliciana's Odds and Ends. He'd never been there before but rumor had it she carried many products catering to the area's newly arrived Portuguese community. When Feliciana saw Rogerio and all the equipment in his bundle buggy, she knew exactly what he was looking for. She said in a lowered voice, signaling with her hand:

"The *alambiques* are in the back behind the chairs. I just got two new ones in, real beauties, fresh from Lisbon."

When Rogerio got to the back, the place was so cluttered he could hardly see a thing. Then he saw a stack of rickety old chairs piled on top of one another, and directly behind them

– the *alambiques*. He was much impressed. They were fine-looking with big round punched copper pots, all hand-worked, the seams perfectly soldered, and with brass thermometers. He chose the bigger of the two, which could hold twenty-one gallons easily. Feliciana offered delivery services. She said her husband had a pick-up truck and would be available later that day. She asked for his address, to which Rogerio replied:

"11A Bank Street."

"11A?" Feliciana put her hands on her hips and shook her head. "What kind of number is 11A for a house?" Then as if having given it some consideration, "Oh, I get it, your house number is really 13, but they changed it to 11A because 13 is an unlucky number and no one would buy it. So, you fell for that old trick, did you?"

As Rogerio walked out the door, Feliciana called after him in a sarcastic voice, "Good luck with your 11A! You'll need it! Hah, hah, hah!"

Out on the street, Rogerio tried not to think of Feliciana's biting words. What did she know anyway, meddlesome old woman. He lived at 11A and the number was on the door to prove it, and at night it even lit up. His mail was delivered to 11A, all his identification said 11A, when he went to vote it was 11A. Everything about the house was 11A and not 13. He felt assured.

Heading for the fruit market which was on the next corner, Reginald ordered several crates of grapes, five sacks of sugar, packets of yeast among other things, and asked to have them delivered.

As evening approached, closing up his store, Reginald couldn't stop thinking of Rogerio and his unusual purchases. What was he planning to do with all that paraphernalia? No question, it all pointed to one thing – moonshine. And Reginald didn't even know about the *alambique* yet. The minute it got dark he would head over to Rogerio's house and check it out. Never before had there been a bootlegger on Bank Street and he felt compelled to find out more.

At last nightfall. The moon came up a blood red. Rogerio's house was a solid-looking Victorian with tall double-paned windows, a shingled roof, and a broad veranda with a wrought iron railing. In the front yard was a vegetable garden consisting of cucumbers, tomatoes and peppers, and next to it a grape arbor. The house was unlit, except for a faint light coming from the basement. Reginald hurried toward it but surreptitiously, like a cat. Getting down on all fours, he was easily able to see inside.

It was dingy in there and looked much like a dungeon. The floor was a poured concrete and the walls were shelved with wooden racks on which stood empty bottles and various sized jugs. A single light bulb dangled from the ceiling. Rogerio was there and he was washing what appeared to be a rag in the laundry tub, which he then wrung out and hung on a line to dry. A few minutes later he walked over to a big stainless-steel container and started filling it up with grapes. He mashed them up with some kind of kitchen utensil. Proceeding to crush a tablet on a largish dinner plate, adding sugar, he then mixed it into the crushed grapes. Covering the pot with a lid, with the light left on, he went upstairs.

"That's it?" thought Reginald, disappointed. "It looks like all he's making is wine. Now he's left it there to ferment. But what about the moonshine? What a waste of my time!"

Then he thought maybe he got it all wrong from the start, maybe Rogerio had no intention of making the high-octane intoxicant. But wait a minute, why would he go out and buy the propane tank and those tubes? There had to be a distilling contraption down there somewhere. Straining his eyes, he couldn't see anything. Getting closer to the window, at once he caught sight of something near the end of the wall, just behind the stairs.

It was a huge pot of some sort and it looked as if it was made of copper, and there was a tube running from the top, connecting it to a largish bucket. And right beside it was a propane tank.

"That's it! That's the *alambique*; he does have a still down there! I was right all along!"

Several days passed and each night that Reginald peeped into the window there was nothing going on. Rogerio was hardly ever there. The *alambique* stood untouched. "Why isn't he doing anything with it?"

Reginald was growing impatient but he kept coming back.

Then finally on the seventh day it happened. Rogerio was stooped over the stainless-steel container with his now well-fermented mashed grapes and he was stirring it with a metal spoon. The *alambique* had since been moved next to the fermented grapes and the propane tank was there too and it was all hooked up. Reginald watched and waited. Rogerio then picked up the grape mixture and poured it through a sieve with cheesecloth into another stainless-steel container, pressing out the remaining liquid until every last drop was extracted. He was obviously making wine and when the winemaking was complete, he then gradually siphoned it into small barrels for aging.

What occurred next utterly astounded Reginald. Rogerio then took the mashed grape mixture from the wine with the skins and even the remaining stems, and instead of discarding it, emptied it into the copper pot of the *alambique*. He added sugar, lots of it, and water, followed by some kind of powders. He then lit the propane tank. As the grapey fermented mass got heated, drops of alcohol could be seen leaving the condenser. Rogerio kept stirring it on and off. He sat on a stool and watched as it went through the distillation process, all the while keeping a close eye on the hygrometer. He sat there showing great patience.

Reginald didn't understand, "But all he's got is pomace in there. Making hooch out of pomace?" He'd never heard anything like it.

Then he remembered what his neighbor Carmela had said to him one day when they stopped to exchange a few words. "We, the Portuguese, don't believe in wasting a thing, not food, not drink. How do you think we make our *aquardente*? But of course, out of pomace; in other words, out of waste."

Trying to imagine what this *aquardente* might taste like, Reginald continued watching. When the distillation was done, he saw Rogerio siphon the liquid into bottles, seal them, and put them on a shelf. He then started in on another batch with what grape pomace he had left. Again, he sat down on his stool and waited for his mixture to reach alcohol level.

At once there came voices and before long four men entered the basement. They were neighbors. Two were wearing tweed longshoreman's caps and the other two dark green work pants and plaid button-down shirts. They appeared jovial and carried with them empty bottles.

"Just in time, amigos! My very first customers, welcome! *Bem-vindos!*"

Rogerio started to siphon the booze into their bottles right away.

One of the men said smiling, slapping Rogerio on the back, "What a service you provide for us, what a service! You are a great man! Whatever you do, just don't get caught. What would we do without you?"

Noela came into the basement carrying a tray of food. She offered the men *linguiça* sausages she had cooked using flaming *aguardente*. The men thanked her and ate with appetite. Rogerio then gave them each a shot. They stayed about an hour kidding, laughing, and talking about the old country.

The next night, just as a dark shadow passed over the rising moon, Reginald went back to Rogerio's house to peep through the window. He watched Rogerio make more of his wine and then put the pomace into the copper pot to be distilled. He saw people, mostly men from the neighborhood show up, and then one day he saw Feliciana with a couple of empty milk jugs. Over the door leading to the basement hung a sign reading: "Cash Only". Soon word got out that Rogerio, who lived at 11A Bank Street in the city's west-end had a little *aguardente* operation going. It did not take long for Rogerio to have a steady stream of customers, and people even started coming from the distant suburbs. They came mostly by night. Money was good, and Rogerio's pockets were filling up quite nicely and tax free.

Luckily for Rogerio, the police didn't show much interest in Bank Street, and when they drove around the area, they found no reason to take a look.

Late one night when there was a break between customers, Rogerio sat on his stool as if taking a moment to relax. Things had become so busy of late he hadn't found the time to even catch his breath. If business were to carry on at this rapid pace, without question, he would soon have to invest in a larger facility, maybe get extra help. He had much to consider.

Continuing to sit there, suddenly for some reason he got up and walked toward the wall beneath the staircase. He proceeded to play around with the plaster as if to loosen it up. As it turned out, there was a secret door there about the size of a porthole and he soon had it wide open. He pulled out what looked like a wad of bills.

"What on earth?" thought Reginald, who was at the window again. "Money, and lots of it!"

Rogerio could be heard counting, "One hundred, two hundred, five hundred, a thousand, two thousand, six ... "

Yes, it was now very clear, Rogerio's operation was growing at a rapid pace, and to add to it, he was becoming quite the big spender. It so happened his oldest daughter, Daniela, was getting married in a few months and her dream was to have the biggest and most lavish wedding. Rogerio had every intention of flaunting his new-found wealth. His daughter's wedding would be a hundred times more costly than Nuno Magro's daughter's down the street, and unlike Nuno, he would have an open bar. Everyone in the neighborhood would be invited, and for a wedding gift he was planning to present his daughter and her new husband with that house they'd been eyeing at the end of the street.

In the meantime, customers kept pouring in and they were now not only showing up by night but by day as well. There was a line-up outside Rogerio's house that stretched half-way down the block and on weekends as far as the variety store. To ease the flow of traffic, Rogerio's wife had set up a little area in the yard with tables and chairs, a sort of mini café, where customers could wait their turn relaxing and chatting. For a small fee, she offered up snacks and espressos. As far as neighbors were concerned, they tolerated the extra traffic on the street mostly because they didn't want to make waves.

Eventually, it got to the point Rogerio was simply unable to meet the demands of his forever growing customer base. Sometimes he ran out of the *aguardente*, and running out was not good for business as it only made his customers unhappy.

Then one day he'd heard there was a new business in town set up by two brothers, Angelo and Breno Velez, and they owned a large unmarked truck that was really a mobile distillery. What a great idea! The brothers drove around delivering *aguuardente* mostly to community-minded sports bars and restaurants. To relieve the demands on his enterprise, Rogerio got in touch with them and put in an order.

One evening as Reginald was relaxing on his veranda taking in the cool air, a big white truck showed up on Bank Street and stopped before Rogerio's house. It happened to be the Velez brothers with their mobile distillery.

"What's going on now?" Reginald got up to have a look.

Two men emerged and almost at once started pulling out a hose and dragging it along the side of Rogerio's house. They dragged it all the way to his basement window. Soon after a pump started up.

"They're pushing out hooch? No!" Reginald couldn't believe his eyes. "How brazen of them, and with such a flagrant violation of the law!"

Days passed and business at Rogerio's bustled. With the help of the Velez brothers, he no longer ran out of product. His customers couldn't have been more pleased.

Things got so busy, Rogerio had to extend his hours. Living the good life, that his world might come crashing down on him, was something Rogerio never considered. But crash it did and no one saw it coming, not even Rogerio himself. It crashed with a bang. And it was all thanks to, of all people, Reginald, though through no fault of his own. Here's how it all came to be:

One evening, as Rogerio was putting grape pomace into his already-lit and running *alambique*, for some reason he started to think about Feliciana and what she had said to him about the number 13. He could almost hear her nagging old voice ringing in his ears.

"11A is really 13 and 13 will bring you bad luck, you wait and see."

He couldn't help but laugh. "That stupid woman, to say such a thing and to me of all people. Can't she see I'm having the best of luck? My family is happy and healthy, the police never bother me, and I have customers galore. And she herself comes here once a week to fill up. Things couldn't be better! The number 13, hah!"

At once there came a noise from the window. It was strange but very pronounced. Rogerio stiffened, he listened. It was a sort of knocking sound and then as if the shuffling of feet. There was someone out there. His body tensed. He would go have a look. Pinning himself up against the wall, he crept slowly toward the left pane. One step, then another, he was almost there.

At first, he didn't see anything but looking more closely what he saw completely startled him. He let out a gasp. There was a face out there and it was staring right at him. Who could that be? An intruder? A burglar? Suddenly, the face looked familiar, like the face of a neighbor, of that strange little man down the street, Reginald. But how could that be? And why would he, of all people, be out there in the dark, peeping through his window? It absolutely made no sense.

Then one of the eyes on that face, as if out of nowhere, started glowing and it soon began to flicker. Before long it grew to double its size. Rogerio, at first thought he was seeing things but then he became convinced what he was seeing was real – not only was the eye growing bigger but it looked sinister, dangerous, even threatening. No, it couldn't be! May God help him! It was the evil eye! It was the Devil himself!

"*O diablo!*" Rogerio cried out and his blood ran cold.

Quickly making the sign of the cross, shouting out a Hail Mary, running upstairs as fast as he could, he hollered for his wife, "Noela, Noela! Quick, get the salt! The evil eye, it's here! I just saw it! It's in the window!"

Noela came running to see what was going on. She was alarmed to find her husband white as a ghost and shaking. She pulled him into the living room and got him to lie down. Putting a cold compress on his forehead and rubbing his feet, she tried to calm his nerves.

"I saw the evil eye, Noela; it was there in the window. Big, round, bulging, like a frog. It was blazing, staring at me. And now I have the hiccups. We're doomed, Noela, we're doomed."

(Allow me to take a moment to explain something here. Truth is, though Rogerio had indeed seen a frightening-looking eye in the window, it was not an evil eye by any stretch of the imagination. What he had in reality seen was a perfectly natural phenomenon – it was the light of the moon playing tricks on him.)

Rogerio by now was in complete delirium. He lay there on the couch short of breath, sweating, trembling. He forgot completely that in the basement his *alambique* was still lit and running, and he also forgot the words of warning from his grandfather: "Never, not even for a split second, leave a working still unattended."

Noela thought of making her husband some tea because tea always had a soothing effect on him. As she made for the kitchen, at once she smelt something. The smell was very strong. It smelt like smoke. Had she left something burning on the stove? She went to take a look. It wasn't coming from the kitchen. Then she realized it was coming from the basement. She fell into a panic. She thought of the *alambique*.

"Fire! Fire!" Then in Portuguese, *"Fogo! Fogo!"*

She ran to the phone and called the fire department. Barely a few minutes passed and there came the sound of sirens. When the firemen opened the basement door, a flash of yellow-orange came at them and then from down below the sound of shattering glass. As it turned out the *alambique* had overheated, causing the alcohol to erupt from the top of the structure and to spew clear alcohol several feet into the air. Everything was getting burned. The firemen finally put out all the flames but the damage was extensive.

Soon more sirens came but this time it was the police. Two officers entered Rogerio's house, and handcuffing him, read him his rights. They escorted him outside and pushed him into the back of their cruiser.

Neighbors, including Reginald (who had long since returned home), wanting to see what was going on, crowded the street. All were sad to see their good neighbor meet with such an unfortunate end. Feliciana, having heard the news from one of her customers, came rushing to Bank Street. Of course, she'd seen it coming from the start. Waving her arms, shaking her head, she shouted to Rogerio as he was driven off.

"Didn't I tell you? Didn't I tell you 11A is really 13?"

Noela got charged too. Wiping away tears with a handkerchief, led by a police officer, she could be heard saying under her breath, "Dear God, what now?"

★

The next morning at breakfast Reginald was listening to the radio. The broadcaster made the following announcement. "Breaking news: West-end bootlegger, Rogerio Ribeiro, becomes author of his own demise, he blames it on the evil eye."

Taking a sip of coffee, Reginald was surprised to hear about Rogerio on the news and so early in the day. But what puzzled him most was mention of an evil eye. How did an evil eye fit into the picture? He paused a moment and tried to recall events of the previous night; after all, he had been there the entire time. But he didn't remember anything unusual or anything about any evil eye either. Then it struck him.

"But of course, that's it! When Rogerio looked out the window last night he saw me. He must have zoomed in on one of my eyes. It was *my* eye he took for the evil eye. So that explains why he suddenly started going so berserk. How strange it all is. Oh, dear me."

Considering heading over to the jail to visit Rogerio and to explain to him what had really happened, in the end he decided against it. It was a complicated matter after all, and the news, if anything, would only further unhinge him. He decided best to leave well enough alone. Instead, he turned off the radio and poured himself another cup of coffee.

Chapter 14

Nick the Dick

It was barely June and there was a heat wave. Reginald was sitting on his veranda having a scotch. It was considerably cooler there on the veranda than on the street where the pavement was as if on fire. In spite of the heat, there was much going on. Children were running around, playing, laughing, and spraying each other with water hoses; women were standing round, gossiping, waving hand fans; and men were busy charging up barbecues. When it started to grow dark, and with mosquitoes coming out, everyone disappeared inside. The streetlights went on and a pale moon rose up over the rooftops.

With no one left, Reginald felt lonely and sad. What he wanted more than anything is what all the other men on the street had, a wife and a family. He didn't want to be the odd-man out. But his prospects didn't look good. He had no meaningful relationship, not even casual companionship, he had nothing of true value. Women never looked his way and if they did it was either with indifference or with utter contempt. Though strong emotions swirled within him and almost on a daily basis, he continued to repress everything for fear of getting hurt.

Closing his eyes, he began to doze, and just as he was about to nod off, suddenly something out of the ordinary happened. It didn't seem real. Was it real? A woman appeared before him and she was beautiful with buttery blonde hair, sparkling eyes, and a warm smile. Where did she even come from? The woman took him tenderly by the hand and started to lead him someplace. It was as if she wanted to be alone with him. In a complete quandary, Reginald was only too ready to go along.

But who was this woman and where was she taking him? Somehow, she looked familiar and suddenly he realized who it was – it was Gloria from high school. She still lived a few doors down but now with her husband, Nick, having inherited her childhood home from her parents, who moved back to their native Italy several years ago. Strangely, she looked exactly the way she did in school when she had been a cheerleader. All the boys including himself had been madly in love with her.

Reginald thought back on his high school days. But it brought bad memories. He thought of one incident in particular:

He was standing in the hallway outside the library and Gloria came by. Without knowing what possessed him, he shouted out to her like a fool, "Gloria, I love you!"

Gloria was stunned by his sudden display of adoration and there came a look of disgust to her face. She said back to him, "What? You love me? Are you kidding? Imagine, a little hunchback like you. And how far do you think you'd get with me? Not very! Hah, hah, hah!"

And now after all those years, here she was, that same Gloria, but taking him by the hand, leading him somewhere, wanting to be with him. She was telling him she was sorry, that in high school she'd been wrong, and that she should have given him a chance.

He couldn't figure any of it out, it all seemed so incredible. Then at once Gloria wasn't there anymore; she disappeared completely. Where did she go? Had she even been there with him? He was completely mixed up.

"Gloria! Gloria!" he called out.

Looking round, he found himself alone in the middle of the street. It was dark but the streetlights gave off a whitish light and shadows stretched along the houses. The question of where he was going agitated him though he was not quite aware of how agitated he actually was. Before long he realized he was of all places in front of Gloria's house. What was he doing there? And how did he even come to be there? Her house was fine-looking, two stories high with bay windows and flower boxes on the sills. And her lawn was the most manicured on the street because every Saturday her husband Nick cut the grass and pulled weeds – if he wasn't working, that is.

Reginald was jealous of Nick because Nick had Gloria, and it was Nick's life he wanted. Back in high school, why couldn't Gloria have chosen him? However awkward he might have been, given the opportunity, he would have proven to her that he was a good and dependable human being, that he was smart, that he had a big heart. But, of course, he never stood a chance with her, not then, not now, not ever. He was grotesque-looking, as horrible today as he was yesterday.

And Nick was everything Reginald was not – tall, handsome, debonair, and with a high-profile job. Always well-dressed, he was husky but not fat, and he worked out regularly at the gym. Though Nick had to travel a lot for work and was frequently out of town, his well-paying job afforded them two cars, a cleaning woman, and tutors for their daughter, Chloe. It was no secret both Nick and Gloria had a penchant for the finer things in life and they took every opportunity to flaunt their riches, especially to their neighbors. Nick even had a Rolex watch but some claimed it was a knock-off. Gloria herself ran a small online business from home, and on its own it was lucrative enough and added nicely to the family annual income.

But sometimes Nick and Gloria had fights and it was mostly over money. Although there was plenty to go around, at the end of each month for some reason there was always a shortfall, which didn't make sense, especially to Gloria.

Nick, it was no secret had a penchant for the ladies. But all that bad behavior had come to an end when he got married, he even swore on his mother's grave. He boasted to his friends he was the most faithful husband around.

Gloria wanted to believe him and trust him, and she did. That he might be guilty of any pernicious conduct was the farthest from her mind.

The two had met in community college right after high school, where they both studied business administration. There was a strong chemistry between them and after only a few dates of movies and candle-lit dinners they knew they were made for each other. Their aspirations were the same: work hard, make a lot of money, live well, and spend. They completely remodeled their house and then traveled extensively – Europe, Asia, the Caribbean. When they married, they agreed to have no children as that would only put restrictions on their free and easy lifestyle. However, when Gloria accidentally became pregnant with Chloe, they welcomed their new daughter with open arms.

Tonight, Gloria's house stood dark as if no one was home, which was unusual, as normally there was someone there. But then Reginald noticed a light coming from a back room. He assumed Gloria was with her husband (if he wasn't away on business, that is) and Chloe, either watching television or playing some video game. He thought he'd go have a look.

To his surprise Gloria was alone, and she didn't look very well. She was sitting on the sofa, looking very much beleaguered, with her head buried in her hands. She was hardly moving. Then she got up and went toward a small end table by the door, where her phone was. Picking it up, she tapped in a number. Her voice was uneven.

"Hi, Francine, it's Gloria, Chloe's mom. Is Chloe there by any chance? No? Well, she was supposed to be home a few hours ago and it's not like her not to call. It's getting late and I'm worried. I thought she might be with you. Her last exam, you ask? It was yesterday. Well, thanks; if you hear from her please let me know."

Gloria paced the room. Then back to her phone to check her texts. There was no message from her daughter, and when she went on her Facebook page and her other accounts, there was no activity either. Where could she be? She wanted to call her husband, to alert him, but no, better not as he was in a meeting tonight and wouldn't appreciate being interrupted – he would just say she was overreacting anyway. She checked her phone again. No text messages, no missed calls. Getting more and more anxious, she didn't know what to do next. Maybe she should jump in her car and go to some of her daughter's hangouts; maybe she should call the police. She contacted a few more of her friends but it was all the same – no one had seen or heard from her.

Then suddenly the phone rang. It gave Gloria a start. The ring sounded shriller, louder than usual, and it had an almost sinister tone to it. An awful sensation passed through her and she could feel the beating of her heart. There was something wrong she was sure of it, something had happened to Chloe, an accident, a car crash. She was afraid to answer it. Preparing for the worst, hardly able to breathe, she put the phone to her ear.

"Hello," she said.

There came no answer.

"Hello," she said again.

Still nothing.

Then she heard what sounded like muttering but it was far away and it was full of static. She couldn't make anything out. She became confused.

"Chloe? Chloe? Is that you? Is there something wrong? Chloe, answer me!"

There came more muttering, more static. By this time, she figured it obviously wasn't Chloe. About to hang up, right at that moment something came at her so disturbing, so shocking there was nothing in the world that could have prepared her for it. It wasn't her daughter on the other end but rather a man and she could now hear him breathing, laughing, making weird noises. The man was recognizable to her: it was her husband.

"Nick?" she called into the phone, "Nick, is that you?"

Nick didn't seem to hear her but he was talking to someone who was obviously with him. His voice was low and raspy-sounding. This is what he was saying, "Brush up against me; yes, like that. Oh, baby, do it again."

Then there came a woman's voice in the background, giggling, groaning, "Ah … I love you when you do that to me. Don't stop."

Nick again but this time louder, "Come on, baby, just keep doing it; come, baby, come."

Gloria dropped the phone. She couldn't move for five whole minutes. Her head was in a spin. Then she started to cry and she couldn't stop. Burying her face in her hands she was upset, hurt, and then anger set in.

"You son-of-a-bitch!" she screamed. "You fucking piece of shit!"

As it happened, she had got a pocket-call, in other words, an unintentional call coming from someone's pocket with that person having no idea they've made a call. In this case, of course, it was Nick.

Reginald, still outside the window, tried to get a better look. Of all moments, what a moment for him to be there! But he felt sympathy for Gloria and all he wanted was to go to her and put an end to her pain. If only he could crawl through the window, take her in his arms, hold her, comfort her. He muttered to himself, "She should have chosen me. I would never have betrayed her like this, I would have worshiped the ground she walks on."

Suddenly, Gloria's phone let out a ping. It was a text message from Chloe. Chloe! She had completely forgotten about Chloe! She read aloud: "Hi Mom, sorry for not calling. Turns out I have a teaching job at the university. It was a last-minute deal and I start tomorrow. Lost track of time. Am staying on campus for the next few weeks. Am excited. Not to worry. Fill you in later. Love you, Chloe."

Gloria threw herself onto a chair, her head throbbed, and she felt a shivering in her legs. It's a good thing her daughter wasn't home after all, what a mess that would have been. She looked round the living room. Everything stood as it always stood, the sofa, the coffee table, the chairs. By the door her eyes landed on a photograph of herself and Nick on Centre Island, and they were smiling, their arms wrapped around one another. She couldn't bear to look at it, it made her sick to her stomach. Getting up, ripping it off the wall, hurling it across the room, she watched it break into hundreds of pieces. And she didn't stop there. She took a swing at the floor lamp, then turned the coffee table upside down and kicked it with her foot. Her life was falling apart, her marriage was over, and a few seconds was all it took.

At that moment footsteps resounded from outside, then the sound of a key being turned. It was Nick. Before long he entered the hallway. His suit was crinkled here and there and he looked disheveled. He called out as if nothing, "Gloria, I'm home. Sorry, I'm so late, but that meeting went on longer than expected. I brought you a pot of sweetheart roses, I know how much you like them."

Gloria stood there and watched him, utterly disabled. A minute passed, then two. About to come at him, she was having difficulty matching the thoughts in her head with the words about to come out. Finally, she said in a voice that was not her own, "Where were you?"

Nick didn't like the look on Gloria's face, it made him uneasy. He half-laughed, "I told you, I was at the office."

"Really? And who was there with you?"

To Gloria's chagrin, Nick didn't answer. She repeated the question, "Who was there with you?"

"Oh, just Jerry and Mike. We were doing some last-minute revisions on the Delaney account I told you about. It's all going down tomorrow morning."

Gloria swallowed hard. Intense rage came to her eyes and as much as she tried, she couldn't restrain herself. She started shouting:

"Liar! You weren't with Mike or Jerry. I know where you were because you called me, yes, you pocket-called me, and I heard everything – I heard about your hard cock, your girlfriend's big ass, you disgusting son-of-a-bitch!"

Nick stood back; the color drained from his face. He became hot all over, and not in a good way. About to deny everything, seeing it would get him nowhere, he fessed up.

Gloria couldn't stop, "You bastard, to think I started trusting you again!" Then, "So now it all makes sense. All those late nights.

Those out-of-town meetings. So, that's where all the money's been going!"

Nick remained silent and avoided looking at her. Finally, he sputtered out, "Things just got out of hand. I didn't mean for it to happen, really, I didn't. It was stupid of me. I'm sorry."

"'Sorry?' That's an empty word."

Nick seemed to want to say something more in his defense. Finally, he blurted out, "She doesn't mean anything to me. It won't happen again. Please believe me."

The flush on Gloria's cheeks only grew more marked and her chest rose and fell. All she wanted was to push this hurtful person as far away from her as possible, she wanted to smash his head in, kill him. She cried at the top of her voice, "Fuck you!"

Nick was in a nervous state, he had never seen Gloria like this, and the determination in her face frightened him. This time he knew he had gone too far, he could feel divorce in the air, and it wouldn't come cheap either. He needed a drink.

Gloria knew her marriage was over. As she stood there, suddenly, there was no longer any grief, pain, or anger left in her; it was all gone. She felt nothing. It was as if an enormous weight had been lifted from her shoulders. Nick was a liar and a cheater and she was done with him, she couldn't get out of there soon enough.

Snatching up her purse and jacket and a few personal items, without giving him a second look, she walked out the door. She was going far and she would never come back, though first, of course, she would see her lawyer.

But there was one last thing she had to do. Heading for the shed at the back of the house, grabbing a can of spray paint off one of the shelves, she started for the street. She looked for Nick's BMW Z4 with its leather interior and customized paint job. There it was parked in front of the Martinelli house. A smile strayed on her lips. Walking over to the passenger side, which faced the street, pressing the nozzle, she started to spray paint:

"Nick is a dick. He cheated on his wife."

She then got into her own car that happened to be behind his and drove off. She would never return to Bank Street, she would start a new life, maybe she'd go to Italy for a while to be with her parents. Chloe could come later. She wouldn't call Nick or text him; she would leave it for her lawyer to work out.

★

That night Nick tossed and turned and he hardly got any sleep. Gloria was gone; she'd left him and she wouldn't be back. He was experiencing a particular form of anxiety that was irritating, and the anxiety would not leave. She would milk him dry; he could see it all coming. That stupid pocket-call, why hadn't he been more careful? The house would be sold, the bank accounts emptied, there would be spousal payments on top of that. What a relief Chloe was no longer a dependent.

Finally, morning came. With a bad headache, making a pot of coffee, Nick took a painkiller but it didn't help. He had to be in top-notch shape today, as there was that important meeting regarding the Delaney account. It would be starting in less than an hour. Dressing, patting down his hair, looking in the mirror, he thought he looked presentable enough, given all he had been through. He couldn't be late. Walking out the door, already in his car, he started up the engine and drove off.

As he turned onto Dufferin Street, he noticed a small group of people standing at the bus stop, his neighbor Reginald among them. For some reason they were staring at him, pointing, laughing, and making jokes. "What's that all about?" he thought to himself. Then a couple of women along the sidewalk gave him the finger. When a car passed, it honked, then another honked, and then someone shouted through an open window, "Hey, Nick is a dick!"

"What's going on with everyone today, and how'd that guy even know my name? Did I hear him right? Did he say what I think he said?"

Nick became utterly confused. Looking round, he checked his rear-view mirror to see if there might be something strange or out-of-the-ordinary with his car. No, there didn't seem to be. Then it was not long before he figured out why he was getting all that negative attention. It was his BMW Z4. People were simply jealous and it was jealousy driving them, as it was not usual to see such a high-end luxury car in the area.

Soon he made a right on Dundas. Passing Maciuk's Smoke Shop, he caught sight of owner Mike standing on the sidewalk, watching the cars go by, something he routinely did when there were no customers to tend to. Upon seeing Nick's car, adjusting his glasses, Mike, for some reason, started showing excitement, jumping up and down, pointing, as if trying to tell him something. "What's with Mike today?" Nick wondered. As he was about to pull over to find out, he realized he had to keep going because if he didn't, he'd be late for his very important meeting. He'd ask Mike about it later, on his way home, when he'd stop to get cigarettes.

Continuing to Bay Street, finally Nick pulled into the office parking lot. He noticed his boss and Mr. Delaney already there by their cars embroiled in conversation. Both were short, stout and clean-shaven and could easily have been related, though Mr. Delaney was clearly the older of the two. When they saw Nick, they waved to him.

Nick pulled up passenger-side and with the window rolled down called out in good humor, "Good morning, gentlemen! I hope we're ready to start up that new partnership; I'm ready to go."

The men smiled broadly. Just as they were about to say something in return, they caught sight of the side of Nick's car. They each shifted uncomfortably and cleared their throats. Not quite knowing what to say or do, they stood there as if they could not make out why they were filled with such embarrassment. Nick became puzzled then worried. Why were they looking at his car so strangely? What was going on? He thought maybe he got a scratch or worse yet a dent of some kind. Getting out, he walked over to check it out. When he saw what was written, color drained from his face. He stood there shrugging, bobbing his head, looking like an ass.

Then Nick's boss gave Nick a direct stare and the stare was so harsh, so piercing it was as if a knife cutting right through him. Without a word, Nick's boss and Mr. Delaney swung around and started for the building. Nick's boss was patting Mr. Delaney on the back and saying something to him. Nick could hear it clear as day: "I'm so sorry about this. It's really unfortunate. Please accept my apologies."

And just like that, like a house of cards everything came crashing down around Nick. He knew his wife all too well and now he was afraid, more afraid than he'd ever been. She would show him no mercy.

Jumping into his car, heading down the street, first thing was first: he needed to get to a paint-and-body shop ASAP. There was one about a mile down the road. Almost there, suddenly something unexpected happened, and it was certainly not in Nick's favor. There'd been an accident, a delivery truck had hit a streetcar and all traffic was stopped. Both lanes were blocked and the police hadn't yet arrived.

"Dammit!" Nick shouted and banged his fist on the steering wheel.

People gathered to see what was going on, talking, arguing, gesticulating excitedly. But when they saw Nick's car and what was written on the side of it, suddenly they lost interest in the accident and focused only on him. Laughter broke out, then came jeering, various expletives, even knocks on his window. Soon chanting broke out, "Nick is a dick!". Nick became angry but mostly with himself – shit, why didn't he have his windows tinted when he had the chance? He wanted to crawl under a rock and disappear. And then, to make matters worse, who should he see sitting on the disabled streetcar but that snoopy neighbor of his, Reginald. And now that snoopy neighbor was looking straight at him smiling away and waving.

When at last the accident cleared up, Nick couldn't get out of there fast enough. He went speeding down the street. Finally, the paint-and-body shop! But he was five minutes late, it had just closed for lunch.

"What the hell? What kind of business closes for lunch?"

He broke down and cried. Everything was going against him. And he knew this was just the beginning. Gloria was only getting started.

Chapter 15

Cats

Today was Christmas and Bank Street stood blindingly white. It had snowed since early afternoon and though it was terribly cold at least the wind had died down. A few cars lumbered by and those parked on the street had about a foot of snow on them. Some neighbors had come out to shovel their walkways but when Gerry from Number 29 showed up with his new snow plow and offered to do the entire street, everyone happily accepted and disappeared inside.

Almost all the houses were decorated in imaginable colors and there were elaborate wreathes on front doors. In one yard there was a sleigh with nine reindeer; on another a lavish nativity scene with life-size figures; and on yet another, an inflatable Santa Clause almost as big as a house. Everywhere little bright lights lined eves troughs, encircled trees, and ran along the edges of verandas, some blinking every few seconds.

And if that wasn't enough, the smells of Christmas cooking filled the air – turkey, goose, stuffing, fried cod, roasted chestnuts, gingerbread. Visitors coming and going with giftwrapped parcels under their arms and large trays of food wore broad smiles, and carolers brought with them merriment and yule tide cheer. Bank Street was absolutely shimmering.

Christmas, as one might expect, was a difficult time for Reginald but as a child he had always loved it – the ornamented tree in the living room, the presents, the aroma of his mother's freshly baked mincemeat pies. What he loved most, even in his later years, was going with his parents to midnight mass at St. Anne's Anglican Church over on Gladstone. To him St. Anne's was the most beautiful church in the world, built in the neo-Byzantine style with its stain-glass windows and artwork by members of the Group of Seven.

But when his parents were killed in that freak car accident a few years back everything changed. Aside from Rocco and Susana, quietly living with Franco and Mamma Mia, there was no one in his life, no surviving relatives, not even some distant cousin somewhere overseas. Now he dreaded everything there was about Christmas – the food, the presents, and he couldn't bring himself to go back to St. Anne's either, even though it was just a short walk from his house.

He did, however, always have a Christmas tree, tall and full of decorations, which he placed in the front window of his house. Mostly he did it for the benefit of his neighbors. What he really wanted was to give the impression he was celebrating just like everybody else.

Sitting in his living room on the sofa with his head bent, there was a solemn quiet everywhere and the room felt stuffy. He had microwaved himself a frozen turkey dinner with mashed potatoes and cranberry sauce but he wasn't hungry. The television was on and the voices made it sound as if there were people in the room with him but there was no one there. Reginald was a lonely individual, and he was even lonelier on what was supposed to be "the most wonderful time of the year." He looked at a Christmas card he'd received from one of his suppliers: *Dear Reginald, best wishes to you and your family. May you feel this happiness all year round.* Christmas always placed him even further away from everyone. What he wanted most was to be happy, to find significance in his dismal existence, to spend Christmas with someone, anyone.

He thought of going out and doing a bit of spying; maybe that would take his mind off things. Though he was well aware the windows would be for the most part shut tight given the current weather conditions, he thought he would give it a try anyway. If he could at least watch people moving around, even that would be better than nothing.

Wrapping a scarf around his neck, putting on his coat and hat and felt-lined boots, he made for the street. For no particular reason, he headed in the direction of the park. The snow was now coming down harder and faster and it was obviously not about to let up any time soon. Passing several houses, just as he had expected, there was not a single window even slightly open, and to make matters worse, most of the panes were fogged over and snow lay thickly drifted on the sills. It was impossible to see anything through any of them. A deeper feeling of depression came over him, everything was frozen and dead around him. He decided to give up and go home.

Then suddenly Number 42, one of the smaller houses, caught his attention. There was a light coming from the side but it was whitish and ever so faint. At first, he thought nothing of it, then in a strange kind of way it beckoned him. Hastening to have a look, he came upon a smallish window protected over top by some sort of fiber glass awning, as if to shield it from rain or snow. For such a small window it had an exceptionally broad sill, a mere board really, as if someone had haphazardly nailed it there. A thermometer attached to one side read minus ten degrees Celsius. To Reginald's astonishment the window was opened a crack and what's more it had no curtains. He was able to see straight into a kitchen.

But there didn't seem to be much going on, save for a woman over a stove mixing something in an oversized pot. She was somewhere in her sixties, and her movements were so mechanical and the whole scene so uninteresting, Reginald considered turning away. Then the woman started smiling and humming away, and chopping up what looked like a pile of almonds. Obviously, she was preparing Christmas dinner, but strange to say, there was no one there and it was already getting late. Reginald began to wonder.

"Who could she possibly be making dinner for?"

He then noticed a big, fat cat asleep on the stove, then another on a chair, and still another in a cat-bed by the door. Then a scrawny Siamese jumped into the sink and started scratching himself.

Reginald knew the woman's name; it was Hedda Heppenheimer. He also knew a bit about her life. She was relatively new to the neighborhood, having moved in barely a year ago. Widowed, with two grown children living somewhere outside the city limits, she was of Germanic background and spoke with somewhat of an accent. With her husband deceased, she had moved to Bank Street to downsize from her large suburban home.

Clearly, she had a liking for cats. Reginald had sometimes seen her sitting on her veranda with one on her lap or one wrapped around her neck like a fur collar. By the door, she always kept a bowl of cat food and sometimes milk. Every time Reginald passed her on the street, she looked unkempt and seemed in a hurry. She was friendly enough and always offered up a smile, but for the most part it was as if her mind was someplace else. There was something vulnerable and wanting in her face and she seemed withdrawn into herself.

Just yesterday Reginald had passed her on the street. She was heading home from the variety store, pulling a bundle buggy behind her over the packed snow. The bundle buggy was filled with cans of tuna, a couple of cartons of milk, cheese, and two oversized bags of cat food. Her load was so heavy she could barely get it over the curb. Reginald had offered to help.

"Hello, Hedda, allow me to give you a hand."

Hedda was as if she didn't hear him and she seemed agitated, "No, no, it's fine. Thank you, I can manage."

She then dragged the buggy up her porch stairs and opening her front door disappeared inside.

Reginald continued to look through the window. His hands were red and blue from the cold and his feet were starting to freeze. Pulling his hat down over his ears and tightening his coat collar, he tried to keep warm. Snow lay thickly accumulated everywhere – on the ground, on the boughs of trees, on the rooftops.

Hedda was now fussing over the table. It was unusually long and wide and could easily seat up to twenty people.

Reginald was puzzled, "What is she doing? But there's no one there."

Spreading out a white embroidered tablecloth, she then started laying out dishes, cutlery, and glasses. In the middle, she placed a traditional red poinsettia and next to it a bowl of chocolates. Taking a *stollen* out from the cupboard, she began to sing "O Tannenbaum" but ever so quietly.

Then the phone rang. It was her daughter. She put it on speaker phone.

"Mother, hello. Merry Christmas. I'm sorry I'm running late. Snow has been falling the whole way and there's heavy traffic. It's been a while since we've seen each other, I know, I know. The kids, you ask? No, they're at home with David, both in bed, with a bad cold."

A brief pause.

"Anyway, I'm calling to say I'm not far now. I should be there in about an hour. And I have a surprise for you; you may not like it much at first but you'll thank me later."

Hedda was overwhelmed, "A surprise? For me? Oh, my."

Hanging up the phone, there was still much for her to do. She wanted everything to be perfect. She hadn't seen her daughter in over a year and she was very excited, though she was disappointed about the grandchildren. And then her own babies came to mind. Oh, dear, she still had to get her babies ready.

Hedda quickly started sweeping, dusting, wiping the stovetop, doing all the last-minute chores. If anything, she wanted the kitchen to be spotless, to demonstrate to her daughter that she was well, and that she was taking care of herself.

At once a cat with a bushy tail jumped up onto one of the chairs, then another on a stool, then a third on the table. When one jumped up on the counter where Hedda was busy at work, she shooed him away.

Reginald couldn't help but say to himself, "She sure has a lot of cats." Then he started to count them, "One, two, three …" He came up with eight in total, no nine, then ten.

When Hedda suddenly opened the door to her living room, what Reginald saw utterly astonished him. "Wow," he exclaimed to himself. It was a Christmas tree and from where he stood it looked magnificent. Reaching the ceiling, it was brilliantly lighted and glittered with at least a hundred bright ornaments. On the top was a star with multi-colored jewels. Reginald couldn't help but admire its beauty – it was even bigger and more impressive than his own tree, it was that grand. If only he could get a closer look.

Then he heard Hedda call out: "Here, kitties, kitties, Apricot, Frazier, Goldy, Rufus ... Come, my little ones, come to mommy. Time to start in on your milk."

At once a black cat came trotting into the kitchen, followed by a slate blue-gray short hair, then a calico, then a domestic long-hair. Cats started coming in by twos, threes, then a whole army of them emerged. There were cats everywhere, big cats, fat cats, small cats, even kittens. They jumped onto the table and started lapping up milk Hedda had poured into little bowls from a jug. There must have been at least fifty of them.

"Well, I'll be," Reginald couldn't stop gazing. "She's crazy for cats. She's a cat lady!"

As he stood there in the cold, suddenly a large powerfully built cat with snow on its back jumped up onto the sill and started scratching at the window as if trying to get inside. But the opening wasn't big enough. Then a second cat with white spots emerged and leaped up next to him. They both began yowling and howling, one louder than the other. Reginald, fearing being discovered, tried to drive them off.

"Go on, get! Scat!"

Hedda, catching wind of the noise, looked to the window. Walking toward it, Reginald, not wanting to be seen, without thinking, jumped back. But he tripped and fell into the snow. Hedda opened the window wide and let the cats in. She scolded them as they came in.

"You naughty boys! How on earth did you get out anyway? Why you could have frozen to death out there. Go on, drink your milk before it gets cold."

As she was about to close the window, she caught sight of something in the snow.

"Who's there?" she called out. Then looking closer she saw it was Reginald, her neighbor. She became suspicious, "What are you doing here? You're trespassing. What do you want?"

Reginald, getting up, brushing the snow off his shoulders, tried to come up with an answer. Finally, he blurted out, "Actually, I was just passing by and I saw your two cats on the sill. They looked cold. I wanted to help them. I was about to go knock on your front door."

Hedda looked at him from under her brows as though she didn't believe him. Then her face showed a change of expression, "Well, if what you say is true, then I suppose I really should thank you."

Reginald smiled faintly, "I'm sorry to have bothered you. Merry Christmas."

He turned to go.

Hedda caught him up but there was hesitation in her voice.

"No, wait! I just got a thought. It's Christmas after all and no one should be alone on Christmas. We're having an aperitif right now, waiting for my daughter to arrive; she's driving all the way from Burlington. Maybe you'd like to join us? I hope you like milk."

Reginald was very cold standing there, his hands were frozen, and his face was coated with crystals of frost. He could sure use a nice warm drink about now and the prospect of milk sounded appealing.

"Thank you. I don't mind if I do."

Normally, Hedda didn't allow people into her home, but today being Christmas, she thought she'd make an exception. Leading Reginald into the kitchen, bringing out a chair, she sat him at the table next to Rufus and Goldy. Leaning forward, she whispered as if imparting a confidentiality, "Rufus and Goldy. They're inseparable. Brother and sister, from the shelter over on River Street."

Pouring milk into a bowl, she passed it to Reginald and then filled one up for herself. She started lapping it up like a cat.

Hedda then proceeded to complain, "See Jasper over there, the brown one with the broad face? He picks fights all the time. No matter what I do I can't get him to behave. I'm at the end of my ropes."

Reginald looked over at Jasper. He did indeed look like a bully, sitting there with his head cocked, his chest all puffed up, as if he was something.

Then a pregnant orange tabby emerged and went straight to Hedda, rubbing up against the side of her leg. Hedda began to talk to her in gibberish as she stroked her backside. "Oh, you, you, Miss Minnie, Mama's silly little girl. Meow, you say? Well, meow yourself! Meow, meow, I say."

"Meow," the cat answered back.

Reginald kept quiet and said nothing. Not knowing quite what to think, he tried to ignore Hedda's bizarre behavior.

Hedda said to him, "My cats are lovely wouldn't you agree? They're my babies. I love them all so much and they love me back. I rescued them, every last one of them, and now they're safe here with me." At once her face became sad and she rubbed her eyes, "But poor Bonnie and Clyde, they just got too old. A shame you never got to meet them. They died within a day of each other, but they're together forever now in my freezer."

Reginald noticed several of the cats were scratching themselves and one was licking an open wound. At once the smell of urine and fecal matter came up from the floor boards. He held his breath.

Hedda now talked hurriedly as if she was bothered by something, "Yesterday, what a day I had. I spent the whole time online looking over animal websites. I found several cats that need rescuing right away. They'll be euthanized if I don't get to them. Tomorrow first thing I'm heading out to the shelter. But I do hope the snow stops; it's so hard to get around with all that snow."

Reginald looked at her seriously. For a brief moment she appeared so ordinary to him, like any other person, as if picking up three or four cats to add to her already fifty was the most normal thing. He tried to be of help.

"You're going to the shelter tomorrow you say? Yes, tomorrow is a good day to go. According to the weatherman, the snow is supposed to stop overnight. The streets will be cleared by morning, I'm sure."

Hedda poured Reginald more milk.

The two sat in silence five maybe ten minutes. Hedda started up.

"I'll have you know I don't normally care for human company but you seem all right to me. You're different from the others, you don't give me funny looks. And I like that you drink milk."

Then as if out of nowhere, Hedda started mixing meowing sounds in with her speech, as if it was part of her everyday. This is what she said, "Maybe you'd like to *meow* visit us again sometime, be a *meow* regular visitor. We can sit and chat. *Meow*. We're mostly *meow meow meow* ..."

Reginald smiled awkwardly and then shifted in his seat. Though the woman he was sitting with obviously had an unusual cat habit and seemed controlled by it, truth be told, he was rather enjoying her company. He would certainly consider her kindly offer. Yes, he said, he would be happy to come again.

Getting up, Hedda walked over to one of the cupboards and pulled out a tin of cat food. Opening it up, she started eating it with a spoon as though it were people food. She went on with her mouth full, "I like this neighborhood quite a bit, friendly people for the most part. There are a few kids down the street. I pay them to go and find strays. They always come up with something."

She indicated with her spoon, "See Bentley over there, the white shorthair? He came the other day with near frostbite on his paws. I had to wrap them up with bandages."

Hedda then for some reason started up on her deceased husband.

"My Diedrich's been dead for almost two years now, from a heart attack. He worked as an engineer at an electrical company. We were happy together and the children were happy too. But that was long ago. The children don't come around anymore. They say I'm a cat hoarder and that I'm overwhelmed by my hoarding. But it's not true; they don't understand. I rescue cats and I give them love. What's wrong with giving cats love? Diedrich would understand, though he never cared much for cats."

Reginald noticed Hedda's sweater was full of cat hairs and stains but what struck him most was Hedda's own hair. It was pulled back and loosely braided made to look like a cat's tail. He decided it best not to take further notice of her eccentricities.

Suddenly, as if out of nowhere, Bentley sneezed, then Jasper coughed, then two tabbies chased each other across the floor.

At that moment there came a knock on the door and it was rigorous.

Hedda's face lit up. She clapped excitedly, "That must be my daughter. Finally, she's here!"

Getting up, wagging her finger at her cats, she gave them a stern warning, "Now listen all of you: I want you to be on your best behavior. If any one of you acts up, then no treats. Do you hear?"

As she made for the door, Reginald followed close behind. But first they had to pass through the living room. It was a huge mess and in an unlivable condition. Reginald could hardly breathe, the room smelt like one big litter box. The Christmas tree, looking more beautiful from afar than up close, had beneath it not presents but huge overflowing boxes of kitty litter. There was fecal matter on the floor, and the little throw rug by the sofa was covered in vomit. Loads of old clothes, towels, and various rags were piled up on top of one another in different places and some were wet with urine. There was dust build-up everywhere.

Hedda's daughter was standing on the veranda wearing a heavy woolen coat almost to the floor and there was a checkered shawl around her neck. Her nose and cheeks were red from the cold and her hair had a bit of frost. She was tall, taller than her mother, slender, and very pretty. But there was an odd look in her eyes. Hugging her mother, when she went to speak, she did so with effort as though performing a duty.

"Good to see you, mother; it's been a while. Merry Christmas."

Hedda was thrilled to see her daughter. Quickly introducing her to Reginald, she couldn't wait to bring her into the kitchen and show her all the preparations – the meal, the Christmas tree, the little bowls of milk.

But her daughter stood as if rooted to the spot. She obviously had no intention of going anywhere inside. There was a firm, serious look on her face.

Hedda could feel something was not quite right. A rush of alarm passed through her.

As it happened, her daughter indeed wasn't there for Christmas, rather, she had something of a plan going, a plan that was about to turn her mother's life upside down.

Then came a buzz of voices from the walkway. There was a small group of about three or four people. At first, Hedda thought they might be Christmas carolers, but then she became unsure. Looking closer, she noticed they were all wearing strange white uniforms and for some reason they had masks on their faces. And she noticed they were each carrying something. It looked like crates, of all things, and not just any crates but cat crates. At once, their voices became louder and to Hedda they sounded frightening, sinister, threatening. She froze. She cried aloud:

"Animal control!"

Her daughter tried to calm her, "Mother, I want you to listen to me. You have to understand, we're here to help."

A look of sheer terror came to Hedda's eyes and her voice shook, "My babies, my babies! Don't take my babies!"

The animal control authorities had a search warrant and they were already inside the house. The conditions were deplorable and they soon determined the house was a health hazard and should be condemned. It took them several hours to find all the cats. Hedda got charged with animal cruelty.

★

Hedda was soon gone along with her daughter, the cats, and animal control.

Reginald was now all alone; one minute the house was full of life and activity, now there was no one there. It made him sad. He then decided he was hungry. Ignoring the "condemned" sign that had been posted on the door, remembering all the food in the kitchen, he decided he would fill up some plates to take home to eat. It was Christmas, after all. Going round back to avoid the living room, picking up a plate, he started filling it up with everything he could – turkey, dumplings, red cabbage, sausages.

At once there came a movement at his feet. He thought at first he was imagining it but then it came again. Looking down he was taken aback at what he saw.

"Miss Minnie!" he exclaimed.

As it happened, animal control had failed to find Miss Minnie, who had been all the while hiding in the pantry behind a sack of potatoes. Reginald picked her up and stroked her behind the ears. She purred vigorously and slipped out her tongue.

"You silly little kitty," he said to her.

Though he wasn't a cat person by any means, he found himself taking a liking to Miss Minnie. He decided to take her home with him.

Making a soft, comfortable bed for her in the corner of his kitchen, he filled up one bowl with milk, another with sardines, as he had no cat food. She came to following him wherever he went, upstairs, downstairs, to the basement, even out into the yard. And when he was sad or lonely, she curled up on his lap.

Several days passed. Miss Minnie gave birth to six kittens all orange just like her. Reginald kept three and gave three up for adoption.

And suddenly he understood where Hedda was coming from — maybe having cats wasn't such a bad idea after all. But certainly not fifty! Ten, he concluded, would be a much more reasonable number. However, unlike Hedda, he would take his cats to the vet for regular check-ups, give them baths, and clip their nails. Though he was a man of many bad habits, luckily for him, cat-hording was not one of them.

Tomorrow, he decided, he would pay the animal shelter a visit.

Chapter 16

The Mouth Painter

Several doors down from Reginald lived a man by the name of Pavlo. Pavlo happened to be an artist and by no means was he an ordinary man. He was tall, rugged-looking, and his shoulders were broad and strong. He radiated masculinity and his big blue-gray eyes drove the women on the street wild. With a wad of thick black hair atop his head, he was bigger and more handsome than other men, and he had so much charisma when he walked it was as if the pavement shook beneath him.

Not surprisingly, all the neighborhood men were jealous of Pavlo, and no matter how hard they tried, like spending more time at the barber shop or lifting weights to build up muscle tone, they could never come close to being his match. Amongst themselves, to boost their own egos, they would mock Pavlo and share nasty comments about him. These are the sorts of things they would say:

"That Pavlo is an artist? What kind of job is that for a man?"

"He paints pictures all day long, for God's sake! How does he do even *that*?"

"Carpentry, construction, road work, now those are man-jobs! But he couldn't do any of those even if he tried, not with those hands of his anyway! Hah! Hah! Hah!"

The women, of course, saw things differently. Pavlo to them was everything the other men were not – cultured, refined, well-bred. He obviously had an appetite for experience and it was as if he was forever searching for ways to fill that next canvas. He was gentle and kind, and the expression on his face was always brimming with the joys of life. The women loved that he did not have working-man hands, red, blistery, and leather-like. And he did not indulge himself in crude activities either such as arm-wrestling, soccer, and/or fist-fighting. No, he was so unlike the other men. It would be fair to say, for the women at least, Pavlo was a constant distraction.

Pavlo spoke with a heavy Eastern European accent and some suspected him to be Russian, but actually, he was Ukrainian, from Kolomyia, a town in the heart of the Carpathian Mountains. Though Bank Street had at one time been filled with Eastern Europeans, even a few hailing from Kolomyia, most had since moved on to the suburbs with only a handful remaining, of which Pavlo was one. He now looked totally out-of-place among the wave of newcomers even though he had lived there longer than most.

No doubt, Pavlo was different and he dressed differently too. Unlike the other men, who normally wore durable work pants, checkered shirts, and heavy steel-toed boots, Pavlo almost always had on loose-fitting pants and a peasant tunic which he belted at the waist. And those tunics only added to his sweeping allure, especially when unbuttoned, exposing a very chiseled chest.

When Pavlo met people along the street he would greet them all, even those he didn't recognize; first, he would smile and make eye contact, then he would nod and say "hello" or "how do you do?" always putting great feeling into it. He was self-confident and readily talked about his Carpathian homeland, the people, their way of life, and their attitudes toward the lowlanders. Sometimes he even cracked a joke or two because mostly he was in good humor. He was quite extroverted, a personality trait not typically associated with mountain people, and his laughter was both infectious and sincere.

The men listened begrudgingly to his stories, but the women couldn't get enough, his voice was so deep.

But there was one thing that set Pavlo apart from other men and it was the most obvious thing – he had no arms. Yes, that's right, there was nothing there.

Though one might argue his being armless could easily have taken away from his overall appeal, on the contrary, it only added to it. The women started dreaming, fantasizing about what it might be like to be with a man with no arms, some even lost sleep over it. This is what they said amongst themselves.

"I can't even begin to imagine what he's like in bed."

"Arms, who needs arms?"

"Did you ever look at the size of his feet? Oh!"

And now for the big question – how was it Pavlo came to have no arms? Everyone wanted to know. Pavlo was only too ready to tell his story.

"When I was eight years old, I was sent to stay the summer with my grandfather on his farm outside of Brody, which is north of my hometown Kolomiya. This was just after the Second World War. One morning in a field I tried to catch some butterflies. I spotted the most beautiful one sitting on a stalk of flax. As I raised my net and started toward it, suddenly beneath my feet there came a strange clicking sound and right after that a huge thunderous bang. Before I knew it, I was in the middle of an explosion and the explosion was so powerful it hurled me up into the air. It felt as if I was being electrocuted. Then I fell to the ground. My eyes were closed but when I opened them, I saw one of my arms in the ditch, the other hanging from a tree. Next thing I knew, I was in the hospital in Brody. I had nightmares. The doctor explained later that I had stepped on a landmine left by the Russians. I was lucky to be alive."

Pavlo continued.

"As a child, even before my arms were blown off, I loved art and I painted everything I saw like trees, animals, flowers. And now I am a professional artist, but mostly I paint nudes."

No question, Pavlo was a professional artist and also prolific in his work. Neighbors had seen male and female models come and go on a regular basis, and they had watched buyers walk off with framed canvases, large and small.

But how on earth did he paint with no hands? they all wondered. Some said he used his feet, others said prosthetics, but no one knew for sure. They dared not ask because they didn't want to appear rude.

If there was one person who could find the answer to that question, it was Reginald. Being the skilled peeper that he was, all he had to do was go over to Pavlo's house and look through his studio window. But truth be told, it wasn't as simple as that. It so happened, every time Reginald passed by, Pavlo's windows were either closed or the curtains drawn, and if there ever was a crack it was never big enough for him to see anything inside. It was obvious Pavlo went to great lengths to guard his privacy.

One bright, sunny afternoon with the sun high in the sky, something unforeseen happened on Bank Street, and it happened right out in the open for all to see. Pavlo pulled up in a cab and with him was a woman who was his new girlfriend. Everyone ran out to see. She was tall, extremely attractive, and with a beautiful repose. The two seemed more together than any two people could be and they clearly had eyes only for one another. It was obvious they were in love. Though the women in the neighborhood were jealous of what was unfolding before their very eyes, at the same time they couldn't help but be happy for Pavlo getting lucky in love.

It was ten-year-old Alfonso from Number 7 who first came to notice something out of the ordinary, and it had to do with the new girlfriend. He shouted for all to hear:

"Hey, look everyone! Pavlo's new girlfriend, she's just like him, she has no arms!"

And indeed, it was so. Pavlo's girlfriend, whose name was Louisa, just like Pavlo, had no arms. But she suffered from Amelia, a rare disorder, born with no arms but lucky for her it was an isolated defect with all other body parts intact. She, too, was a painter and the two had met at a club for armless painters, though, unlike Pavlo, her preferred subject matter was landscapes. When Pavlo first laid eyes on her, she had affected him to such an extent it made his heart flutter away. He adored her through and through and now all he wanted was to paint her in the nude.

One evening as dusk approached and the trees, houses, and gardens all merged together, Reginald set out on his nightly prowl. There was a slight breeze and the air was lofty and sweet. He decided to head in the direction of the variety store. Passing by Pavlo's, expecting nothing but darkness, lo and behold what did he see? A wide-open window and it was without curtains, too. And it wasn't just any window but the window to his studio. "I don't believe it!" Music emanated from inside – a mix of trembita, fife, bagpipe, and Jew's harp – all instruments of the Carpathian highlanders. Keeping to the wall, without so much as a sound, Reginald could hear a woman's voice. It was Louisa but she sounded frustrated.

"Please, Pavlo, if you don't mind, leave the window open, yes, like that; the smell of your oils is so getting to me, I've got a bad headache already."

"I think it's better to close it. You'll be fine, I'm sure. Besides, I swear I heard a noise out there."

"A noise? Don't be silly, there's nothing out there; you have such an imagination, really!"

Reginald, now beneath the window, dared not breathe for fear of being discovered. Peering from the edge of the pane, he could pretty well see the entire room. It was long and narrow with upholstered chairs in chintz, and by the door there was a beat-up old table with a can of mineral spirits on it. On the floor lay a matted rug with geometrical patterns and in the corner against the wall were several unfinished canvases.

As Reginald's eyes wandered, suddenly he came upon something completely unexpected. It was so extraordinary at first he thought he was seeing things. But no, it was real, very real. It was amazing, no, better than amazing, it was out of this world, a gift from God! Propped up on a high-stool was Louisa, and not just any old Louisa but a stark naked one. He couldn't believe his eyes. What a marvelous beauty she was with her firm, round breasts the size of cantaloupes and her kernel-white legs so long and slender. He'd never seen anything like it. She sat there perfectly still, passive, and graceful in her energy. That she had no arms made her all the more worship-worthy, like a Greek goddess, a Venus de Milo.

Then he noticed her backside was set against a full-length mirror, and her backside reflected in that mirror couldn't have been lovelier. It excited him to no end to be able to see the naked front and the back of her both at the same time.

All the while Pavlo was busy with his paints. He stood before his easel and studied Louisa. On his face was the perfect look of happiness, and he was obviously reveling in her engaging form – her muscle tone, her bone structure, the texture of her skin. She sat in the best possible pose not stirring or moving a muscle. The painter in him regarded her only as a model with sex the farthest thing from his mind. Bending over his little work table, lowering his head over a jar filled with brushes of various sizes, he picked one up with his mouth.

"So that's how he does it!" Reginald suddenly remembered why he had come to be there in the first place. "He paints with his mouth! How absolutely astonishing!"

Pavlo proceeded to dab his brush into some paint on his rich palette. After a few seconds, he started moving his brush across his thus-far blank canvas. He dabbed for more paint. His technique was complex, his strokes soft and gentle. He was silent as he worked and Louisa was silent, too. Starting in on her mirrored backside, Pavlo then picked up a knife between his teeth and almost with a sense of violence proceeded to apply thick slabs of white and cream and then streaks of brown. He worked every muscle of his mouth and he worked thoroughly.

About to start in on Louisa's hair, which she had piled up on the top of her head, at once Pavlo detected a movement in the mirror. It was the strangest thing. After a minute it came again. And then he realized the movement was not coming from the mirror itself but, rather, from the window, which happened to be, along with Louisa's backside, reflected in the mirror.

"There's someone out there!" he said to himself. "Someone's watching."

Continuing to gaze at the mirror, trying to make sense of it, at once, he saw half a head emerge and then a whole head, then a set of big, black, bulging eyes. He stood back. Why would someone be at his window and at this late hour? A prowler maybe? The head then rose up and moved ever so slowly toward the middle as if trying to get a better look. At once Pavlo recognized who it was. It was Reginald Rutley from down the street. He'd heard rumors about him, that he was a peeping Tom, a voyeur of sorts. Now he was seeing it for himself, that it was true.

Pavlo thought of confronting him, maybe even calling the police, but then something made him stop. He noticed there was an unusual look on Reginald's face, almost like that of an animal, and he was gazing at Louisa, hungrily, lustfully, as if wanting to eat her up. How unsettling that look was, but, yet, at the same time, how fascinating. The artist in him more than anything wanted to capture that face and put it in his painting.

Pavlo dared not move for fear of scaring the intruder off. He rendered the face quickly. First, he gave it some dramatic undertones beneath the eyes, then applied several dabs of black and brown with a hint of gray to the cheeks. This unexpected subject matter so enthralled him, he painted as if in a state bordering on ecstasy. He completely forgot about Louisa, who was still in her pose, careful not to move.

After an hour or so the session was over and Louisa casually slipped off the high-stool. Feeling stiff and cramped, she stretched her back then her legs. With a soft cotton robe over her shoulders, she sauntered over to the painting to have a look. Her face darkened when she saw it. It was not what she had expected; in fact, the painting rather shocked her and there was an element of danger in it she hadn't expected. It was supposed to have been a simple nude study of her but for some reason, she was a mere shadow off to the side, hardly even noticeable. Someone else had taken over the painting, a man, and he was centered, looking through a window. His face stood out vigorously and he had terrible, glowing eyes, and they were as if ogling her, consuming her. The whole scene disturbed her and she couldn't help but wonder what prompted Pavlo to come up with something so unsettling. How did this strange man even get into the painting in the first place? And yet it all seemed so real. She was completely confused. She wanted to question Pavlo directly but knowing his artistic temperament decided to go about it in a roundabout way.

"There's so much passion in your work, Pavlo. Your strokes are thick and very skillful and you put so much depth into your coloring. But that man, whatever possessed you to put a strange man in with my nude? It makes me uncomfortable."

When Pavlo did not respond, she threw in randomly, "What do you intend to call the painting anyway?"

Pavlo gave it some thought. He said after a moment, "'The Peeping Tom'."

Louisa gave a bit of a shudder but tried to hide her feelings. Wanting to learn more about the strange man, Pavlo was unwilling to open a conversation too soon.

The two artist-lovers soon forgot about the painting and the strange man. They conversed about things inconsequential, and as they joked and laughed, their bodies moved close together. They spoke of their feelings and impressions of things, and suddenly it was as if no one else existed except themselves. She kissed him on the cheek and told him she loved his mouth and he kissed her back and told her he loved her feet (she painted by foot).

Pavlo then walked over to the window and sticking his head outside, looked first to the left then to the right. There didn't appear to be anyone out there, at least not anymore. With what little bits of arm he had, he closed the window and drew the curtains.

★

It took Pavlo a couple of weeks to finish his painting. The canvas, standing three feet high and two feet wide, was the result of the greatest inspiration and art. Rather than hanging it in his studio, carefully picking it up (he had on his prosthetics that day), he put it in his shoulder bag and made for the street. He was on his way to Reginald's house. He had a surprise for him and he couldn't wait to show it. Turning into his walkway, knocking the door with his boot, he waited patiently.

Barely a minute passed when Reginald appeared on the threshold. Astonished at seeing Pavlo standing there, he didn't know what to say or do; he felt rather awkward as there had hardly ever been a word exchanged between them. When a vague smile came to Pavlo's mouth, Reginald fancied he caught a flash of mockery.

Pavlo spoke first, "Good morning, Reginald. You're probably wondering why I came by. Actually, I'm here on a sort of business matter."

Reginald licked his lips, an involuntary gesture, something he did when he was nervous. "A business matter?" he repeated. "But what sort of business could you possibly have with me?"

Pavlo watched Reginald closely. "The fact is I have something to show you. It's in my shoulder bag. Yes, do take it out, please. It's a painting. I think you'll find it interesting."

Reginald proceeded to pull the painting out of the bag. But why should the painter come to him of all people with one of his works? True, he had an appreciation for art and it was commonly known on the street, but still, it didn't make any sense. However, when he took a look at the canvas, his body froze. He became gawky and awkward, and then his face turned a tomato red. The painting was of a man and the man's head was pressed up against a window, looking at a nude model. But the man was more than *looking* at the model, he was ogling her, as if hungering after her. And it wasn't just any man, it was a very recognizable one – it was him! He was overtaken with such shock and embarrassment he could hardly contain himself. Trying to say something, only incoherent sounds came out. Feeling utterly humiliated, he wanted only to slam the door and run away.

Luckily for Reginald, Pavlo was in a great hurry that morning. He had a busy day ahead of him. As it turned out, he was having a joint art show with Louisa the very next day and had to get to the gallery before noon to help set things up. With his painting back in his bag, already on the street, he called out to Reginald, winking his left eye:

"I'm glad you like the painting, Reginald, I was so worried you wouldn't. I'll be showing it tomorrow at the Propeller Gallery just off Queen Street, it'll be hanging by the front door. I've already invited all the neighbors. There'll be wine and cheese. Things kick off at six-thirty. Hope to see you there!"

As Pavlo headed down the street, the morning was a fine morning indeed. He couldn't help smiling. If anything, he was feeling a guilty pleasure, a kind of schadenfreude. Never had he enjoyed himself so much as on this day. Then he started wondering about tomorrow. Would Reginald show up? Though he was hoping yes, his guess was probably no.

Chapter 17

Margarida

It was a cold, muggy evening, the sun about to set. There was a slight wind and there came a dampness in the air. A quiet mist was moving in and around the houses, and soon the leaves would be falling off the trees. The autumn atmosphere was everywhere. It felt like rain and before long it started to drizzle.

Three girlfriends, Margarida, Rory, and Tanya, all fifteen, were walking home from the corner store. They were talking loudly, cracking jokes, and laughing. They each were very different from one another: Margarida was the badass, smoked pot and stole from stores; Rory played the banjo and meditated; and Tanya liked writing stories. The girls passed an old woman with a cane then a small loose dog of the mongrel variety, then a boy on a bike. Before long they came upon a yard with a plum tree and it was full of plums.

"Would you look at that?" Margarida picked a plum and took a bite. "Yum. It's really sweet. It tastes just like from my grandfather's orchard back home." She started to fill her pockets with the deep blue-purple fruit.

At once a noise erupted from the house. A man's head popped out of a window and he was waving his fists furiously. It was Reginald. "Stay away from my plums you little thieves. They're not yours to pick!"

Margarida was quick to shout back and she couldn't have been ruder, "Chill out, will you, old man? Your tree's hanging over the sidewalk anyway. It's a public space as far as I can tell. I can pick all I want."

"You're a mouthy little thing, aren't you. I know who you are; you're the kid from down the street. Where did you grow up anyway, in a barn? You should mind your manners."

Margarida stuck out her tongue and made a face. "You should mind *your* manners! Hah! Hah! Hah! You and your stupid tree!" She threw her unfinished plum and knocked Reginald in the head.

Tanya fell into a panic, "Margarida, what did you just go and do? You hit the street psycho; he's nuts. Come on, let's get the hell out of here before he does something like kill us."

The girls flew down the street screaming, laughing, and flailing their arms about.

They came to Margarida's house. It was smallish, two stories high, and made of red brick. A bit rundown, obvious attempts had been made to keep it together: the veranda stairs had been repaired, the roof patched up, and a couple of windows replaced. Margarida and her parents lived on the first floor, which was accessed by a side door, and upstairs they rented to a young couple with a baby to help pay the bills.

"You guys can come in if you want," Margarida offered. "There's no one home. My mom's at work and my dad's out of town. We can eat, watch TV, play video games, do whatever."

As the girls went inside, little did they know Reginald had followed them but he stayed far enough behind so they wouldn't notice him.

It was raining now and pretty hard but Reginald wasn't too worried as he had on his raincoat and galoshes, and he didn't forget his umbrella either. What he wanted was to find out what the girls might be up to, especially that trouble-maker, Margarida. He seldom looked in on young people and this was his perfect opportunity. Finding a window off to the side, he was not only able to see the entire living room but also into the kitchen.

The girls were sitting at the table chatting, arguing, filling up on napoleon squares Margarida's mother had brought home from the bakery where she worked. There was a bowl with bananas as well but the girls took no interest. The kitchen was rather small with painted wooden cupboards, fake marble countertops, and a patterned linoleum floor. By the fridge there hung a photograph of a young woman holding a baby. The woman was smiling and she was very pretty with dark hair and eyes.

"Is that your mom?" Tanya wanted to know.

"Yah, that's my mom and me."

"Is that in Portugal?"

"Yeah, actually in the Azores, on São Miguel Island, that's where we lived."

"So, what was it like living in the middle of the Atlantic?" Rory drew forward.

"I don't remember much, we moved when I was nine."

"Nine? Nine's not that young. You must remember something."

Margarida fidgeted and there came a strained look to her face. Her eyes wandered but she said nothing

The girls sat a moment in silence.

Margarida then pulled a packet of cigarettes from her jacket pocket, lit one up, and puffed on it several times. She passed it on to Rory.

Rory shook her head, "No thanks, no cancer for me."

Margarida punched her in the arm. "You're such a dumbass, Ro. Do you ever do anything that's not perfect? And what's all this meditation stuff you're into these days?" She started chanting in a teasing way, "Ommm, ommm, ommm …"

"Oh, shut up!" Rory glared at her. "Just shut up! You have no idea what you're talking about. You should try it sometime. It might do you some good. You're always so high-strung."

No one said anything for the next little while. The rain had grown heavier and started to hit up against the window pane. The girls chattered on. Margarida suddenly turned to Tanya, as if having remembered something.

"Oh, by the way, Tanya, I want my ten bucks back."

"What do you mean?"

"That English paper you wrote for me was a fail. I got an F."

"You got an F? No way."

"Actually, the paper got an A, I got the F. Mr. Mitchell, what a jerk. He said I didn't write the paper, and that if I try and pull a stunt like that again, I'll get detention."

"You didn't tell him I wrote it, did you?" Tanya had a look of alarm. "He'll dock me for sure."

"No, relax. I didn't say anything. But I still want my ten bucks back."

The girls then went into the living room. They played a few video games and later put on a movie. Margarida made some popcorn.

The rain continued. At once there came a flash of lightening, followed by a clap of thunder. Suddenly the lights went out. Everything became black.

"Oh great, no power. Now what?" this was Tanya.

"Man, is it ever dark in here, I can't see a thing," said Margarida.

Tanya again, "It's kind of spooky. It's like there are demons all around us."

"Candles, do you have any candles?"

"Yeah, in the drawer somewhere. That's where my mom usually keeps them. Shit, now where are my matches? Oh, here they are."

Margarida lit a candle and placed it on the little coffee table next to the couch. The light flickered.

Rory opened up her laptop. "Damn, my battery's dead."

"Hey, I know," Tanya had a thought. "Since there's not much to do, we can play cards. Margarida, do you have a deck lying around?"

"Cards? No, cards are lame anyway."

"How about board games? Do you have board games?"

"Board games? Are you serious? Who has board games?"

Then Rory, "I have an idea, let's play psychiatrist. It's a really cool game. I played it at a party once. One person's the shrink, another's the patient."

Margarida rolled her eyes, "Sounds totally dumb, count me out."

Tanya agreed, "Count me out too."

"No, it's fun, trust me. It's like this: the patient lies down on the couch and tells the shrink all her problems. And the shrink tries to help the patient figure things out."

When Margarida and Tanya still objected, Rory was as if she didn't hear them, "Okay, this is what we'll do. I'll be the shrink and you, Margarida, be the patient. And who knows, maybe I'll even uncover some of your dark, deep secrets. Hah, hah, hah."

"Get lost."

"Come on, don't be such a loser."

Margarida finally gave in, "Oh, what the hell, okay, but only till the lights come back on."

At once there came a flash of lightning so bright it clearly revealed the furnishings of the living room – an oversized wing chair, a tiffany-style floor lamp, a television. Margarida lay down on the sofa, which happened to be by the window.

Reginald watched on and with close attention, all the while keeping dry beneath his umbrella.

Rory started, "Margarida, take a deep breath. Yes, like that. I want you to clear your mind and to not think about anything. Now close your eyes. Get comfortable, relax. Deep breath, now exhale. Deep breath again, exhale. You're completely at ease with yourself. Tell me, how are you feeling?"

"I'm feeling fine."

"How was your day at school?"

"Okay."

"Just Okay?"

"Yeah, except for that shithead English teacher, Mr. Mitchell."

"He caught you cheating, is that right? Why didn't you write the paper yourself?"

"I don't know. I didn't feel like it. It was stupid anyway."

"What was it about?"

"It was a book report on *Lord of the Flies*."

"Did you read the book?"

"No, not really."

"How do you know it was stupid then?"

Margarida half got up. She looked impatient, "Oh, this game really sucks. Just so you know, it's not going to work."

Rory ignored her, "Sh. Quiet, lay back down. Eyes closed. Breathe in, breathe out, yes, like that." Then, "Do you love your mother?"

"Yes."

"Do you love your father?"

"Of course."

"Describe to me the happiest day of your life."

A smile strayed on Margarida's lips.

"It was my birthday and my parents bought me a bike. It was blue and white and had a wicker basket and a big horn."

"Was that in the Azores?"

"No, it was here, in our old house on the other side of town, they made a big party for me in our backyard with lots of my friends."

"How old were you?"

"Eleven."

"Did you have a cake?"

"Yes, a big chocolate one."

"So, you were happy?"

"Yes."

"But what about the Azores, were you happy in the Azores?"

Margarida at once became quiet. There came a strange, tense moment. Her lower lip twitched.

Rory carried on.

"Where did you live in the Azores?"

"On São Miguel Island. In a house by the sea. There was a small beach and my mother let me play with my dolls on the rocks."

"Did you have a big family there? Cousins? Aunts and uncles?"

Margarida suddenly stirred and there came a terrible expression to her face. She started muttering something but in Portuguese.

"Margarida, what are you saying, I don't understand."

Margarida kept on.

"Margarida, stop fooling around. Speak English. Tell me what you're saying."

"Okay."

"Okay, what?"

"Okay, I'll tell you."

"Tell me what?"

"It was Uncle Filipe."

"Uncle Filipe? What do you mean? Who is Uncle Filipe?"

"Uncle Filipe, he wasn't really my uncle, I just called him that."

"So, who was he then?"

"He was an old friend of my father's from when they whale-hunted together on the high seas."

"What about him?"

"He was always smiling; he was fun and he liked to make jokes. He often brought me presents: a stuffed animal, a train set, a doll. Then one day … "

"Then one day what?" Rory straightened her back.

"When I was seven years old, he came to our house and told me he wanted to take me for a ride on his brand-new fishing boat. My mom said okay, so off I went with my Uncle Filipe."

"What did his boat look like?"

"It was a shrimp trawler, white and with a closed cabin. And there was a downstairs part to it too."

"What happened next?"

Margarida hesitated and there came something peculiar in her hesitation.

Rory repeated the question.

"What happened next?"

Margarida's voice faltered. "Everything happened. That's the day I died."

Rory didn't like where Margarida was taking this. She waited for what would come next.

"Uncle Filipe gave me candies. He showed me how to use the nets and later he showed me the wheel and all the steering mechanisms. Then he told me to come with him to the cabin below because there was something special waiting for me down there."

Margarida paused briefly. She couldn't stop fidgeting with her hands. Then barely audibly, "That's when he became all weird and a horrible shine came to his eyes. He started telling me how pretty I was and that my hair was soft like silk."

"And what happened after that?"

"He pulled up my dress and began touching me all over. I didn't know why he was doing what he was doing. I went numb. It was like the most sickening nightmare ever in my life. It hurt so bad and he wouldn't stop. I tried to get away but he was too big and strong. And I was trapped on the boat. It was all so disgusting."

Margarida was now shaking and twitching convulsively. Tanya covered her up with a blanket.

Margarida struggled to go on.

"He laughed like a savage. He told me if I told anyone he would take my mother on his boat, throw her overboard and let her drown. I didn't tell my mother or anyone. I didn't want him to kill her."

Tears welled in Margarida's eyes, "And the whole time I could hear the waves hammering against the boat, and I just listened to the waves – crash, smash, crash, smash. And there were gulls screaming in the air."

Tanya and Rory didn't say a word. A dreadful, unspeakable scene had just been revealed to them and they gazed at one another trying to figure out what to do. Their friend was in such a painful state. What they wanted more than anything was to leave but nothing could induce them to do so. They wished they had never started this stupid game in the first place.

At once, as if out of nowhere, there came a loud bang, followed by a pronounced cry. It came from the window. Tanya and Rory froze. Something or somebody was out there. At first, they thought it might be a burglar, then decided it most likely was a raccoon trying to get into one of the garbage bins. But of course, it was Reginald spying on them. As it happened, he accidently slipped and banged his head against the pane. Not about to take any chances, Tanya and Rory hurried to close the window. Then they pulled the curtains.

Shut out, unable see or hear anything, Reginald cursed under his breath, "Dammit! And right at the most critical moment!"

There was no point in him staying any longer, and, besides, he was starting to get cold, having been out in the wet all this time. And his head was sore too from that bang. Making for home, he couldn't stop thinking of Margarida. A great sympathy for her rose within him and his mood was gloomy and sullen; he couldn't help but live and breathe her every bit of agony. He hardly knew her but he cared so much. He cried out loud: "How awful this life can be!"

It was not long before anger set in. "I'll find that bastard and when I do, I'll kill him. I swear I'll kill him!"

As Reginald turned into the walkway of his house, at once the electricity came back on. Going inside, he took off his rain gear and put a kettle on to boil for tea. Sinking into a chair, he tried to clear his mind but no matter how hard he tried, he couldn't. Everything Margarida had said was so disturbing, so overwhelming, he couldn't believe it, and he was afraid to believe it.

Back at Margarida's the shrink game was over. Tanya and Rory were so completely troubled by all they had heard they wanted to say something but didn't know how to start. It was shocking to them how their friend could have spoken so freely about something so frightful. They couldn't understand why she had chosen to tell them today of all days, why not yesterday or a week ago or even a month ago? They had known Margarida for a few months now and not a word, not even a whisper.

The girls decided to go to the kitchen and get a drink. They told Margarida to get up but for some reason she remained supine, her eyes closed. She wasn't moving.

"Come on, Margarida, get up. Let's get some soda."

No answer.

Rory poked her in the arm. "Margarida, get up."

Still no answer.

Tanya then gave her a shake, "Margarida, stop fooling around!"

When still there came nothing, Tanya suddenly filled with alarm, "Something's wrong! Why isn't she moving? It's like she's in a trance. Rory, what did you do to her?"

"What do you mean, what did *I* do to her? I didn't do anything! I just asked her a bunch of questions, you heard me."

"You've been into all this weird meditation and transcendental stuff lately. You put her in a trance."

"A trance? What do I know about trances?"

"Oh my god, I think you hypnotized her!"

"Hypnotized her? Are you crazy?"

"Oh no! What if she never wakes up?"

"We need help. We have to find a hypnotist somewhere, someone who knows what to do."

Tanya thought quickly, "Hey, I know. Up on Dundas there's a psychic. She's usually open late. You know, the one by the fish store. We can ask her."

"A psychic? Are you kidding me? Those psychics are all just a bunch of scam artists. She'll sell you some potions for a few hundred dollars and tell you they'll get rid of the demons."

Tanya then came up with another idea and she was decisive about it, "Okay then, we have to get her to a hospital, there's no other way. They have specialists there; they'll know what to do with her. We'll have to call an ambulance."

Rory paced the room, "Oh, my God, we're in so much trouble, maybe we'll even get arrested. And what are her parents going to say?"

Suddenly something occurred to Tanya, "Where's your laptop? Hurry, plug it in. There must be some information online on how to get people out of hypnotic trances. Maybe we can do it ourselves."

"I don't know if that's such a good idea. What if we make things worse? We need someone who actually knows what they're doing."

"It can't hurt to try."

Looking over several sites, at last Tanya found one that seemed straightforward enough. She read aloud: *"At first talk to them in a normal conversational tone. This will bring them out of hypnosis and back to everyday consciousness. But do it gradually and not suddenly. Increase the pace and energy of your voice. Use their name more prominently and start talking to them about something before you hypnotized them."*

Tanya looked up, "Let's do it. Let's do what it says."

Rory started right away. She kept her voice steady: "Margarida, about your English paper. Why did you get Tanya to write it for you? Mr. Mitchell's not stupid. He could tell it wasn't your writing."

Margarida lay rigid and speechless. Several minutes passed. Rory continued.

"*Lord of the Flies* is actually an okay book. You should try reading it sometime."

Margarida's breathing started to increase and then her head moved slightly.

"Look, it's working!"

Rory went on, "Margarida, you picked plums from Reginald's tree. Tell me, why did you throw one at him?"

No answer.

"Margarida, I said why did you throw a plum at Reginald?"

Margarida slowly opened her eyes. She smiled faintly, "Because it was fun, and he's creepy."

"What did they taste like, those plums? Do you remember?"

"Sweet, they tasted sweet like honey."

Margarida sat up. Rubbing her eyes, she looked around, "What's going on? Where am I? And why are you two staring at me like that? Did I fall asleep or something?"

"Yeah, something like that."

"Do you remember anything that happened?" this was Tanya.

"What do you mean?"

"Well, you said a lot of things."

"I did? Like what? I don't remember."

"It was all pretty crazy. You talked about the Azores, about your mom, about the beach, and about a boat."

Margarida stiffened, "About a boat?"

"Yes, and about a man, your Uncle Filipe."

"Uncle Filipe?" Margarida tensed and her mouth quivered. Struggling to remember, she couldn't recall saying anything to them about Uncle Filipe. Had she forgotten? No, she couldn't have said a thing because Uncle Filipe was hidden deep within her and she would never have let him out. Then she noticed her eyes were damp with tears and her mascara was running. Had she been crying? She looked at her friends confusedly.

"What's been going on? Is this some kind of joke?"

At once there came a silence and it was oppressive. Tanya and Rory exchanged glances. They couldn't imagine what was going through their friend's mind. They wanted to help her but didn't know how. All they could do was sympathize and be there for her.

Finally, Rory said with a special carefulness, "It's getting late; Tanya and I should really get going. If you need anything Margarida just call us. See you tomorrow."

Margarida didn't say goodbye; she didn't even raise her head. When her friends left, she burst into tears.

★

Though it had long since stopped raining, the next morning was still overcast. When Reginald awoke, he was restless, and it was a mournful, probing kind of restlessness that had been with him all night. Margarida remained heavily on his mind and he couldn't help but relive those appalling scenes she had so vividly described. He was in no mood to drink coffee or eat breakfast. He wanted to do something for Margarida, something to make her feel better, to show that he cared, if that was at all possible. But he was a stranger to her after all, and he certainly wasn't about to overstep any boundaries. Soon he came up with an idea and it cheered him up.

Going to the cupboard from under the sink he pulled out a basket. He then went outside to his plum tree and started picking the fattest, juiciest plums he could find. He would go to Margarida's before she left for school.

With his short legs moving at an astonishing speed along the pavement, he got there just in time. Placing the basket by her door, ringing the bell, he hurried away so she wouldn't see him.

When Margarida came to the door there was no one there. Seeing the basket of plums, her eyes lit up at once. But who could have brought them? Then she realized they could only have come from one person, from that strange little man down the street – Reginald. But why would he care to bring her plums, especially after she'd knocked him in the head with one? Maybe he wasn't such a creep after all, she decided. Taking the basket inside, she placed it on the kitchen table and then left for school.

Chapter 18

Murder on Bank Street

Two of Reginald's neighbors, Beatrice and Anna, had come into his hardware store. Though Beatrice knew Anna was there, Anna had no idea Beatrice was, and, to add to that, Anna had no idea Beatrice had purposely followed her in there. As it happened, Beatrice had something up her sleeve, something so menacing, so nefarious no one could have ever imagined what it could possibly be. And unbeknownst to Reginald, it was he who would be at the center of it all. Beatrice's intention was, by way of Anna, to get to Reginald and have him fall into a trap she'd been setting. If all went according to plan, everything would play itself out that very night. So, when Beatrice "accidently" bumped into Anna in the small appliance section, that's when everything started going into play.

Beatrice spoke first but she looked over her shoulder to Reginald to see if he was listening. He was.

"Hi, Anna. Fancy meeting you here."

"Hello, Beatrice. How goes it?"

"You'll never believe it."

"Believe what?"

"Have you seen that new woman who moved into Number 41?"

"You mean Desiree? Yeah, I've run into her a few times. She seems nice enough. What about her?"

"Well, let me put it this way, she's not your average everyday working woman."

"What do you mean?"

Beatrice raised her voice.

"She's a sex-trade worker."

"A what?"

"A sex-trade worker."

"No way!"

"Yes."

"How do you know?"

"I've been watching. I've been out of work several weeks now and I have a lot of time on my hands. I sit on my porch and I see things."

"You're out of work? I'm sorry to hear."

"No big deal. I have something in the works, and it looks like it will be going through. Anyway, about Desiree. The men, they come to see her day and night, but mostly they sneak round back through the laneway."

"The laneway, you say? Oh!"

"And if that isn't enough, they each stay maybe an hour, maybe two, sometimes just fifteen minutes. One goes in, another goes out. Quite the business she's got going on in there, if you know what I mean."

Reginald, who was all ears by now, moved closer, pretending to be busily wiping the counter.

"And you wouldn't believe who I saw coming out of there yesterday."

"Who?"

"Gus."

"You mean Gus from number 4, the construction worker?"

"Yes."

"No!"

"Yes."

"And Harvey too."

"Harvey? As in Molly's Harvey?"

"Yep."

"Really?"

"Really."

"And not to forget Julio."

"Julio? Oh no, not Julio too!"

The women exchanged a few more words of gossip, then went to the counter to pay for the items they had come in to buy, Beatrice a coffee pot, Anna a plunger for her toilet. Reginald punched in the coffee pot first, and giving Beatrice her change, then started in on Anna's plunger. As he bagged the purchases, completely unaware of anything going on, he couldn't help but smile to himself, grateful for the bits of information that had come his way. He had no idea there was a scheme in the works and that it would be a scheme so extreme even the police would have to be called in. And, to make matters worse, he had no idea it was set to happen in a matter of hours.

With Beatrice and Anna long gone, Reginald was counting the minutes to closing time. He couldn't wait to get over to Desiree's house to see for himself what was going on there. Beatrice's and Anna's little conversation had more than piqued his curiosity. He would check out the laneway, where, supposedly, all the action was taking place. Still, he couldn't believe it – Desiree, a sex-trade worker? Why hadn't he picked up on that before? He had passed her several times on the street and there was nothing odd about her, nothing to rouse his suspicion. She was very pretty, and, true, maybe her clothes were a bit on the tight side and her face too made up, but a sex-trade worker? Sex-trade workers were down on Queen Street, in the dark, dingy taverns and shady hotels, but on Bank Street?

At last the time came to lock up his shop. Hastening down Dufferin, it was already getting dark. A heavy mist settled over the rooftops and the air became thick and muggy. Lights were on in most of the houses he passed and the smell of meatloaf filled the air. Coming to Bank Street, there was no time to stop at home, not even for a bite to eat.

As he passed by Beatrice's, at once he noticed a faint light in an upstairs window. Somehow, he got the strange feeling he was being watched. Was there someone looking down on him? He was sure there was. Was it maybe Beatrice? When he tried to get a better look, there was nothing out of the ordinary. He decided it was probably just the night light playing tricks on him.

Heading for the laneway, now only a matter of steps away, he would creep into Desiree's backyard and try and find an open window. The prospect of having an X-rated scene unfold before him gave him such a thrill he couldn't stop thinking about it.

The laneway was narrow and dark, much darker than he expected, and he could hardly see where he was going. Old wooden garages lined up in a row and the surrounding shrubs were barely visible. Desiree's house was the third one on the left, he was almost there. As he made for her gate, as luck would have it, he noticed an open window on the lower level, and there was a light flickering from inside as if from a candle. Curtains were blowing in the wind. He could hear the music of Louis Armstrong.

As he started along the stone walkway that led to her back door, his foot suddenly became snagged by something and he was met with quite the crash. A burning came to his knees and then blood trickled down his legs.

"What the hell?" he struggled to get up.

From his jacket pocket he pulled out a flashlight he was in the habit of carrying and proceeded to inspect the ground. He suspected maybe a fallen branch or a twig but what he saw was more like a piece of water pipe or maybe a broom handle. He became confused; if only he had more light. Touching it, he found it cold and squishy but in a weird sort of way.

"What can it be?" he said to himself.

Then he jumped back in horror and screamed.

"An arm, it's a human arm!"

He could scarcely breathe and his heart gave a jump. Flicking his flashlight toward the fence, he saw the arm belonged to a woman and she lay stretched out on a patch of grass overgrown with weeds. Half-naked, her body was streaked with mud and blood and there were signs of bruising on her legs and abdomen. There were stab wounds on her chest. She was dead, she'd obviously been murdered. Though Reginald had seen dead people before, never before had he seen a murdered one.

When he turned his flashlight onto the woman's face, he was shocked to learn who it was. It was Desiree! Her lips were split and bloody and it appeared her nose was broken. He fell into a panic. Taking out his cell phone he started to call 911. A crime had been committed and he needed to report it. As the phone barely started to ring, suddenly he changed his mind and hung up.

"Are you stupid or what?" he chided himself, "Calling the police? They'll be all over you in a minute. They'll want to know: what were you doing in the laneway in the dark? How was it you happened upon the body? Why did you go into the victim's yard in the first place? Did you know the victim? Yes? No? Then – did you murder her?"

"What should I do? What should I do?"

At once, he made the decision to get the hell out of there and fast before someone should spot him. Taking to his heels, making for the street, suddenly, to his great dismay there came the sound of sirens. And they were coming fast. Before long two police cruisers pulled into the laneway, followed by a black unmarked car. Reginald, pinning himself up against one of the garage doors, became dazzled by the flashing lights.

A police officer got out of the first cruiser. His gun was aimed. He shouted:

"Freeze! Hands up!"

Reginald put up his hands.

The officer did a quick pat-down but found only a flashlight.

Two other officers climbed out of the second cruiser, and wasting no time, searched the surroundings. They looked briefly along the fence, in and around the garages, and behind the garbage bins. They then went into Desiree's yard. It was not long before one of them called out:

"We found the woman's body! Just like the caller said. Looks like she's been stabbed, dead maybe an hour."

Reginald could feel his stomach tighten. The words *just like the caller said* hit him like a ton of bricks. That meant someone had called the police! Someone knew about Desiree's murder, and not just about the murder but that he, Reginald, would be there at this very moment. He started to get worried. Someone had been watching him. He was being framed! But who would do such a thing? Then it struck him – but of course, the murderer himself!

A homicide detective in a pin-striped suit with a blue and yellow tie came forward. It was Detective Henderson. Not much over forty, slender, and with a slight limp to his right leg, he went straight into Desiree's yard to check things out. It was much worse than he had expected. The woman's stab wounds were very deep and it looked like one had gone straight through her heart. After a few minutes, he walked up to Reginald as if already having convicted him. He asked arrogantly.

"What's your name?"

"Reginald Rutley."

"Where do you live?"

"At twenty-five Bank Street."

"What are you doing here at this late hour?"

Reginald wasn't prepared for the question, even though it was the most obvious one to ask. He had to make something up and fast. He swallowed hard.

"I was out for a walk."

"A walk? Do you make this laneway journey often?"

"No, um, you see, I saw a cat chasing something and I was, um, curious, so I followed the cat."

"A cat you say?"

"Yes, yes, a big yellow tabby."

"What was this tabby you saw chasing?"

"I don't know, that's why I followed it. To see."

He looked at Reginald as if he didn't believe him. He narrowed his eyes.

"Were you aware there was a dead body on the premises?"

Reginald could hardly articulate.

"No. Yes, no, I … um … "

The detective then noticed drops of congealed blood on his trousers. He asked pointing, "How did that happen?"

"I tripped and fell. I scraped my knees. They started to bleed."

"There's blood on your shirt too, a lot of it. How did it get all the way up there?"

"It must have got smeared somehow."

The detective arched his left eyebrow, "Nothing you say adds up. Why don't you start from the beginning? Let's go back to the cat."

Reginald broke into a nervous laugh, "All right, as you wish. There was a cat and the cat was chasing something. I chased after the cat and when it ran into Desiree's yard, I followed it. That's how I ended up there. Then I tripped over something and when I went to check out what it was, I saw an arm, and it belonged to a woman, a dead woman. It was Desiree's."

"What else did you see?"

"I saw she was all roughed up and had stab wounds in her chest. There was blood everywhere. I think that's how I got this blood all over me, when I fell."

"How well did you know Desiree?"

"Not very well at all. She moved here a few weeks ago."

"Were you aware she was in the sex trade?"

"No, yes, actually, I only found out yesterday."

"Were you a client?"

"No."

The detective narrowed his eyes, "Are you sure? Not even once?"

"No."

"Did you see or hear anything unusual tonight?"

"No, I just heard music coming from her house. It was a Louis Armstrong tune."

A moment of silence. Then it came, the dreaded question:

"Did you, Reginald Rutley, murder Desiree?"

Reginald froze. He knew he was about to face the conflict of his life.

"No, I did not murder Desiree."

The detective went on.

"Well, Reginald, I'm sorry to say, things aren't looking very good for you right now. This is the way I see it. I think you're lying. I say you knew Desiree and on a more intimate level. The two of you obviously got into some kind of spat and you physically attacked her, hence the bruises on her. She ran out into the yard and you chased after her but not before grabbing a knife, possibly from the kitchen. You stabbed her in a fit of rage, maybe even passion, you murdered her. It's only a matter of time before I get to the bottom of things. I've seen it all before."

Reginald could hardly grasp any of what the detective was saying, his words were so harsh, so beyond comprehension. He was no murderer; why, he couldn't hurt a fly let alone a human being. The cruelty of Desiree's murder was unfathomable to him. About to defend himself at once he realized how seriously compromised his situation truly was. He was now a suspect in a murder case, and as a suspect anything he said or did could be used against him in a court of law. He vowed from here on in to watch his every word.

The detective proceeded to read Reginald his rights. Handcuffing him and leading him to his cruiser, he then shoved him into the back seat and closed the door.

Meanwhile, a forensic team arrived with a photographer, followed by paramedics, then came TV reporters with camera crews.

The neighbors were already thronging around the cordoned-off yellow tape reading "Crime Scene Do Not Cross". A murder had been committed on Bank Street and that didn't happen very often. Everywhere was noise and conversation and people were shouting in groups together and jostling each other. All were met with fear and disbelief, stunned by the tragic news of Desiree's untimely death. But no one could believe it, that Reginald Rutley, the seemingly harmless little hunchback from Number 25, owner of Rutley's Home Hardware, was the murderer.

Anna was in the crowd too and so was Beatrice, and Beatrice happened to be standing next to Gus. Gus was taking the murder very hard. Gasping and shuddering, every few minutes he dabbed his eyes. He was all choked up and this is what he was saying but half to himself, "Desiree, murdered, my God! What am I going to do now? What am I going to do now?"

Luckily for Gus, Beatrice was right there to console him. Rubbing his back, she could be heard whispering into his ear:

"There, there, Gus; it's a hard blow, I know. The police have a suspect, let's just hope the killer's brought to justice. Come to my place later if you have nothing to do. I'll make things good again, maybe even better. I promise."

Had not everyone been so preoccupied with the murder case at hand, they would have noticed a considerable change in Beatrice's appearance, actually, it was more like a metamorphosis. She was quite dressed up, but in a provocative sort of way, and her clothes seemed thinner, skimpier, cut lower in the front, and her heels were very high. She had on blue eyeshadow and heavy mascara, and her lips were painted a bright red. There wafted from her the strong scent of perfume, but it was her hair that really stood out, done up much like Desiree's, flipped and curled in the front and hennaed to give it that lush orange hue. Had anyone bothered to take a look, Beatrice could easily have been mistaken for Desiree. It was quite the freakish thing.

As Beatrice continued to calm Gus, at the same time her gaze wandered. She was on the lookout for someone. She was searching for Harvey certain he too would need some comforting. Oh, there he was by the fence, sobbing, gasping, shuddering much in the same way as Gus. Happily, his wife Molly was nowhere to be seen. She would saunter over to him, place his head in her bosom, and whisper in his ear, same as she did with Gus, "There, there now, Harvey. Come to my place if you have nothing to do. I'll make things good again maybe even better. I promise."

Her next plan of action was to search out Julio.

The three men, Gus, Harvey, and Julio were something special and very serious to her because she knew what easy conquests they would be. They would help her get things up-and-running, they would be her very first clients.

Finally, after an hour, it came – the body bag. Carried by two paramedics, they could be heard speaking to one another.

"Poor woman, she was so young."

"Yes, such a frightened look on her face, what a violent way to go. What did she see before the end, I wonder?"

"She saw her killer, no doubt."

"Yes, that she did."

"It's never easy, something like this."

"No, never."

The paramedics carefully placed Desiree in an ambulance and then shut the door. It sped off to the morgue.

Reginald was driven off too but to the police station where he was put in a holding cell. Allowed one phone call, he called his lawyer, who agreed to see him first thing in the morning.

The cell was cold and damp and his cot thin and rickety. Reginald tossed and turned all night, unable to sleep. He tried to collect his thoughts. That he was being charged with murder was all so unthinkable to him, so unreal. He'd been set up, there was no doubt in his mind but who would do such a thing? He racked his brain trying to figure it out.

At once, it struck him. Remembering the scene in his hardware store that morning, it all started to make sense.

"Beatrice! Of course! She's the one who set me up! She'd been watching me, studying me. It was not some plain coincidence that led her into my store this morning. No, not in the least, and she made sure I overheard her little conversation with Anna. It had all been carefully crafted. She used Anna to get to me. She caught me peeping in on neighbors a couple of times and figured I'd be an easy target. And she had watched me from her window tonight, I didn't imagine it. She knew where I was headed because she was the one who set me up to go there. I fell right into her trap, like a rabbit into a snare."

Then he became unsure.

"But Beatrice, the murderer? Why on earth would she want to murder Desiree? What motive could she possibly have?"

The more he thought about it, suddenly he remembered seeing her from the patrol car. She was dressed strangely, wearing very much unlike anything she normally wore – a figure-hugging dress, heels four inches high, and her hair all done up colored a bright orange. Why, if anything, she was looking more like Desiree than Desiree herself. What struck him most was that she had this strange, malignant look in her eye and it was very much her own. And why on earth was she standing next to Harvey and why was Harvey's head in her bosom? There was definitely something more going on than met the eye.

Outside the cell door there came footsteps, then the rattling of keys. Reginald was expecting his lawyer but instead Detective Henderson showed up. He looked disheveled and under his arm he carried a blue folder. Unshaven and with his eyes all puffy, holding a cup of coffee, it was clear he had been without a break all night working on the case. He spoke reluctantly but to the point.

"Well, Reginald, it looks like you're in luck. Results from forensics just came in. A few things don't add up and you'll be happy to know they're in your favor. There are footprints coming from Desiree's house, hers and that of a third party – it appears that of her killer. The foot size is smaller than yours and with a thin heel, which suggests a woman. The blood on your shirt is Desiree's but it's consistent with your story, that you tripped over her arm and fell. We found your partial imprint in the grass."

Then from under his brows, sternly, "But I want you to know, there's still much evidence connected to you though not enough to convict you, at least not yet. I believe somehow you were mixed up in all of this and I intend to prove it. But for now, you're free to go, only don't go too far, and don't leave town either."

Reginald felt a sudden intense, indescribable relief and his anxiety and agony of mind lifted. There was not enough evidence to convict him. He couldn't believe it. He was free to go!

Out on the street, jumping on the streetcar, he headed for home. He couldn't stop thinking about the detective. How presumptuous he was, so unpleasant, and with such a great opinion of himself. He acted as if he knew everything, but catching at straws was what he was doing, obsessing with details. Reginald was determined to prove him wrong, and while he was at it, he would prove his neighbors wrong too because they also had him pegged guilty.

But didn't the detective say there were footprints suggesting that of a woman? Reginald thought a moment. This little bit of information was most definitely a relevant lead in his investigation. He had been right all along. Beatrice! The footprints did indeed belong to a woman and that woman was Beatrice. When it got dark, he would go to her house and try to find answers.

It was eight o'clock and the sun was down. The empty street could be dimly discerned through the lingering mist and black clouds hung motionless from the sky. Mosquitoes buzzed here and there and leaves rustled in the soft breeze. In the distance a night bird called.

The lights were on in most of the houses Reginald passed, and looking round, he could see nothing menacing in any of them. But there was a tension in the air. A murder had been committed on Bank Street, and as far as the neighbors were concerned, though a suspect was in custody, the suspect's guilt was yet to be determined and the killer or killers might still very well be on the loose.

Already at Beatrice's, Reginald hid behind a bush and listened. Tonight, he couldn't have been more careful. He hardly made a sound. No one knew of his release and he wanted to keep it that way, at least until the crime was solved.

At once, he heard footsteps coming up the pavement. They were heavy, even, and deliberate, and they were coming up fast. A man emerged, tall, well-built, wearing a loose-fitting shirt, dark trousers, and looking very Mediterranean. He was whistling and under his arm he carried a bottle of booze. It was Gus. When he came to Beatrice's, he mounted her veranda stairs and rang the bell. Beatrice opened the door and stood for some time looking as though expecting him. She let him in. Gus walked into the living room and sat on the sofa.

Luckily for Reginald, several windows were wide open, and from where he stood, he could see everything, including a semi-erotic painting of a woman half-undressed on the wall. There wafted some sweet scent like maybe rose or lilac bought at a bath and body shop, and then there came the music of Louis Armstrong.

"How strange," thought Reginald, "that's the same Armstrong tune I heard coming out of Desiree's house the night of her murder."

Beatrice was talking but her voice was so small and distant Reginald could hardly hear. Pouring some wine, now speaking louder, looking straight at Gus, she came off as rather business-like.

"Gus, I want you to know I have certain standards and specific rules. No heavy drinking, no vulgarity, and no rough-housing. Now that Desiree's gone, I've stepped in to do her work."

Barely having finished, her expression suddenly changed. Peering at him from the corner of her eye, she started to cry but it couldn't have been more artificial. She then choked on her words as if for effect. "Desiree, poor dear Desiree, she didn't deserve such a brutal end! And that little hunchback of all people, who would have thought?"

Gus, overwhelmed with grief, not picking up on Beatrice's disingenuousness, sobbed and shivered away. He said wiping away tears, "You're right, she didn't deserve any of this. Poor Desiree, may she rest in peace."

At once Armstrong's rendition of "All of Me" came on. Beatrice, as if regaining herself, got back to the business at hand. Reaching for the coffee table, from a pile she took hold of some kind of brochure. It was printed out on a home computer and carelessly stapled together. On the cover was a drawing of a naked woman lying on a furry rug showing the curves of her back. She handed it to Gus.

"It's my price list. Look it over. Take your time."

Gus scanned the first page.

Hand job $50

Blow job $100

Quickie $150

Gus studied the list. He was having trouble choosing. Turning to Beatrice for guidance, she said nothing as she sat there motionless in her see-through dressing gown that was a little bit torn. At last he opted for number five, a thirty-minute session for $175. He said almost apologetically, "I'm sorry, I'm being conservative by my own standards. But I have every intention of upping things once we get better acquainted."

Beatrice was keen on getting started. Sitting on his lap, kissing his neck, his mouth, she went on to assert herself. She couldn't have been more alluring in the faint light, and soon the two fell into impetuous passion. There was much between them but not love.

In the meantime, Reginald, still at the window, couldn't help but become roused. He too had imperative sensual needs, and Beatrice was managing to take care of him at the same time, though she didn't know it. If only he could be in Gus' place. Beatrice's eroticism so enticed him, he contemplated paying her a visit himself, maybe even later tonight. She was making him forget why he had come to be there in the first place. He forgot he was on the hunt for a killer, that he himself had been accused of that horrific crime, that he had spent the night in jail – he forgot about the detective, the police officers, his lawyer, he forgot about everything.

Then, completely out of the blue, something strange happened. Catching sight of Beatrice's white naked skin that was whiter than ivory, he became confused, so confused he didn't know what to think. Somehow it was not Beatrice he was seeing but rather Desiree. But how could that be? Had Desiree come back from the dead? Was he putting one over on himself? And then to further complicate things he heard Gus cry out:

"Oh, Desiree! Desiree! Again! Again!"

Pulling out his opera glasses, which he purposely brought with him, as clear as day, he could see it was Beatrice after all.

As if a comrade-in-arms, he wanted to call out to Gus and to alert him, "Hey, Gus," he wanted to say, "it's Beatrice you're doing not Desiree. Beatrice is only messing with our heads!"

And then suddenly it struck Reginald – Beatrice's motive:

"That's it! Beatrice wanted Desiree dead so she could take over her identity, she wanted her business, she wanted it all for herself. Back in the hardware store, didn't she say to Anna she had lost her job? Well, now she had one and quite a lucrative one at that, one where she could play by her own rules.

"But murder?" Still, Reginald found it hard to believe.

With Gus and Beatrice wrapping things up, zipping up his pants, it was obvious Gus had had a helluva time. Out on the veranda, bumping into Harvey, the two men exchanged glances, then awkwardly looked away. Harvey hurried into the house while Gus made down the street into the darkness.

Beatrice took care of Harvey in much the same way she did Gus, but because Harvey opted for number eight, he got a lot more for his money. At a cost of $275, she not only took him upstairs but kept him there for a full hour.

When Harvey at last was done, in came Julio, who wasted no time in picking the 'house special'. After forty-five minutes in the basement, he came up happy and singing: "What a great world this is, it's marvelous!"

It was now well past midnight and the air had grown heavy and damp. Beatrice was calling it a night. She started straightening pillows on the sofa, locking doors, and blowing out the candles.

Reginald, still at the window, knew he ought to go home. Obviously, nothing was going to happen, she was wrapping things up. But then he had a change of mind: he vowed not to leave until he got what it was he had come for. He needed evidence. And sure enough, before long, things started to unravel.

Beatrice was sitting on the sofa with her legs kicked out in front of her. She was relaxing as anybody would after a lengthy day's work. Louis Armstrong was playing in the background.

Tonight had been a success, all her seductive ideas had taken root and become reality. What a great little enterprise she had going for herself: she was her own boss (no pimp to be found), she established her own hours, everything was already set up and running – and all thanks to Desiree. She quickly did some mental math, "Let's see now, $175 from Gus, $275 from Harvey, another $250 from Julio, that's already $700, and for just over two hours' work!"

'Mack the Knife' suddenly came on. She sang along, "The shark ... pretty teeth ... Jack the Knife ... the knife ... the knife."

Then she burst out laughing and she couldn't stop, but it was a disdainful, sinister laugh and her face became distorted. Getting up, she walked to the middle of the room and stood there as if looking for something. She bent down. Seizing one of the floorboards with both hands, jiggling it, with some effort she pulled it up. Under the board was a small hole, and in that hole lay something long and silver. It was a knife!

Reginald adjusted his opera glasses. He could see the knife was about ten inches long and it was stained with a red substance.

"Blood! It's the murder weapon!"

Pulling the knife out, stroking it several times, Beatrice proceeded to rock it as if it were a baby. There was an intense almost unbearable look of joy on her face and she was smiling malevolently. She began to talk to it.

"Well, well, my little knife, not to worry, all our tracks are covered. How brilliant of us! No one will ever think of coming here looking under the floorboards. And that homicide detective, what was his name again? Oh, yes, Henderson. He thinks he's so smart, handcuffing that pathetic little hunchback and putting him in the back of the cruiser as if he was capable of murder! Hah, hah, hah!"

Reginald watched with wide open eyes. He could hardly believe it. He had just cracked a real live murder case and the murderer was right there a mere few feet away. But he needed to stay calm. Pulling out his cell phone, snapping a couple of shots of Beatrice with the knife, he couldn't call the police station fast enough. He asked to speak to Detective Henderson. He explained everything to him, that he had been suspicious of Beatrice all along, that he had been secretly watching her, and that he now had solid evidence she was not only Desiree's murderer but that she had set him up.

The detective was reluctant to hear Reginald out; after all, Reginald was his prime suspect and he was building a case up against him. About to hang up, when an image of Beatrice with a blood-stained knife flashed on his screen, he agreed to come at once.

Within minutes several police cruisers arrived and stormed inside Beatrice's house.

Beatrice refused to talk even though there was now solid evidence against her. It wasn't till two days later that she confessed to the murder, but she would plead not guilty by reason of insanity.

★

Reginald was exonerated. Having cracked a murder case and single-handedly brought on a new kind of sensation within him, one of pride and self-confidence. He even started feeling a little triumphant. He had just done what Detective Henderson and the entire police department were incapable of doing – catching a killer. Sinking into an armchair, closing his eyes, a light pleasant drowsiness came upon him, and he began experiencing unspeakable delights as if in a dream. He fancied neighbors coming round – Anna, Mamma Mia, Marissa, Lily, Big John, Christy – all apologizing for misjudging him and for calling him a killer. Then they would congratulate him on his keen detective work. Gus, Harvey and Julio would be there too, but, understandably, with mixed feelings, Beatrice taken away from them and so soon after Desiree.

At once Reginald started to envision himself a celebrity of sorts, of possibly getting interviewed on the radio or being on social media. Everyone on the street, no, in the entire city would come to know that he, Reginald Rutley, solved the Bank Street murder case. He waited with happy anticipation for his time in the spotlight.

But, as it happened, things did not turn out the way he'd hoped. All his dreams came to an end and one blow is all it took. In the day that followed, this is what appeared in all the newspaper headlines: *"Bank Street Murder Solved. Homicide Detective Charles Henderson Does it Again – With Tip from Annonymous Source."*

Chapter 19

Fancy Feast

Reginald was taking a leisurely stroll along the street. Suddenly there came a scream so loud it made him stop dead in his tracks. It was as if someone was being tortured, chopped up into a million pieces. Then it came again.

"Eeeeeeeeeeeeeeeeeeeeeeeek!"

The scream was coming from Number 50, from the Bendetti house. It sounded as if it was Mr. and Mrs. Bendetti going at each other, something they did often. But this was impossible, hard to believe, never had they gone at it to this extent.

Then again.

"Eeeeeeeeeeeeeeeeeeeeeeeek!"

A window near the back was open and Reginald hurried there to have a look. Expecting to come upon some kind of awful, ghastly scene between the middle-aged couple, what he found instead completely confounded him. There was Mrs. Bendetti but she was alone with no Mr. Bendetti anywhere in sight, and she was standing on a chair, shaking, hyperventilating, flailing her arms about as if out of her senses. Her dyed black hair was a big mess, her blouse was half undone, and her fluffy pink slippers had slipped off her feet and fallen to the floor. The chair she was standing on looked rickety as if about to collapse beneath her.

"What the devil?" Reginald moved closer.

Then suddenly Mr. Bendetti appeared in the doorway and he was out of breath. Roly-poly, not a day over fifty, with hairy arms and crooked legs, he stood there dripping wet and with no clothes on; yes, that's right, he was buck-naked. As it turned out, he'd been taking a bath, and when he'd heard his wife scream, with no time to lose, he jumped out of the tub, and barefoot, run down the stairs to see what was going on. On his face was a look of alarm.

"Bianca, what's wrong? And what are you doing up on the chair?"

Bianca could hardly articulate. She was crying and pointing, "It's over there! It's over there!"

"What's over there?"

"It's a … It's a … !"

"It's a what?"

"I can't say it! I can't even say the word!"

"What word?"

"A mouse, for crying out loud! A mouse! It went under the sofa. Just get it out of here and fast!"

Mr. Bendetti, well aware of his wife's rodent phobia, knew if he didn't do something immediately, she would only further rile herself up. He gave the sofa a shove. And sure enough, out came the little creature, squeaking and squealing, scampering across the floor.

"Catch it! Catch it!"

Grabbing hold of a throw pillow for lack of a better weapon, Mr. Bendetti chased after it. He tried to give it a good whack but the mouse was quick on its heels and made for the credenza, where it slipped into a crack and disappeared.

"You let it get away!" Mrs. Bendetti was in anguish. "How could you!"

Mr. Bendetti urged his wife, "You've got to calm down, Bianca."

"Calm down; what do you mean, calm down? There's a mouse in the house and you tell me to calm down?"

"You've got to get over this. You'd think it was some giant monster taking over the world the way you're carrying on. You're not rational."

"Not rational?" Bianca flared, "A mouse in the house and I'm not rational? Where there's one there's a hundred! This is all your fault. You were supposed to seal up those holes around the house weeks ago. How many times did I have to tell you?"

"I said I'd get around to it."

"When, in ten, maybe twenty years?"

"There you go again, nagging me to death. Maybe if you didn't nag me so much, I'd have done it a long time ago."

"Well, if you'd done it a long time ago then I wouldn't have had to nag you, would I?"

"If that's the way you see it, then patch up the holes yourself."

"Oh, you, you! Our poor daughter, to have such a father!"

The two continued another five minutes.

Then without warning Mr. Bendetti flung himself around and stormed out of the room. Among other things, he was getting cold and needed to find his robe.

Mrs. Bendetti, still on the chair, so incensed by her husband, completely forgot why she was up there. Then she remembered the mouse. Looking round, jumping down, as fast as she could, she ran up the stairs to her bedroom and banged shut the door. She would be safer up there.

Not long after, Mr. Bendetti returned to the living room clothed. He was grateful his wife was gone – at least now he'd have himself a bit of peace and quiet. Though he was annoyed by her hysterical behavior, at the same time he agreed with her insofar that they had a mouse problem. He even repeated to himself, "Where there's one there's a hundred."

Considering what to do, suddenly the phone rang. It was their daughter, Andrea. He put her on speaker phone.

"Hey, Dad, how are things. Just calling to say hi. The kids, you ask? Yes, they're fine, they're doing their homework right now. Jim's fine too. How's mom?"

"Mom? Things aren't the best with her right now. She's not in a very good mood."

"Why, what happened?"

"She saw a mouse."

"Oh no."

"I tried to catch it and when I couldn't, well, you can imagine what happened then."

"So now what?"

"I've got to come up with something."

"Like what?"

"A trap, poison, maybe a cage, you know, the humane kind."

"Um, Dad, none of those are good choices. If mom sees anything dead or alive, she's going to fall off the deep end completely."

Silence fell over the room, the two were as if trying to think of what to do. Then Andrea got an idea, "Dad, I've got it! A cat; get a cat!"

Mr. Bendetti straightened his back. "A cat you say? Why, of course, why didn't I think of that? A cat just might be the perfect solution. And I know exactly where to find one!"

"What do you mean? Where?"

"You know my neighbor, Reginald, from a few doors down, that odd-looking little hunchback? Well, he has a cat and her name's Miss Minnie and Miss Minnie's supposed to be the best mouser around. It's been said her mere presence is enough to scare them all off, and if she happens to catch one, she'll eat it on the spot. And she's guaranteed to never leave a mess. She has quite the reputation around here. I can ask to borrow her for a few days. Yes, I'll go see Reginald first thing in the morning."

Saying goodnight to his daughter, Mr. Bendetti, feeling as if all his problems had just been solved, poured himself a drink.

The next morning, he got up nice and early and set off for Reginald's house. The sun was already up over the rooftops and there was hardly a cloud in the sky. It was looking to be a fine day. Turning into Reginald's walkway, cutting across the lawn, he rang the bell. Reginald, of course, was expecting him, having learned everything the night before. But he made out as if surprised to see him.

Mr. Bendetti started in on his mouse problem right away. When at last he finished, Reginald said to him, "You're looking for a cat, you say? Yes, I have the best cat for the job. Miss Minnie's her name. You're welcome to borrow her for a few days. She'll get right to it, I assure you. Her mere presence will scare the mice off and if one happens her way, she'll gobble it up just like that!"

And so, with Miss Minnie under his arm, happily, Mr. Bendetti set off for home. As he came through the door, his wife was standing at the top of the stairs. She had just woken up but was too afraid to come down.

"Not to worry, Bianca. Soon our mouse problem will be over. I want you to meet Miss Minnie, she's on loan from Reginald, and she's exceptional. I've even heard neighbors talk. Rodents don't stand a chance with her around. She scares them off and if she catches one, she eats it up."

Bianca clasped her chest. She was thrilled by the news. Having a general, overall liking for cats, especially orange tabbies, of which Miss Minnie was one, coming down the stairs, she reached out and petted her behind the ears. Miss Minnie purred softly and then meowed.

Mr. Bendetti, looking lovingly at his wife, had more reassuring things to say. "Later today I'm going to patch up every last hole there is around the house. It's going to be sealed completely."

Mrs. Bendetti was exceedingly pleased with how things were turning out and she was even more pleased her husband was taking the matter seriously.

Miss Minnie, now on the ground, knowing there was a job to be done, headed straight for the living room. With her ears pricked up and her belly low to the floor, she plopped herself down by the credenza. With one eye on the vent and the other on the baseboard, every few minutes she turned round to check the sofa. She had her hunting area completely covered.

"Well, Bianca," said Mr. Bendetti delighted, "it looks like we're in the best of hands. I believe this is cause for celebration. How about dinner tonight at Roma House?"

As evening approached and Mr. and Mrs. Bendetti set off for the restaurant, Miss Minnie continued her vigilantism in the living room. The clock ticked over the mantel, the floor creaked now and then – it was just a matter of time.

Over a candle-lit dinner, Mr. and Mrs. Bendetti talked, laughed and sipped red wine. They were getting along splendidly tonight, as on occasion they did, but tonight it was all on account of Miss Minnie. They couldn't have been more pleased knowing she was solving their problem without them even having to lift a finger.

Back on Bank Street with Mr. and Mrs. Bendetti gone for the evening, Reginald wondered how Miss Minnie was making out. He thought he'd pop over there to have a look.

As on the previous night, he went to the side of the house and peeped through the window. And sure enough, there was Miss Minnie crouching, waiting, looking at any moment to let loose her violent predatory self. She was doing what she was brought there to do, stake out the grounds, wait, and then go for the kill.

And suddenly there came a movement from beneath the credenza. Miss Minnie, lifting her head slightly and raising her back, got into position. With her keen sense of smell and acute hearing, she looked fierce and frightening. Her teeth couldn't have appeared sharper and her jowls more powerful. At last, out came an unsuspecting mouse. Miss Minnie watched attentively. Then with short, quick movements, she made forward, paused briefly, then again made forward. The mouse, suddenly catching wind of danger, scared out of its wits, made a swift turnaround back to the credenza. But it was too late, Miss Minnie was ready to pounce, and pounce she did. With the creature already in her mouth, she started batting it sharply with her paws as if to wear it down. To finish things off, dropping it briefly, she gave it a quick bite to the neck, then set the dead animal on the ground.

Soon another mouse emerged, this time from under the sofa, and Miss Minnie was only too ready to again demonstrate her fine-tuned hunting skills. Then a third mouse came out, followed by a fourth, all of them meeting the same sad, violent end.

"Mrs. Bendetti was right. Where there's one, there's a hundred," thought Reginald, stretching his neck, trying to get a better look. "And they're so brazen, those mice. Either that or just plain stupid, coming out in the open like that, not afraid of a big cat like Miss Minnie."

And there was Miss Minnie, piling up the carnage. But how strange. Why wasn't she eating up her kill the way she always did? And what's more she was showing no interest. What was going on with Miss Minnie?

Reginald became confused. He couldn't figure it out. Then it struck him:

"Fancy Feast! That's it! It's because of Fancy Feast! Ever since I brought those tins home from the grocery store as a test-run, she's refused to eat anything else. And now, with all that deliciousness waiting for her at home, why would she eat rodents, tasteless as they are, raw with not even salt or pepper on them? So, what now?"

He started worrying what Miss Minnie might do next. And sure enough, to his horror from her pile of corpses with a mouse in her mouth she started for the stairs and marched straight up.

"No, stop!" Reginald cried out. He knew exactly what her intentions were. "She's going to Mrs. Bendetti's room. She's going to share her bounty; she's going to drop the mouse off at her door!"

When he saw Miss Minnie come back down, pick up another mouse, and then go back up, he fell into a panic. Banging on the window, he tried to get her attention.

"No, Miss Minnie, don't do it, come back. Mrs. Bendetti will absolutely die from fright; she won't take kindly to any of this!"

Reginald realized the only thing left for him to do was to somehow get himself into the house, to get at those mice and clear them out. Poor Mrs. Bendetti, he wouldn't wish such a thing on his worst enemy. He thought of forcing the window open somehow and getting himself in but then reconsidered as Mr. and Mrs. Bendetti wouldn't appreciate having to do repairs. Going round to the front, he tried to open the door, but it was locked. The side door was locked too. Looking up, he contemplated an open window on the second floor but he'd have to use a ladder and it looked risky.

Then he heard a car pull up. It was the Bendettis returning home. Afraid of being seen, barely having time to think what to do, he jumped headfirst into a clump of bushes.

Mr. and Mrs. Bendetti came out of their car talking and laughing, oblivious to all that was going on in their house. They had had a splendid evening and were in high spirits. Mr. and Mrs. Bendetti both were a little tipsy. The last thing on their minds was their mouse problem, so confident were they that it had been solved. When they stepped into their living room, they couldn't have been more delighted. There was Miss Minnie spread out on the sofa, swishing her tail, licking her paws. Obviously, her work had been completed.

Mr. Bendetti placed his hand gently on his wife's shoulder, "You see Bianca, you have nothing more to worry about. Miss Minnie took care of it all; she's everything they said and then some."

Mrs. Bendetti breathed a sigh of relief. So grateful was she to Miss Minnie, she went to pet her first on the backside then on her tummy.

"We'll keep her here a few more days," remarked Mr. Bendetti, "I'm sure Reginald won't mind. And then we'll invite him to dinner as a thank you."

Mrs. Bendetti couldn't have agreed more, she even offered to make a pot of her special minestrone. Rubbing her eyes, she said she was tired and would go to bed. It had been a long day after all. She asked her husband if he too were tired, to which he replied, "No, you go ahead, I think I'll stay up for a bit. There's something on television I want to watch. I'll be up soon."

"Goodnight then." She gave him a quick peck on the cheek.

"Goodnight."

Turning on the hall light, Mrs. Bendetti started up the stairs. When she came to the landing she turned left to her room. As she was about to take hold of the knob, at once she stepped on something and it was the strangest thing. It felt soft and mushy and even a little bit wet. "What could it be?" she thought. She had no idea. She couldn't recall having dropped anything earlier that day but maybe her husband had. Looking down with the intention of picking up whatever it was, when she saw the pile of dead rodents, she screamed a scream as never before heard. It was so loud, so penetrating, it was as if all the windows in the house were shattering. Her skin went completely white, she started to wheeze, and her pulse became rapid. She fell to the ground, fainting.

Mr. Bendetti came rushing up the stairs to see what was going on. He saw his wife lying on the ground, hardly breathing. She looked badly injured. Then he saw the pile of rodent corpses next to her.

"Oh, merciful heaven!" he clasped his chest.

Picking her up, he carried her into the bedroom. He put her straight on the bed, placed a pillow under her head, and covered her up with a duvet. First thing was first. He needed to clean up the mess.

But his mind was on Miss Minnie. He was furious with her. She was supposed to have scared the mice off, and if she was to have caught one, she was to have eaten it, and right there on the spot. Isn't that what Reginald had promised? But clearly, that was not the case. He would not tolerate her in his home a minute longer. Was she even aware of the damage she had done? But she was a cat after all. If he was to take issue with anybody it would be with Reginald, misrepresenting his cat the way he did. And the nerve of him to speak so highly of her capabilities. Scooping Miss Minnie up in his arms, late as it was, he set off for Reginald's house.

Reginald, still in the bushes, climbed out and followed Mr. Bendetti but at a distance so as not to be seen. He fretted over the scene about to unfold.

When at last Mr. Bendetti reached Reginald's house and knocked on the door, Reginald didn't answer because, of course, he wasn't there. Coming up from behind, pretending to have been out for a walk, he was determined to keep things civil. He called out with almost exaggerated politeness, knowing full well all hell was about to break loose.

"Hello, Mr. Bendetti. A fine night to be out for a walk. So, I see you're bringing Miss Minnie back to me and so soon. I hope she's done a good job for you."

Mr. Bendetti was obviously in terrible exasperation. When he went to speak it was with such anger, he put emphasis on almost every syllable.

"A good job, you say? Hah! Because of your cat, my wife's having a mental breakdown. Lies, you told me nothing but lies and it's reprehensible, absolutely reprehensible! Miss Minnie doesn't scare mice off and she doesn't eat them either! No, she catches them then piles them up, dead! Yes, she piled them up in front of my wife's room. Now, the situation is worse than ever! My wife's going to need therapy!"

Reginald listened to Mr. Bendetti intently and uneasily and he dared not utter a word.

Mr. Bendetti went on several more minutes but with venomous phrases, and he used language so obscene Reginald could hardly believe what he was hearing. Then it became apparent Mr. Bendetti was about to do something outrageous. And sure enough, raising his arms over his head, firmly holding onto the by-now yowling Miss Minnie, with all his might, he hurled her straight at Reginald.

"Here's your Miss Minnie. Keep her, she's all yours."

Then Mr. Bendetti had but one last thing to say to Reginald: "Bah!"

Making down the street, hurrying back home, his only hope was that his wife had not yet regained consciousness. What he wanted beyond all else was a drink and a few minutes of quiet to collect himself. He very well knew, once she would waken, he'd never hear the end of it.

★

Back at Reginald's house, Miss Minnie was in the kitchen meowing with all her ability. It so happened she was hungry, actually, starving would have been a better word for it. She hadn't eaten all day, having been stuck in the Bendetti house as she was. What she wanted more than anything was her newfound favorite food – Fancy Feast. Rubbing up against the cupboard, meowing, she was well aware that's where Reginald kept it stored.

When Reginald came in, he opened up a tin and set it down for her on the floor. She ate heartily. Having finished, licking her paws, she made across the room to her cat bed. Curling up, producing several low deep trills, she fell asleep.

Making himself a cup of tea, Reginald could only think of the Bendettis. He felt sorry for them but more so he felt answerable for all their suffering. Had he not introduced Miss Minnie to Fancy Feast, she would have settled their whole mouse business quickly and efficiently, and everyone would have been happy. But because of him, Mrs. Bendetti's mouse phobia had gone completely off the rails, and now it was up to poor Mr. Bendetti to find ways to cope with her terrible condition.

Yes, it was all his fault. He, Reginald, should have seen it coming.

Turning off the light, heading for bed, he had but one thought and it troubled him: "Poor Mrs. Bendetti, will she ever be the same again?"

Chapter 20

The Drunk

It was two in the morning and Andy, unstable on his feet, was making his way down Bank Street. He was going home. Actually, he wasn't going home to his own house because he didn't have one, rather, he was going to his mother's house, where he'd been living the past year. He had two bottles of whiskey both empty, one in his jacket pocket, the other under his arm. His legs looked as if they would fall off beneath him, he was that drunk. He was extremely thirsty too but that didn't stop him from singing:

What will we do with a drunken sailor?
What will we do with a drunken sailor?
What will we do with a drunken sailor?
Early in the morning

Finally, his mother's house, at least what he thought was his mother's house. Turning into the walkway, half way down, he stumbled over something and fell. He landed face down in the grass and passed out. As it happened, it wasn't his mother's grass he passed out on, rather, on Marissa Hardy's a couple of doors down. Truth be told, the two houses looked so much alike anyone could have made the same mistake.

Marissa was sound asleep in her upstairs bedroom but when she heard the noise it woke her up. Fumbling for her glasses, which she kept on her night table, she went to the window to have a look. At first, she didn't see anything, then squinting her eyes, there on the lawn beneath the street lamp she saw of all things a man. He was lying there unmoving, looking more dead than alive. "What if he's dead?" she thought to herself in alarm. "What should I do?" She was alone in the house and afraid. Should she call a neighbor, the police, an ambulance? When the man suddenly gave a kick with his left leg, she let out a sigh of relief. "Thank God at least he's not dead. Probably just some drunk who's had one too many." But from what she could see, he appeared well-dressed in a suit and tie, not the usual fair for a drunk, and he was wearing shoes of an expensive variety. Taking a closer look, when she saw who it was, she let out a little cry. It was Andy from down the street. An emotion ran through her.

"Sad, so sad."

Andy was in need of help but what could she do? By nature, she was a thoughtful person and had a genuine goodness about her. Making for her linen closet, taking out a pillow and down comforter, in her heavy flannel nightgown, she hurried down the stairs and went outside. She couldn't let him get cold.

Andy was a drunk and she objected to his way of life, yet, somehow, she had a deep human sympathy for him. She had loved him for a long time, in fact, for over twenty years. She and Andy had both grown up on the street together and had gone to the same schools, the same dance classes, and both had played in the community marching band. To her, he was as beautiful today as he had been in his youth, even though his face was now twisted and disfigured and his nose in the early stages of rosacea. Being beside him right now made her confused and excited and she tried to reason her feelings. Concerned about the damp earth upon which he lay and that he might catch a chill, all she wanted was to protect him, to keep him warm. Placing the pillow beneath his head and gently covering him up, she stared at him for the longest time, and she kept on staring.

She couldn't leave him; something was keeping her there. Lowering her body, she lay down next to him and then moved closer. She could see the outline of his chest and feel his male warmth. With her head on his shoulder, she whispered, "Don't move away from me, my darling. It's so lovely here, isn't it?" She could feel his unconsciousness, his breath, and before long she became tingly all over. Little screams broke within her and then she let them go without inhibition. She felt womanly. Her hand traveled through his hair, along his shoulders, and she kissed him lightly on the neck, on the cheek.

Then suddenly a frown came to her face and she drew herself away. He became objectionable to her and everything about him made her angry. She said to him in a scolding way, as if he were awake and listening, "Just look at you. What have you gone and done to yourself, with your life? You've thrown it all away."

But soon her voice changed, "Sleep, yes, it's best to stay asleep; sleep is beautiful and peaceful." She began to sing, "Sleep, baby, sleep, your father tends the sheep."

The idea of loving a drunk overwhelmed her, there was rapture in her heart and there was fear. She lay beside him for what seemed like hours. She couldn't have been more grateful he had landed on her lawn instead of his mother's.

A breeze suddenly picked up and the whole street was as if roused. From Dufferin there came the sound of a speeding car, then a siren, then the honking of a horn. At once footsteps resounded on the pavement and soon after came laughter and animated conversation. Some people were fast approaching, a lively bunch, undoubtedly young people from a party somewhere. Marissa became fearful. She thought to herself, "Oh, dear, what if they see me out here with Andy and in my nightgown! What will they think!" Not wanting to be spotted, picking up, as fast as she could she ran toward her house. Already on her veranda, up against the wall, she waited for them to pass.

She had every intention of going back to Andy. As she was about to do just that, out of the corner of her eye she spotted something across the street, in the bushes. It alarmed her and made her stop. It was a shadow of some sort and it was moving slowly, first to the left, then to the right. She tried to get a better look. Then came the outline of what appeared to be a head, then shoulders, then a torso. It was a man and he was looking straight in her direction. "Who could that be?" After a minute, she recognized who it was, she should have known. It was Reginald, that pesky little busybody from down the street. He'd been watching the entire time, and what's worse, he had seen her lying next to Andy, rubbing up against him, kissing him. She felt completely and utterly humiliated. Running inside her house, slamming the door behind her, she ran upstairs to her bedroom and drew the curtains.

The next morning when Andy got up his face was flushed and heavy-looking and his hair was disheveled. Still intoxicated from the night before, his need to drink was so great there was no shame in him. Still believing he was at his mother's house, he shouted as he made his way to the front door:

"Hey, Ma! Fix me a drink, will you; and not a beer this time but something with a bit of punch. Like maybe vodka; yeah, a bit of vodka would go down nice about now."

He appeared hardly to know what he was saying and he seemed unaware that he had spent the night on the lawn.

Marissa heard Andy's voice and came to meet him. There wafted from him the smell of booze. Keeping her eyes fixed on him, she tried to bear herself as if nothing had happened. She was relieved to see he had no recollection of the previous night.

Marissa was the same age as Andy, a little over forty but she looked older. She had never married and had lived most of her adult life alone. She was not beautiful by any means and age was catching up to her. Already her brown hair was streaked gray here and there and little crows' feet appeared beneath her eyes. With a pointy nose, a very small chin, and a long, skinny neck, it could easily be said she was homely looking.

"Ma? Ma, where are you?" Andy looked round, then entering the house, started down the hall to the kitchen. He sat down.

Marissa followed close behind. Pouring coffee, she said quietly, "You're mixed up. This is not your mother's house, it's my house."

"Your house?" Andy banged the table with his fist. "Hah! Your house, well, I'll be damned!"

Marissa was unaccustomed to having a man in her house. Looking at his thick black hair, his black eyes, she couldn't help notice the size of his chest. She put her hand on his arm and said with a quiet scorn, "You're drunk; you're still drunk from last night."

"Drunk?" Andy burst into a kind of booze-induced arrogance, "Drunk, you say? Well, you're right about that, drunk I am. That's the way it is with me. Drinking makes me happy, and it gives me a warm, fuzzy feeling inside. Besides, I made a commitment to drink, and drink I will."

Marissa watched Andy steadily without moving or drawing her face away. She couldn't help come back at him with some degree of disgust, "You're soaked in booze; you are an addict."

Andy laughed, "Hah, an addict, you call me an addict? Well, the joke's on you! You're wrong, all wrong. I'm no addict! It's like this, I have a new doctor and he put it all together for me. He said I'm not really a drunk but that I have a disease of the brain. Yes, a disease right here in the old noggin."

He pointed his finger to the side of his head as if a gun.

Marissa ventured to look boldly at him, "You say you have a disease of the brain? Is that what you call it? That's the most ridiculous thing I've ever heard, and I don't buy it for one minute. All you're doing is removing the stigma and personal responsibility from alcoholism. You drink because it's an act of will."

Andy stood up briefly. He took issue in what she said. "An act of will, you say? I hate to disagree with you but I prefer to agree with my doctor, that I have a disease of the brain. And he knows best because after all he's a doctor and you're not."

Marissa held firm her opposition, "So, you really believe you have a disease? I say, how can you have a 'disease' when this 'disease' of yours comes in a bottle, you buy it in the liquor store, and you pay taxes on it. Some disease! All you are doing is showing signs of weakness. There is no safe amount of liquor to the system. If there's a disease that you have, it's called alcoholism."

Andy kicked out his legs. He turned the conversation, "Hah! Look at you, little Miss Marissa. I never realized you were such a feisty little thing. But why do you have to be so damn mean, not to mention, sanctimonious? You're a prude, yes, that's what you are, nothing but a prude. I remember even in high school you were a prude."

He came closer. She let him. He took her hand in his. He went on quietly, "You want to know a little secret? All right, I'll tell you. But sh, don't tell anyone. Back in high school I used to think you were kind of cute and a bit hot too, even though you were still a prude. Actually, it was your boobs that did it for me. Yes, your boobs because they were so big. Now you know, I had a thing for your big boobs. But why did you keep running away from me? And why were you always so condescending?"

Marissa did not respond. She gazed at him in astonishment. She was trying her utmost to grasp his words in full. She had no idea.

Andy waved his hand, "Well, those days are all gone now, all gone. I threw them away, but you threw them away too just like I did. I'm a wreck. But you, just look how you've let yourself go, your hair, your clothes. Such a waste, such a waste."

Marissa flushed with embarrassment and her feelings were hurt. She averted her eyes.

Andy fidgeted with his pant pocket, "Do you mind if I smoke? No?" Striking up a match it did not take long for the smell of cigarettes to mix in with the smell of liquor. He continued to go back in time, "Yes, I remember in high school you were always kind of nerdy, at the front of the class all the time with your nose in a book. Your clothes were such a mess some days and you never wore makeup like the other girls. You were different, and I always thought you were pretty but in a weird kind of way."

Marissa did not answer, she was thinking. Several minutes passed, "But you just only teased me. You had all those pretty girls around you. And later you went on to marry Connie Maddison who was every guy's dream girl. The two of you were the perfect couple. Then you became a drunk and now you're divorced."

Andy screwed up his mouth, a bitterness came to his voice, "Fifteen years, we were married for fifteen years. She never had enough. Not enough money, not enough clothes, not enough furniture, not enough anything. I worked and worked and it was never enough, I worked myself to the bone. I even bought her a big house in the burbs. She never had time for me either, always busy with something or other, her job, her pet projects, the kids."

Andy fell briefly silent. A look of regret came to his face. "I might have married you instead, Marissa. You were probably the sort of woman I needed, modest, frugal, sensible. Maybe not the best looker, but if there ever was a woman who could have kept me in line that would have been you. Yes, you would have done a loser like me a world of good, a world of good, I say."

Andy's eyes wandered. His movements became restless. Getting up he started opening drawers, poking his head into the kitchen cupboards, peering under the sink.

"Hey, you wouldn't happen to have a drink around here, would you?"

Then he became agitated, "I can't believe it, not a drop anywhere! What's the matter with you anyway? You should have at least one bottle of something somewhere; most normal people do."

He then became loud and obnoxious and started shouting abuses, "What an uptight old maid you've become, Marissa. You should take a few drinks to loosen yourself up. Look at you sitting there in that ugly old sweater with your hair piled up on the top of your head like a bird's nest. Why don't you freshen yourself up, fix up your face? You look like a hag, an old hag!"

Marissa looked overwhelmed with embarrassment. Hiding her face in her hands, she broke into tears.

Andy sat for a long time plunged in thought. He felt sorry for what he had said, and when he started up again, his insolent manner was gone. "I apologize, Marissa. I didn't mean to be nasty. I just want to help you, really, I do. It's not too late; you can still find someone. But let me give you a word of advice. Promise me one thing – make sure he's not a drunk like me."

After a moment a kind of earnestness rose in him, "Marissa, I need for you to do me a favor. Be a sweetheart, go to the store and get me a six-pack. I'll pay you back later."

Marissa sat pale and grave before him. If anything, she would not get him that beer; she would not condone his behavior.

A stuffiness came over the room and it was oppressive.

Andy narrowed his eyes, "You think I'm pathetic, don't you. Well, you're right, I am pathetic. You want to hear what I did yesterday; do you want to know why I'm all dressed up in these fancy clothes? Well, I had a job interview with a car dealership up the street, for a sales position. Yes, I said 'sales'. But can you imagine, me going for a job interview? What a joke! Hah, hah, hah! Well, I didn't make it. I ended up meeting some of my buddies along the way and they took me drinking instead, to that strip joint over on Queen Street. Yes, I got pissed. And what happened next, you ask? No, you don't want to hear, really you don't."

His voice was now slurred, "I'm a drunk; that's all I am. The more I pour into myself the drunker I get. But not to worry I still have some sense and memory, at least for today. Oh, I'm so thirsty. Go get me that six-pack, will you, please."

Marissa sat painfully silent. There came a passion and yearning to her face and she tried to hide it. She watched as his chest began to heave. She could not grasp the thought of him leaving.

Andy caught her staring at him, "Oh, I see what you're doing; you can't fool me. Don't go and love me, if that's what you're thinking, don't be getting any crazy notions. It's too burdensome to love a booze-chugger like myself. I would only ruin your life. Ask my ex-wife. I brought her nothing but misery, I drank everything away, all my wages; I wasted her life for drink. She wanted money, money, money, but all the money went on drink. I'm so sorry to her, I'm sorry to my kids, I'm sorry to you, too. I'm just plain sorry."

Marissa watched Andy attentively. She could see his shape, the shape she had loved all these years. If only he knew how strongly she felt despite everything. She drew nearer. She asked him, "Why do you drink?"

"Why do I drink? Hah, hah, hah! You're too much, you really are. Come here and I'll tell you, but it'll be our little secret. Promise? It's because I have Satan in me."

Marissa clasped her chest, "Oh, to say such a thing! Is that how you explain it? Satan? But the drink is killing you; can't you see that it's killing you?" She stared straight in his eyes. "I don't believe you have Satan in you, I don't believe it for one minute. You drink for a reason, though I don't know what it is. Maybe something happened to you when you were young, maybe something from your childhood, something horrible, like a nightmare."

A constrained silence followed.

Through the open window there came the sound of the wind, then there came a strange scratching, as if someone was out there. Marissa went to have a look but found nothing.

"A nightmare you say? Yes, you're right, it was like a nightmare, a really terrible nightmare. And she knew, she knew all along."

Marissa touched his shoulder, "Andy, what are you saying?"

Andy was as if someplace else. His eyes were strange and glowing, "She knew and she didn't help me. It was Ma; she knew everything."

Marissa tensed, "Ma? Your Ma? What are you talking about? What did she know?"

"She knew, let's just leave it at that."

"You mean ... Oh, my God, No! But who?"

Andy was rocking back and forth and his eyes were half closed. He seemed to be crying. After a moment, collecting himself, he tried to pretend as if there was nothing the matter.

"Ach," he said, in an attempt to make light of everything. "Just listen to me, going on, talking nonsense."

Marissa's face worked with compassion. This woke in her the spirit to fight for him. She said in a gentle tone, "You could get help. You can still live a good life. And what about your son, your daughter? You can do it for them. I could help you."

Andy laughed, "You help me? It's too late for me. I'm a gonner, can't you see? There's no limit to my drinking powers either."

At once his face changed and turned a tomato-red. He became abusive again, "Why do you keep sticking your nose into my affairs anyway? You really think you're so above it all, don't you? Go away, leave me alone. Mind your own business!"

Marissa gazed at him with a sad but serious face and tears trickled from her eyes. She was unable to move. Then more tears but now she held them back. What she wanted more than anything was to fling herself on his neck and to kiss him all over. She knew she needed to protect herself from him, but couldn't. He was bad news. *I love you* she tried to say with her lips drawn to quivering. If he let her, she would forgive him for everything and she would let him see she was feminine, a woman, and there was a sensuality about her.

Andy forgot a moment where he was, it was as if his mind went blank. Then he remembered the drink.

"If you don't get me that six-pack, I'll just have to go and get it myself. Or better yet, I'll tell Ma to go get it. Ma! Hey, Ma!" he called as if she was right there in the room with them.

Picking up, he made across the room to leave. When he came to the door, suddenly it was as if he remembered something. Turning around, he said with a smile:

"Last night I had a dream about you. You were lying next to me on the grass somewhere, maybe in a park. You were pressing your body up against mine, then you started kissing me. Yes, you were kissing me softly right here on the cheek. You held me tight. Imagine that, you holding me tight. What a dream that was, what a dream."

Marissa froze; her heart throbbed and sank. A sense of hopelessness and helplessness passed through her. She could hardly breathe.

Everything became quiet. And suddenly it was as if Andy hadn't been there, hadn't been there at all, as if he too had been just a dream.

She could hear him singing from the street but it was quickly fading.

What will we do with a drunken sailor?
What will we do with a drunken sailor?
What will we do with a drunken sailor?
Early in the morning

Chapter 21

The Red Mustang

It was an early spring afternoon and Reginald was mowing his lawn, the first mow of the season. He still had hedges to trim, his vegetable garden to weed, and seeds to sow. But he was already feeling exhausted and needed a break. He decided to take a drink of lemonade he had prepared for himself on the veranda. Noticing Miss Minnie curled up on one of the chairs, her paws covering her face, he took a seat next to her.

A few cars drove by followed by a boy on a scooter and later a young man on roller blades. Birds were lounging up on the power wires and passers-by could be heard chattering away along the sidewalk. Across the street two magnolia trees were in full bloom and daffodils were coming up everywhere. A lovely scent filled the air and the day couldn't have been more pleasant.

The lemonade refreshed Reginald and soothed his throat. Sinking his head on the back of his chair, kicking out his feet, he started to nod off – a minute, maybe two and he would be out completely. Then suddenly, as if out of nowhere, there came a roaring, blasting sound, so loud, so thunderous it was as if the entire ground was shaking. Springing up from his seat, looking around, he tried to determine the cause of the noise. Miss Minnie jumped up and bolted to the back of the house. Neighbors came running out to see what was going on.

A bright red two-door Ford Mustang came rolling down the street. Shiny, modern, it looked as if it had just come off the new car lot. But it was the muffler making all that horrible noise. Clearly, the muffler had been replaced with aftermarket pipes to make it louder than the stock exhaust. And to make matters worse, the radio was on full blast.

Sylvester Kasun from Number 14 was sitting behind the wheel. Large and of considerable strength he had dark hair and still darker eyes, and though not the best-looking guy around, he did manage to fill the car nicely. He had just turned twenty-three and lived with his parents but he had his own apartment in their basement. Though he hardly ever paid rent, on occasion he did cover the utilities such as water, gas, and electricity.

To his parents' great disappointment, he'd dropped out of business college a few months back. Wanting to make money instead, he got a job at a men's clothing store up on College Street. Wages were not all that great, but since he didn't have many bills to pay, it was more than adequate. And now, thanks to a very reasonable monthly payment plan at the car dealership, he was able to afford a brand-new Ford Mustang.

Finding a parking spot in front of his parents' house, turning off the engine, he sent his gaze over all the people that had come to gather. He couldn't have been more pleased. Not one person looked on with indifference. Just as he had expected, save for a few, all were in awe and wonderment of his new car. He filled with a feeling of pride and joy.

A neighbor called out from across the street.

"Hey, Sylvester, where did you get those hot new wheels?"

Then another.

"Some pipes you have going there; the noise goes right through you!"

Then a woman but with a scowl.

"I hope you don't go roaring through the neighborhood all hours of the night. There must be laws against pipes like that!"

Sylvester paid no attention to the several negative comments, as they were only coming from a jealous place, he was sure. This was his moment to shine and he wasn't about to let anyone spoil it for him. Walking through the crowd, he headed for his parents' house. Giving his car one last quick look-over, he disappeared inside. He was getting hungry and could use a little something to eat. Inside, his mother was already in the kitchen preparing lunch. A tall, stout woman of Croatian blood, today was her day off from the chocolate factory where she worked on an assembly line. She hollered when she heard her son come in.

"Sylvester, soup's on the table!"

As he sat down, she looked sternly at him, "Was that your new car I just heard out there? Oh, my. To waste money like that, and to drop out of school. Your father is ready to put his foot down. You can't be living in our basement forever."

Sylvester took a bite of his sandwich, "Not to worry, Mother, I have a plan."

"A plan? You always have a plan. I've heard enough of your plans." Waving her hand, she walked out of the room.

Sylvester felt bad upsetting his mother but at the same time he felt she didn't understand him or even, for that matter, try. If only she new what it meant to him owning a Mustang, how important it was. Quickly gulping down a glass of milk and practically swallowing his dessert, all he wanted was to get back to his car. When he came onto the veranda, sitting down on the steps, he could do nothing but stare. A few onlookers still remained. He could hardly believe it but he was now owner of a Mustang, and not just any Mustang but a Boss 302, second generation. With its strong edges, sharp lines, and beautiful detail, it was a beast of a car, a classic with muscles. He then started to consider all its special features – a powerful V8 engine, nineteen-inch wheels, aerodynamic elements. Pure technological advancement is what it was, a car like no other, and it was all his.

Suddenly the sun, coming out from behind a cloud, hit upon the far edge of his hood. Was that a smudge he was seeing? Getting up, craning his neck, he tried to get a better look. It certainly looked suspicious. Yes, it was a smudge! Someone had touched his car with their dirty fingers! Hurrying into the house for a damp cloth, within minutes he returned and started wiping the smudge down. But he couldn't get it clean enough. Blowing on it, he further polished it up.

Barely having finished, at once there came a splattering sound from the back of the roof. What he saw practically sent him into a state of arrest. A bird had pooped on the far-left corner and the poop was now dripping down his rear window. He needed to clean it up fast before it would start eating away at the paint, as poop had a tendency to do. But the damp cloth was not enough. Rushing to the shed which was at the side of his house, getting a bucket and filling it with water from the hose, he started washing it up.

It was at that moment he noticed Georgiana coming down the street, the pretty new girl from Number 10. In a light jacket of a magenta shade, off-white trousers, and a thin cotton blouse, she couldn't have looked lovelier. Sylvester had passed her by a few times on the street but had never worked up the courage to say anything to her other than a "hello" or "good day". Today he would try and make conversation. She noticed his car right away.

"Hey, nice car. Did you just get it? I absolutely adore Mustangs, especially red ones."

Silvester beamed, "You're new to Bank Street, aren't you? How do you like it here?"

"The street's great, people are great too. And I can easily walk to work, I waitress over at Café Rosa." Then with her eyes back to the car, "Your Mustang must feel great on the road, like a real sports car."

Sliding her fingers along the side of the door, she then leaned on it slightly.

Sylvester drew a deep breath. He remained still and tense. Georgiana was touching his brand-new car and he was not pleased; he didn't want her or anyone even coming near it. Holding himself rigid, about to give her a talking to, in the nick of time, she pulled away.

"I would love to go for a ride sometime," she smiled.

Sylvester couldn't believe it. Was he even hearing right? She was practically throwing herself at him, of all people. He asked her out to the drive-in later that night.

"Sure, I'd like that a lot."

"It's a date then. Pick you up at seven?"

"See you at seven."

As Georgiana walked away Sylvester could see she did so with every sense of her body. He couldn't help but feel all fired up. How easy it was to be popular now that he had a Mustang. And Georgiana was no ordinary girl. He was excited for seven o'clock.

Sitting back down on his veranda, he resumed staring at his car – the gentle curves, the sleek lines, so athletic-looking, designed for adrenaline-pumping performance. What a car, indeed!

Then he began to imagine what his evening with Georgiana would be like, he at the wheel, she, chattering, laughing away, her long brown hair blowing in the wind. The two of them would draw much attention. The whole street would see them speed off.

At that moment his thoughts were broken by the sound of children racing down the street on bikes. One of them, a girl, howling and screaming, was zigzagging all over the place. She was shouting to her friends, "Hey, look at me everybody, no hands!" Pedalling faster, not watching where she was going, she was headed straight for Sylvester's car. Another second, another two and she would go crashing right into it. But incredibly, at the last minute, somehow, she managed to swerve and miss it by a mere few inches. Sylvester watched in horror. Running to the curb, waving his fists, he shouted after her, "Hey, you dumb girl, next time watch where you're going!"

It was starting to get dark, nearing seven o'clock. Sylvester went inside and began preparing for his date. Showering, combing back his hair, he went into his bedroom and got dressed: a blue checkered shirt, washed jeans, and, in keeping with his Croatian roots, a black bow-tie made of the finest silk. Dabbing on some cologne, he fixed up his collar and then put on his jacket. With one final look in the full-length mirror, he thought he looked quite presentable. Though it was only a few doors down, he would drive over to Georgiana's house as that's what she would be expecting.

Grabbing his car keys from a nail on the wall in his kitchenette, about to step outside, suddenly out of nowhere, there came a great big bang. Boom! Crash! Smash! The windows rattled; the walls cracked. He froze.

"What on earth?"

Then panic set in and his head started to spin. That huge explosion was close by, too close, in fact, it sounded as if it was coming from right in front of his house. All he could think of was his Mustang. He had a very bad feeling. "No, Please, no!"

As he ran outside, sure enough, the scene couldn't have been more devastating. There was his brand-new Mustang, the front-end crushed, all smashed up. And before his car, in a blue-gray sedan behind the wheel sat a young man, a teenager, his own back-end completely destroyed. The young man was Jesse from around the corner and he was pale and shaking.

Sylvester flew at him, "What the hell did you do? You just totaled my brand-new car!"

It did not take long for neighbors to throng the sidewalk. There was a boisterous murmuring among them followed by an almost painful quiet. Then a woman's voice erupted and it was scornful.

"Well, at least now we won't have to listen to those god-awful pipes anymore!"

Jesse, still behind the wheel, tried to speak. After a minute, looking at Sylvester, he blurted out, "I'm so sorry. Shit, I don't know what came over me. I was trying to parallel park and then everything became mixed up. I think I hit the gas pedal by accident."

"You hit the gas pedal by accident?" Sylvester clutched his head. "Do you even have your license? How old are you?"

"I'm seventeen, and, yes, I have my licence. Since yesterday."

"Since yesterday!" Sylvester was now flaring.

Jesse's parents came rushing from down the street, they'd heard there'd been an accident, and like everyone else, wanted to see what had happened. When they saw their son sitting behind the wheel looking shaken and distraught and the two cars all banged up, they pretty well put two and two together. Apologising profusely, they offered to pay for damages but out of pocket, as they would be met with skyrocketing insurance premiums, especially with Jesse being a new driver.

Two tow trucks would soon be arriving.

Sylvester, trying to regain himself, suddenly remembered his date with Georgiana. She was probably angry with him for not showing up. Now that he didn't have a car, he worried how she might react. Would she still go out with him? He could maybe suggest an alternative, of walking up to the Lula Lounge, where there was a Salsa band playing. They could have drinks and do a bit of dancing. Just as he started toward her house, he bumped into her half way. Like all the other neighbors, she'd heard the bang and had come to check it out. Tonight, she looked especially beautiful all dressed up for their date. But when she went to speak her voice was distant, hollow sounding.

"Oh, my, your car, it looks completely ruined. I'm sorry for you, Sylvester. A real shame. Not good for anything now, really."

She stood there perfectly still and warm in the evening light and Sylvester could easily see the pink of her dress. There was no emotion in her eyes only a quiet expression. Obviously, there was something going on in her mind. And suddenly he understood everything, she wanted no more of him than his car. She turned and walked away.

★

The yards on either side began to darken and then a damp fragrance welled up from the flowerbeds. Sylvester became strangely cold. Turning up his jacket collar, with a dull and heavy step, he made down the street. He needed to take a walk, to clear his mind.

Absolutely everything had gone wrong today: his car, his date, and now he had nothing left but that crappy low-paying job down at the clothing store. He felt gloomy. Then for some reason, he started to think of his mother's words, about school.

Maybe he'd go back after all. There was still time to register for next semester.

At once someone let out a cough. Pausing briefly, looking round, Sylvester tried to determine where the cough was coming from. It was from Number 25, from Reginald's house.

"That little busybody!" Sylvester grumbled to himself. "He's probably been creeping around all day, spying on me."

"Get a life!" is what he wanted to call out to him but for some reason didn't.

Hurrying along, with his hands in his pockets, he decided to head down Dufferin to the Gladstone Hotel. He could sure use a nice cold beer about now.

Chapter 22

Reginald at the Art Gallery

Today was Sunday and on Sundays Reginald always felt more lonely than on any other day. On Sundays he was brought to an even colder, darker place, where he struggled with negative feelings. His store was closed on this day, which meant he had time to himself with nothing to do and no friends or family to share it with. Of course, he could always keep his business running and distract himself with customers and inventory, which would at least make things more bearable, but that would mean going against his deceased mother's wishes, who believed Sundays were days meant for rest and rejuvenation. Loving his mother as much as he did, dead or alive, he vowed to always be loyal to her.

Reginald thought hard of what to do. Then he came up with the perfect solution.

"I could go to the art gallery; it's opened all day. I could go look in on the Vincent Laurensz van der Vinne portrait. It always cheers me up."

Vincent Laurensz van der Vinne (or Van der Vinne, as Reginald liked to call him for short) was a Dutch Mennonite painter of the great Dutch Golden Age and also a writer and linen-weaver. His portrait, painted by his friend and mentor, Frans Hals, back in the year 1665, hung in the Old Master Collection of the city's gallery. What Reginald liked was that Van der Vinne wasn't snobbish-looking like the others in the Collection, who were mostly well-to-do and of distinguished backgrounds. Instead, Van der Vinne was forever shabby in appearance, dressed in the same old brown crumpled jacket with a white collar and with his hair always a long, stringy mess. He felt if Van der Vinne were a real, live person he could easily be a friend.

Maybe twenty minutes from Bank Street by streetcar, it was not long before Reginald got to the gallery. With its façade of glass and wood spanning an entire block, entering, paying his admission fee, he went straight to the Old Master Collection. Finding Van der Vinne in the usual place, taking off his cap and jacket, he settled comfortably on a little bench before him. Van der Vinne was as if expecting him, his cheeks a rosy red and his demeanor humble and unassuming. He looked as if about to crack a joke.

The Gallery was filling up with visitors and there were already about ten in the Old Master Collection. Before long, there formed a small gathering of people around Van der Vinne and they began exchanging various details about the portrait painter himself, Frans Hals. One woman spoke with great authority.

"Frans Hals, the greatest portrait painter that ever lived. An artist ahead of his time. Van der Vinne is one of his veritable masterpieces. Observe the very visible brushstrokes, and you can see there are hardly any details in the work, mostly patches of color, smears, and spots. And then there's that glint in Van der Vinne's eye, and that partially ironic grin that never leaves his face. Brilliant!"

A man chimed in, "Yes, Frans Hals was an inspiration to Realists and Impressionists everywhere."

Then a young woman in an orange dress who looked like a student of fine art, put in, "His sense of individual character is simply awesome. He creates life itself, it's as if Van der Vinne were not even a portrait but an actual living, breathing being."

Reginald listened to their conversation and he had an inclination to join in. It so happened, he had his own interesting tidbits of information to share both about Frans Hals and Van der Vinne, and he was sure the small crowd would appreciate his observations. About to speak, the crowd only gave him an extended stare, as if wondering who that strange little man might be and why was he coming at them with his mouth half open. Chattering and laughing amongst themselves, they moved on.

Reginald sank back into the bench gloomy and dejected. He was hoping Van der Vinne's good-natured face would somehow make his loneliness go away. But he only fell deeper into a private world of his own. It made him very sad to be estranged from all those around him, and it was no better here in the gallery than any place else. And Van der Vinne wasn't helping much either. He might just as well have stayed home.

Then the most out-of-the-ordinary thing happened. It was as if there came movement to Van der Vinne's left eye. And it looked real, very real, not the result of light playing tricks with the canvas. Before long, it appeared as though the entire portrait was starting to move – the head, the shoulders, the mouth.

"But how could that be possible?" Reginald watched in amazement. Was he imagining it? Hallucinating maybe? And, to top it off, suddenly it appeared as if Van der Vinne was coming out of his canvas toward him. He was talking too, and his voice couldn't have been more clear and distinct. This is what he was saying and he was saying it straight to his face.

"Reggie, don't give up, my friend, the day is not yet done. There's something coming your way just you wait and see."

Reginald was completely baffled. A portrait coming to life? How can that be? He thought seriously. He must be losing his faculties.

Half closing his eyes, he instantly opened them again then gave himself a shake. Looking about, there was nothing out of place and everything was as before. Van der Vinne was hanging on the wall where he always hung, unmoving, an object of art. Had he imagined the whole thing? But it had all been so real!

A few minutes passed when suddenly Reginald realized he was not alone, that there was someone next to him on the bench. When he went to take a look, he saw a woman sitting there and she was wearing a red dress, red shoes, and she smelt like lavender, very much like the lavender from his garden. She was quite short in stature, shorter than him, with small shoulders, small arms, and small feet that dangled many inches off the floor. He almost mistook her for a child of seven or eight.

He ventured to look more boldly at her:

She had yellow hair that was pulled back in a French braid, and her broad and pleasant face couldn't have had a healthier complexion. She hardly had a neck but the bit she did have was soft and white as snow. With eyes brown and thoughtful-looking and lips the color of raspberries, there was something curiously fascinating about her. But how was it she came to sit next to him? And where did she even come from?

Reginald longed to say something to her, to engage her in some way but he did not dare. Remembering on past experiences with the opposite sex, which always ended badly, he sat there with a strained expression.

The woman shifted slightly, and as it happened, she was not shy by any means, not half as shy as Reginald. She started up a conversation with him right away, and acted as though she had known him a long while, though in fact she was a perfect stranger. It was almost as if she'd been watching him and had designs on him. She spoke loudly and concisely.

"Are you a Frans Hals fan too?"

Reginald felt a flash of fear at hearing her voice, which was sweet, like that of a bird. He couldn't believe she was actually talking to him. It was quite unlike anything.

"Yes," he finally worked up the courage to respond. "As a matter of fact, I am."

The woman couldn't have been more delighted, and it was clear she had every intention of conversing with him further. As it happened, she was relatively new to the city and this was her first visit to the gallery. She had admired Frans Hals' portraits in art books for many years and was now happy to see one in person.

Then assuming a kind of playful, almost teasing manner, as if to challenge him, she started in on a game of words. It was as though she had just made it up.

"Frans Hals, born 1582 – Antwerp."

Reginald caught on at once and was eager to play along. "Frans Hals, died 1666 – Haarlem."

The woman, "Gypsy Girl, his most famous piece."

Reginald, back at her, "Not so, Laughing Cavalier, just as famous."

"My personal favorite, Jester with a Lute."

"My personal favorite, Malle Babbe."

"Malle Babbe?" the woman began to laugh and she said still laughing, "Malle Babbe? That is completely silly!"

Reginald, grasping at once what she meant, laughed too, "You mean sillier than silly!"

Being the Frans Hals fans that they were, they understood instantly that *malle* in Dutch meant *silly* and that's what Malle

Babbe was, silly. They were both silly themselves. Having barely met, already they had so much in common.

But Reginald couldn't help worry because anything could happen next. This amazing woman, this woman who seemed so perfect to him could just pick up and walk out the door, she could be gone from him forever. He felt afraid to think of what might happen next.

A constrained silence came into the room and lasted about two minutes.

But the woman was obviously someone who knew exactly what she wanted and she was naturally assertive and determined. She held out her hand in a friendly way, "I'm Regina, pleased to meet you."

Reginald sat rigid and there was still anxiety in his face. "I'm Reginald."

"Reginald?" she clapped her hands and laughed a little. "Oh my, really? Reginald and Regina! It couldn't get any better than that! Our names are practically the same! I knew when I saw you there was something about you."

"There was something about me?" Reginald could hardly believe what he'd just heard. Could it be there was something remarkable happening?

Regina was truly lovely and he couldn't take his eyes off her. She was different from any woman he'd ever known. What especially attracted him to her was her strong jaw, her snub nose, and her eyes that became even more beautiful when she smiled. He liked her sure, brief speech and her acceptance of herself. The two of them were both people of short stature, so much alike yet so different. He could feel the woman in her, something scintillating and enchanting. A moment ago, he was hopelessly alone and now he'd become a man in love. But the idea made him very much afraid. Could this really be happening to him? Love at first sight? He felt an excitement unlike any other.

Out of the blue, Regina asked if he was hungry and would he like to join her for lunch.

"Yes," he was quick to answer, "I'm starving." Then without thinking, "And I love cheese."

I love cheese? Did I just say that? Reginald was horrified at what had come out of his mouth, he could have kicked himself. Cheese, of all things. What an utterly stupid thing for him to say.

Luckily, Regina paid no attention. She said with zeal, as if the cheese comment was the most normal thing, "Cheese, you say you love cheese? What a coincidence, I love cheese too! We can walk over to Kensington Market, to the cheese shop there."

"Kensington Market? Why that's my favorite place to get cheese," said Reginald happily.

"Mine too!"

"We'll get stilton and camembert."

"And spiced gouda and brie."

Getting up, glancing briefly over at Van der Vinne, giving him a quick nod goodbye, off the two went to Kensington Market. Having a liking for both Van der Vinne and cheese, it was a miracle the two hadn't met before. At the cheese shop, with cheese and bagels bagged and two takeout coffees, they headed for the little park at the south end of the market. Some children were playing hopscotch on the pavement while others were in the playground. Reginald and Regina sat down under the cool of a broad maple and took in the fresh scent of cut grass.

As they ate, they talked. They were interested in everything that concerned the other. Reginald told her all about his life and she told him about hers. She was from a town in the Maritimes called Louisville with a population of about ten thousand, and she had come from a family of little people. Louisville was full of colorful wooden houses, big trees, and there were no fences around any of the yards. When she was born, she was the tiniest baby the town had ever seen, barely three pounds, and in the hospital, she had been placed in an incubator for three weeks. As a child she spent a lot of time fidgeting and was fond of making trouble. At school she was always much shorter than her classmates and they came to call her Midge, short for Midget, but she never took offense, as there was never any ill intent intended. Now as an adult, even with high heels on she stood just over three feet tall.

She'd been married twice but was now divorced, her first husband, Jack, was a little person and her second, Sebastian, a big person, standing at, believe it or not, six-foot-five. Sebastian was a ventriloquist and was still in love with her and wanted her back. She'd been single for about a year now, and though the right man had never come along again, she did manage to have a number of romances here and there. Did she have children? Yes, she had children, a lot of them, but she let forego that little bit of information, for now at least, as it would have been too much to take in. By profession she was a busker and she busked all over the city, though she was considering getting into hairdressing as busking was proving to be not all that reliable. She lived on Ossington Crescent, which was about fifteen minutes west of the market by streetcar.

Reginald was taken by all Regina had to say, and she couldn't have been more thorough and clever. There was something fascinating about her and she was so chatty and witty. He was now quite at ease with her and the two were as if bound together in a close friendship. And the best part was he didn't have to defend his inefficiencies, she accepted him just the way he was. It was all so wonderful.

Somehow, kicking off their shoes, they began to wrestle and play-fight in the grass. As they struggled, with their arms round each other and their bodies pressed closely together, they could feel the other's breath. Suddenly Reginald leaned over and kissed Regina tenderly on the mouth. She kissed him back. Reginald's eyes were wet with tears and so were hers. Things were getting heated. Their lives were going to change forever, Reginald could feel it and he was sure Regina could feel it, too.

The sun was starting to go down; it would soon be dark. Reginald felt proud to be in the company of this compact little woman and his heart was running hot. Dazed by her pink skin, the soft outline of her bosom, he couldn't have been fuller of expectation. He would work up the courage to see her again, to ask her out for dinner next Thursday night. As he was about to do just that, Regina started looking uneasy, as if there was something pressing on her mind. Jumping to her feet, she said suddenly:

"Oh, my, I didn't realize how late it was. I've got to get going."

Gathering her purse and slipping on her shoes, she started across the park in a great hurry. Reginald couldn't bear to see her go and his heart sank. She was running off on him like Cinderella from her Prince Charming. He called after her, "Wait. Please don't go. Can I see you again?"

Regina called back, "No! Yes! No, I mean. Oh, I'm so late!" Then she threw in hastily, "Van der Vinne. Next Sunday, same time same place. I'll be there."

And within minutes she was gone.

Reginald stood spellbound as if it had all been a dream. The park had since emptied and he was now alone. He hardly knew anything about the woman he had just met except she had the face of an angel. Making his way to the streetcar stop, he hopped on the first car and headed for home. Sitting directly behind the driver, looking out the window, shops whizzed by – a men's clothing store, a delicatessen, a pharmacy. The bell clanged now and then, passengers got on, then got off. Reginald had just met Regina and already he was missing her. He had been waiting for someone like her all his life only he didn't know it until today. Strange feelings filled inside him and they were growing stronger by the minute.

That night Reginald didn't feel much like spying on people. Regina continued to play heavily on his mind. He tried to read a book to distract himself, watch a movie, play a video game, but he couldn't focus on anything. He felt as if he was embarking on a new life, one where there was someone in the world for him. Even his house didn't seem so bleak anymore. Finally, he went to bed. And who should he dream about but Regina. He loved her, but did she love him? Why did she run off so suddenly? Was she having second thoughts? Did he do something to set her off? Was there maybe another man in the picture? To wait till next Sunday to see her again felt like an eternity. He had to find a way to see her sooner than that. Then he remembered she lived on Ossington Crescent.

"Ossington Crescent is not too far from Bank Street; I could easily walk there."

He would go there tomorrow night, he decided. He would look through the windows of all the houses there and he would keep looking until he found her. In such a way he would come to be with her even if from the outside, and he might even learn a thing or two about her in the process. But truth be told, he was starting to feel a little guilty about this whole spying business and he worried that if he spied on her and she found him out, she might not take kindly to this invasion of privacy. And so, he made a promise to himself, his spying days were over.

When the next night came, he simply couldn't help himself. Old habits were hard to break. He said to himself.

"Just this one last time and never again."

So, off Reginald went in the direction of Ossington Crescent. With the sun already behind the rooftops, he couldn't have been more inspired by the beauty of the evening. The moon was out, the stars twinkled, and a soft gentle mist rose up from the pavement. Cars passed by every few seconds, and then a streetcar stretched off toward Dundas Station. Tonight, he was a man on a mission and he was feeling hopeful. He was about to look in on the love of his life. He would find her and be near her.

Finally, Ossington Crescent. Except for a slight wind coming in from the north, the street lay still and deserted. There were not many houses there, about twenty in total, all bunched together with largish porches, peaked roofs, and high bay windows. It was a dead-end street and Reginald wondered why it had been called a crescent when there was no curved cycle shape to it and the only way out was the same way in. Looking through various windows, he came up empty. Then suddenly a house near the corner caught his attention. The windows were all blackened but there was a light coming from the basement. As far as he could tell small children lived there, as there were bicycles and tricycles, balls and doll carriages both in the yard and scattered along the walkway. To his surprise, he also noticed a few unusual items such as a unicycle, some juggling rings, a Cyr wheel, and, of all things, a miniature penny-farthing.

"How odd," he thought. "Circus equipment, and so much of it. Circus performers must live here."

At once there came a noise from the basement. He walked up to a screened window no larger than a small picture frame and it was wide open. When he crouched to have a look, he was astonished at what he saw. Everything was topsy-turvy. There were about ten people running about doing unusual, circus-like things, and he noticed right away they were all little people, much smaller even than himself, and some were very young, the youngest maybe five or six.

There was a little boy, who couldn't have been more than eight, whistling and riding around on a unicycle. Another was wearing a magic hat and doing tricks with it. He then observed a girl of about ten, but unlike the others, she was of average size and was pulling things out of her sleeve – a bouquet of flowers, a bird, a silk scarf. There were a couple of dogs there too, very clever-looking, dancing, and jumping through hoops.

"What a spectacle!" Reginald couldn't get enough. Then a red, yellow, and orange banner stretching from one end of the basement to the other caught his attention. It read, "Welcome to Midge's Magic Family Circus".

At once it struck him, "But of course, this is Regina's place. She said she was a busker. She has a circus act!"

And there in the far corner was a smallish dark outline of a woman, the woman he'd been looking for. It was Regina. With her hair tied back, in her face there was something more magnificent than beauty. He was lost to himself in looking at her. She was hula hooping, not with one, not with two, but with three hoops, and one of them was with fire. She was mesmerizing, enticing, and he was amazed at how talented she was.

"So, that's why she ran off on me so abruptly on Sunday – she has children, lots of them!" Then he started counting, "One, two, four, seven, eight. Eight in total!"

What happened next is something he never would have expected. He was finding himself drawn to them, drawn to them all as if they were his own.

Suddenly Regina called out, "Okay children, bedtime, it's almost ten o'clock! Remember the Busker Festival at High Park tomorrow. We have a big day ahead of us. Luckily, we have a good spot, right by the restaurant."

The family made its way up a steep staircase. The basement light went off and soon the house fell silent. Everyone had gone to sleep.

On his way home, Reginald felt an element of rapture, and wild, hysterical sensations kept passing through him. Of all his years spying on people, never had he encountered anything like this. What a show the love of his life had just put on! It was like nothing he'd ever seen. He felt bound to her more than ever, he had been waiting for someone like her all his life and finally he found her.

The next day, Midge's Magic Family Circus, in their big yellow truck, which was especially retrofitted for Regina's diminutive size, pulled into High Park. Unloading all their gear, they started setting up. Century-old trees stood in the background, there were wonderful, sweet-scented rose gardens all around, and to the right a water fountain, where if you threw in a coin it would bring good luck. It was warm and sunny and there was a pleasant breeze coming off the nearby lake.

Before long the park filled with people. And who should be among them but Reginald, though he was hiding in the bushes. Closing up shop for the day, he left a sign in the window: "Store closed due to family emergency, sorry for the inconvenience." Although he promised never again to spy on Regina or anyone else for that matter, it was proving a difficult thing to do. But this would be his one last time, he swore on his mother's grave. "Never, never any more after this."

In the meantime, with everything ready to go, Regina placed a huge glass bowl on the ground for the money collection. She threw in some coins and a five-dollar bill to get things started. She said to her brood, "Let's just hope our crowd today isn't stingy."

A woman in a sundress came by, then a young man eating an ice cream, then a chubby little girl with pigtails. Soon more people joined in and before long a big crowd formed consisting of about fifty people.

Regina, in a clown costume and wearing a clown wig, called through a loudspeaker, "Ladies and gentlemen, welcome to Midge's Magic Family Circus. On with the show!"

Music started up.

The crowd watched attentively. Reginald watched too. First little Cindy came out on her unicycle, followed by her brother Teddy on stilts. Then Jenny (the one of average size) pulled a rabbit out of her sleeve, and later Freddy drove by on his miniature penny-farthing. When Ralphy came out, he amazed everyone with the Cyr wheel, and one of the onlookers wanted to know where he had learned to do that, to which Ralphy replied he had taken a few Cyr wheel courses at a special circus school in Montreal. Mikey had a program of acrobatic tricks, and though his repertoire was not a large one, he did it well and with enthusiasm. Little Lucy and Suzy, who were identical twins, came out walking on their hands, and later the dogs did some fancy jumps and twirls. Regina juggled various objects in the air.

The crowd shook with applause. The family bowed many times.

It was getting late and the sun was setting behind the trees. Regina and her brood were packing up. Reginald needed to get out of the bushes but he couldn't risk being seen. Edging his way onto the grass, jumping behind a tree, then another one, he soon safely disappeared over a hillock to the right of the restaurant. Up and down a few trails, finally he was out of the park. Large brick houses appeared for a couple of blocks, and then when he got to a set of street lights, there came a line of shops and restaurants. Traffic was considerable and the sidewalks bustled with people.

Reginald was feeling happy. It was as if Regina had been part of his life forever and she had never been foreign to him. He wanted to dance, sing, laugh out loud. Tonight, he was over the moon in love.

When Reginald got home, he went straight to bed, though he was restless. There was much on his mind and he couldn't stop tossing and turning. It was only Tuesday night, tomorrow would be Wednesday, then Thursday. Sunday was still far off and he didn't know if he could bear to wait that long. He was yearning to go back to Ossington Crescent and spy on Regina again but he told himself "No!" he was finished with all that, and "No" it would be.

Sunday finally came. After lunch, washing, shaving, and putting on a fine set of clothes, examining himself before a full-length mirror, he thought he looked quite good. Fixing up his shirt collar and adjusting his tie, he went into his garden and picked a small bouquet of flowers – fern mixed with English lavender – and set off for the gallery.

The whole way there, images of Regina floated before him and they would not leave. She was such an inspiration to him; she was more than he had ever dreamed of. But what if she wouldn't be there today? What if it was all over and she was never coming back? When he finally arrived, to his great relief, there she was in the Old Master Collection sitting before Van der Vinne just as she had promised.

"Hello," he called out to her.

Regina, looking up, smiled, "Oh, hello. I was starting to think you might not show up."

Reginald's love for Regina increased by the minute. He marveled at not having to control himself and hide his feelings. Pressing his hands to his heart, going down on his knees, he presented her with his garden bouquet, which she gladly and affably accepted. He said to her without inhibition.

"It's hopeless, what can I do, I love you."

"You love me?" she responded. "I love you too, and I can be happy with you. I know I can."

The two looked into each other's eyes for the longest time.

Right at that moment there came some kind of disturbance from behind. Reginald looked over his shoulder to see what was going on. A group of young people, very small in stature (except for a girl of average height), were misbehaving, jumping around, laughing. They were making such a row it made the Old Master Collection rumble and tumble as if from a nearby train.

That's when a tall, spindly, very officious-looking security guard came rushing in. He'd gotten several complaints from disgruntled patrons about a gang of unruly kids. Dressed in a dark green uniform and black cap, he walked straight up to the trouble-makers.

"Stop that racket at once, I say! This is an art gallery, not some three-ring circus!"

But the noisemaking continued. It wasn't until he blew his whistle that everything fell silent. Then there came not a cough, not a whisper, nor the sound of breathing anywhere.

Regina got up and with a look of dismay, showing unmistakable signs of embarrassment, headed toward the guard. Clearing her throat, she was full of apologies, "I'm so sorry. Yes, they are my children and it's all my fault they got out of hand. You see, I was sitting there before the portrait of Vincent Laurensz Van der Vinne and I completely lost myself."

The guard looked at her from under his brows not in the least bit convinced with what she had just said. Adjusting his cap, throwing back his head, he walked haughtily out of the room.

Regina returned to Reginald and sat almost touching him. Several seconds passed. She said quietly, "Now you know. It's true, those children, they're are all mine, all eight of them, we're street performers, we have a circus act."

Reginald looked at her with a strange timorousness and tried to appear astonished. But of course, he already knew everything, and he even knew each of her children by name: Freddy, Suzy, Mikey …

As it happened, the children had taken a liking to Reginald. They had a gig down by the waterfront in about an hour's time and wondered if he would care to join them. Three of the oldest came up with an idea, "Hey, Reginald, you can be our roustabout."

Reginald raised his brows. He was touched by the offer. He'd never been a roustabout before. He said happily, "A roustabout, you say? Hmm … Yes, okay, by all means, I'll be your roustabout. I would like that very much."

The troup, trotting past Van der Vinne, waved to him as if to say good-bye. Soon they were all out on the street. Piling into the big yellow truck which was parked around the corner, Reginald nestled in the back seat between Freddy and Cindy. With Regina behind the wheel, off they drove toward the lake.

There was change in the air, Reginald could feel it all around him. He was no longer afraid. This was going to be his life and he already had a plan. He would ask Regina to marry him.

Chapter 23

The Street Party

Soon word got out Reginald Rutley was getting married, and not only that but he was joining the circus. Neighbors couldn't stop talking about it. Everyone was wanting to meet the soon-to-be bride. Reginald assured them the love of his life would be at the street party next Saturday night.

Saturday came and everything was raring to go. The evening couldn't have been more welcoming – warm, calm, a full moon, a profusion of stars. All parked cars had been removed and placed around the corner, and three large orange pylons were set up at Dufferin blocking incoming traffic. Chairs and tables lined the street and the tables had on them small bouquets of flowers and scented candles in glass jars. There was a makeshift stage in the middle and a whole sound system was already hooked up. Local talent would be showcased – musicians, dancers, a folksinger, a couple of storytellers. Bunches of balloons fluttered about everywhere, and there was a huge brightly-colored banner stretching from one side of the street to the other reading, "Welcome to the Bank Street Bash!"

The smell of food was everywhere and barbeques were out on the street hissing and spluttering with burgers and hot dogs. Mamma Mia had cooked up batches of spaghetti, linguini, and chicken cacciatore and placed it on a table self-serve style before her house, and Little John had done the same as Mamma Mia but with his Thai fruit carvings, this time of prehistoric animals such as jellyfish, lampreys, and turtles.

And there was more than just food: Lily and her granddaughter, Claire, had set up a table with jewelry and various knick-knacks; Pavlo had some of his paintings on display and offered up free caricature portraits; and Rogerio, having served his time in jail on bootlegging charges, brought out his *aguardente* but disguised in soda bottles. There would also be games, face-painting, sand art and more. The Cabbagetown Jazz Band was getting ready to kick things off.

The street was already full of people and more kept coming. Reginald felt a joyous uplifting of his whole being. His thoughts were on Regina. He had never known anything nor had he ever lived till he met her. She made him happy as a fish in water. She would be there soon. His neighbors would meet her and they would be impressed.

But she said she would be there at seven on the dot and it was seven already and no Regina. Five minutes passed, then ten, then fifteen, and still she was not there. Reginald started to get worried. He shrank into himself and looked uneasily about. Heading toward the pylons, he looked up Dufferin Street to see if she might be coming, but there was no sign of her. He checked his cell, there were no messages either. If she truly felt something for him, she would be there.

He started to think she didn't care and that all along she'd merely been toying with his emotions. And suddenly he saw things as they truly were – how dare he think she or anyone could actually love him back.

Then his thoughts took a turn. What if something unexpected happened to her and this unexpected something was keeping her away? What if she got hurt or one of her kids got sick and she had to go to the hospital?

He felt guilty for mistrusting her.

Carlita, formerly Carlito, noticed Reginald standing there with a sullen look on his face. She was looking very pretty tonight in her long summer dress, dangling earrings, and red painted fingernails. Having become a frequent shopper at Reginald's hardware store and a friend of sorts, she felt obliged to say something to him.

"Hey, Reginald, what's up? Where's that love of your life you've been going on about? Not here yet?" Then shaking her head, "Oh, no, don't tell me she stood you up. You poor thing. I know, it's a pretty shitty feeling. Have been there myself all too many times."

It was not long before Christy and Tanya happened by, Tanya with her six-month old Landseer puppy. Seeing Reginald, they too felt sorry for him but, keeping their distance, they were convinced he had made the whole story up. Christy whispered to Tanya, "Poor Reginald, look at him standing there, it's sad, really sad. There's no Regina, never has been. And to think he almost had us all believing he was getting married."

A few minutes later, Noela, Rogerio's wife showed up. She was holding hands with her five-year-old granddaughter, Bella, who was eating watermelon. She was more sympathetic than the others and her voice was encouraging, "Reginald, we all have our hopes and dreams; there's nothing wrong with dreaming once in a while. And sometimes dreams do come true."

So, where *was* Regina? Was she having second thoughts? Did something happen that was preventing her from being there? Did she even exist?

The truth of the matter was, yes, Regina did in fact exist, and something did happen to her and this something was quite serious and completely beyond her control. Just as she was about to leave her house for Bank Street with her children in tow, who should come knocking on her door but her ex-husband, Sebastian, the one who stood at six-foot-four, and the one who wanted her back in his life. In freshly bought clothes – a light jacket of fine wool, black tapered pants, and a silk tie – there was no question, he was there with a firm purpose in mind.

His appearance caught Regina completely off guard. This was the last person she would have expected and it made her angry, "Sebastian! How did you find me? What do you want?"

"How did I find you? I have my ways. And what do I want? It's simple: I want you."

"Is this some kind of joke? After all you've done? You've got to be kidding!"

"I'm a changed man, what can I say? I made a mistake. Let's get married again."

"Married?" Regina stood back. "You cheat on me, sneak around behind my back, not to mention the whole time ignore the children, and now you want me back? No, never, not in a million years. Your leaving was the best thing that ever happened to me! Go away and don't come back!"

"But I love you. I've always loved you."

"Well, I don't love you, not anymore."

Sebastian then tried to squeeze through the door. "I'm sorry I hurt you, Midge. But you're still my little Midge, aren't you?"

"Don't ever call me that again."

"Please give me a second chance. Everyone deserves a second chance."

"You mean a third or is it a fourth?"

"I said I was sorry, didn't I? Why are you being so cruel?"

"Me, cruel? I'm not the guilty party here, remember? I didn't do a thing. Now, go away, go live your stupid life."

Sebastian thought a minute. He soon came up with another idea, one that was sure to get him into the house. Looking round, he asked, "Where are the kids? Can I at least see the kids before I go? Jenny must be so tall by now, just like her dad."

About to shut the door on him, Regina felt an impulse of pity. Deciding to keep things civil, at least where the children were concerned, she decided to give in to his request. She hollered, "Hey, kids, there's someone here to see you. But no more than five minutes. We're already late enough as it is."

The children were happy to see Sebastian and he'd brought them presents too – a box of chocolates, some toys, and a big bag of gummy bears. They asked him where he'd been for so long, as they had no idea. Though they were well aware of the divorce, the affair(s) had been kept secret. He answered their questions vaguely, "Oh, I've been here and there" and "Working a bit up north, a bit down south."

The children were excited to tell him about Reginald, their mother's new boyfriend. They went on to say that like them Reginald was a little person and he was even willing to be their roustabout. And not only that but he and their mother were planning to get married.

"Married?" Sebastian was obviously hit with a pang of jealousy. He lifted his face. "And he's to be your roustabout too? What do you need a roustabout for anyway? You'd be far better off with a ventriloquist such as myself. Remember how good we had it, how many laughs we used to get? I still have Charlie, he's in my car. What an act we were, what an act!"

The children and Sebastian talked some more. Finally, Regina came in and broke things up. "Time to go, kids! Reginald's waiting. He's probably wondering where we are."

As the children picked up and headed for the door, saying goodbye to Sebastian, they decided to take their circus apparatus as a means of transportation. Riding their unicycles, the miniature penny farthing, and not to forget the Cyr wheel, already on Dundas, they made for Bank Street. The sky was clear and lovely. Weaving in and around pedestrians, singing and laughing, the street lights helped illuminate their way.

Meanwhile, Sebastian made up his mind to follow them in his car. He remained at a distance, so as not to be seen. He had it all figured out: the street party would put Regina in a good mood, such a good mood he would easily be able to win her over. And he would bring Charlie along too because Charlie always brought a smile to her face and made her remember the good times. And then later he'd find that Reginald fellow out and have a word with him. If there was one thing Sebastian would not tolerate, it was another man putting moves on his woman.

Back on Bank Street everyone was in a celebratory mood. An opaque light from the streetlights cast over the pavement and gave a glimpse of people having a good time. Little John was dancing with Mamma Mia, Carlita with her father Miguel, and Angie with Pepe (who had since found out he had a son in little Oliver). The evening couldn't have been finer. A soft breeze coming in from the south was a gentle reminder it was summertime.

But Reginald was miserable. He wasn't dancing, he was sitting at his table with his head down buried in his hands. It was as if he had vanished into the night, as if he wasn't there at all. Regina he was convinced was not coming.

At once there came a commotion from the direction of the pylons, then the sound of a woman and children. Reginald pricked up his ears. He recognized the voices at once. It was

Regina and her family; they had come after all! And Regina was looking so lovely in a burgundy dress belted at the waist and her hair all done up.

Starting toward her, it was then that he noticed a very tall man next to her with big hands, a long nose, and a very pointed chin. The man was saying something to her and following her around. There was definitely something unpleasant about him, and, for some reason, he was carrying a dummy under his arm.

Reginald became confused, "Who is that man and what could he possibly want with Regina?"

Briefly looking round for Regina's children, realizing they had since disappeared into the crowd, Reginald's attention fell back on the man. There definitely was something familiar about him yet at the same time he was certain he'd never seen him before.

Then it hit him. The man looked exactly like Regina's daughter, Jenny, the tall one – the same pronounced features, the same type of hair, the same long legs. And the dummy he was carrying was smiling, though in a very menacing way. Reginald remembered Regina telling him her ex had been a ventriloquist, and though he worked as a shoe salesman by day, he often busked with them nights and on weekends. Reginald got a bad feeling in the pit of his stomach.

"Sebastian! That's Sebastian!"

Reginald became depressed. He had it all worked out, at least he thought he did. "There's only one explanation. Regina's back in a relationship with him. I could see it all now. She's come to the street party to tell me it's over. She'll humiliate me in front of all the neighbors and I'll become a laughing stock! What a fool I've been!"

Suddenly he noticed something odd going on between Regina and Sebastian and it was intense. Regina appeared upset. There was a flush on her cheeks and she was flailing her arms about and shouting. Sebastian, it seemed, was trying to reason with her, stooping to her level, shouting back.

Then Regina, flinging herself around, tried to move away. But before she had a chance to get very far, Sebastian, it seemed, had come up with an idea, one that he was sure would get her to come back. He would use Charlie. Grabbing a chair and sitting down, throwing Charlie on his knee, at once he began working the intricate string mechanism on his back. Pulling one string up, one down, another sideways, before long, Charlie was moving his arms and legs and rolling his eyes. He was calling out like a real live person.

"Regina, please, don't walk out on Sebastian! Don't do that to him! Can't you see he's hurting?"

Regina flung herself around, "Don't you play ventriloquist with me, and don't bother using Charlie to get to me either. It won't work. I told you, I'm done."

"Take Sebastian back, please."

"No."

"But the two of you were so good together."

"*Were* is the operative word here. Tell Sebastian he can go back to Candy, Mandy or whatever her name was, and he can stay there. He has my blessing."

Charlie's brows furrowed to show emotion, "Regina, please, Sebastian's sorry. He says he's been such a dummy."

"Dummy?" Regina fell into laughter. "A dummy, you say? Yes, Sebastian and Charlie, two dummies! What a duo! Hah, hah, hah!"

Sebastian straightened Charlie's back. He had more to say but suddenly he started to cough and he coughed so much he almost choked. His throat had run dry. The problem was his ventriloquism was out of practice; it had been almost a full year now. What he needed more than anything was a drink. Setting

Charlie on the ground, walking into the crowd, he tried to find water, coffee, juice, anything. Finally, he spotted a table with soda bottles on it. Exactly what he was looking for. With no one tending the table (Rogerio was dancing with his wife), he went ahead and helped himself. Grabbing the closest bottle, which was labeled "ginger ale", he took a couple of sips. Screwing up his mouth, he stopped a moment to consider – it was the strangest tasting ginger ale, unlike any he'd ever had before. Was it even ginger ale? He looked at the bottle. Taking another sip, he tried to figure it out. It reminded him of rubbing alcohol, no, of kerosene, no, of something you put in your car. It went down like liquid fire. It was gross, it made him gag, and yet, somehow, he quite liked it. He helped himself to some more.

Before he knew it, his head was going round, everything looked blurry, and he was having trouble standing up. He was drunk. Looking into the crowd, he decided it was high time for him to go find that Reginald fellow. And he knew exactly what he would say to him. He would say: "Fuck off; eat shit and die. Go to hell. Regina belongs to me." After that he would use more bad language.

But the street was so full of people and they were making so much noise he didn't know where to begin. Taking the ginger ale bottle with him, he searched up and down, calling out, "Reginald, oh, Reginald, where are you?"

Passing a group of women, then a group of men, coming up to Mamma Mia's food table, which now stood half empty, accidently he bumped into it. Losing balance, he fell flat on his face. When he looked up who should he set his eye on but Reginald, and he was sitting at a table with none other than his Regina. The two were close to each other, too close for his liking, touching even, and sharing a plate of spaghetti and meatballs.

"Well, well," declared Sebastian, getting up. "At last I found the man I've been looking for."

"What do you want, Sebastian? Why are you even here? Go away," this was Regina.

"So, this is the fellow who thinks he can take Sebastian's Regina away from him. Well, you're out of luck, little man. I won't stand for it; I simply won't stand for it!"

"You're drunk!" Regina moved her chair back and got up.

"Yes, it appears I am drunk though not from booze as you might think, but from ginger ale. What, you don't believe me? Here's the bottle to prove it. Have a look for yourself."

He banged the bottle on the table.

"Please, don't make a scene," Regina begged.

"A scene? Why should I make a scene? I was looking for Reginald and now I found him. I'm here simply to tell him you're mine and I'm hanging onto you. You're not a normal woman, Regina, not a normal woman by any means!"

Turning to Reginald, he became obnoxious and aggressive, "Hey, little man, or should I say wife-stealer. Stay away from my Regina. I'm taking her with me right now and you'll never see her again. If you try and stop me, I'll smash your head in."

Grabbing hold of Regina, flinging her over his shoulder, he started to carry her off.

Regina kicked her feet and screamed, "Put me down, you brute! Put me down!"

A crowd quickly gathered curious to see what was going on. There was a rebel-rouser among them and he looked dangerous. The atmosphere became charged.

Sebastian was now howling and sputtering with rage, "Get out of my way, people! I'm coming through!"

Reginald watched in horror and he didn't know what to do. Such egregious behavior, such foul language. Never had he seen anyone so pugnacious. Regina was being abducted right before his eyes. What could he do? He had to find a way to save her and fast, even if it meant getting himself killed in the process. Mustering up his courage, rolling up his sleeves, he flew at Sebastian in a frenzy with his little fists. "Take that and that you beast! And that, and that!" He punched at him over and over then booted him in the shins.

Sebastian broke into a laugh, "Ouch, you're really hurting me! Really! Stop, I say! Stop! Hah, hah, hah!"

The crowd looked on in horror and waited for what would come next; a few drew closer. They were all well aware Reginald was no match for the man more than triple his size. Fearing the worst, someone called 911.

With Regina still over Sebastian's shoulder, suddenly with his free hand Sebastian reached out and grabbed Reginald by the collar. Holding him in mid-air, he started flinging him back and forth, back and forth with the intention of doing him harm. Reginald kicked and screamed and struck back but with no luck. He was as good as dead. Mustering up all his strength, somehow, he managed to break free and jump onto the table. But he soon found he was no safer up there. With Sebastian now only inches away, he decided his only option was to make a run for it. Then he noticed the ginger ale bottle. Snatching it up, swinging it several times in the air, with all his might, he whacked Sebastian over the head with it. Sebastian was stunned. Rolling his eyes, half opening his mouth, he fell to the ground with a heavy thud. Within minutes he was out cold.

The crowd roared and cheered, even the police, who had since arrived, joined in, "Hooray! Reginald, he did it! He did the big man in!"

All were overcome by Reginald's unexpected and extraordinary display of strength.

Regina fled to him with open arms, "My hero!"

And so, Reginald became the man of the hour, having brought down a man as big as an ape. Taking Regina by the hand, leading her to the stage, he had a big announcement to make. He called out for all to hear:

"Neighbors, I would like to introduce you all to my beautiful soon-to-be-bride, Regina."

There came clapping, whistling, and shouts of congratulations, a few men hurled their caps into the air.

Reginald then called for her eight children to come up and join them, after which they each took a bow. Rocco and Susana, home from college, and who had since learned of their very unusual conception, also came up on stage, happy to join in the celebration.

Everyone was feeling the joy, even those unable to attend. The killer sisters Antonia and Matilde, serving life sentences, sent best wishes; Beatrice, killer of Desiree, also in for life but in another part of the country, texted words of congratulations; and Hedda, the cat hoarder, recovering in a mental health facility, messaged her kindly regards.

Before long The Cabbagetown Jazz Band started up – a tambourine began to jingle, then the strumming of a banjo, then a trumpet. Soon the band fell to playing the Polka and everyone was dancing. Reginald had hardly ever in his life danced and now he was dancing too, twirling round and kicking up his heels. And he was dancing with Regina, the woman of his dreams. The feeling was so liberating, so exhilarating, he couldn't have asked for more. He was bursting with a strange, incomprehensible feeling and it was called love.

★

So, in conclusion to our little story, this is how Reginald's spying days came to an end. He had fallen in love and he was loved back. And it had all happened so naturally and equally. His make-believe days were over and the windows of Bank Street were no longer of interest to him. He wasn't alone anymore or estranged from those around him, he now had a family. They would all have supper tonight together, and they would be together tomorrow and the day after that. He was now like everyone else. It seemed impossible but it was true, and it was quite an ordinary thing after all, not in the least bit extraordinary. And, truth be told, he never expected such an ending, not in a million years.

Acknowledgements

A tremendous thanks to my friends at our Oakville writers' group: Maria Yates, Steve Abbott, Frank Beghin, Ian Robertson, and Mike Przysiezny. Your invaluable comments, criticisms, suggestions, insights, smarts were all so greatly appreciated – and the laughs helped a lot too.

With a special thanks to Maria Yates for that inconspicuous little bottle she brought me one night of her father's very own make-it-yourself *aguardente*.

Credits

"Fancy Feast" appeared in *Feline Fancies* (*The Crimson Cloak Anthologie*s, Book 9) – in support of Los Angeles feral cat non-profit Fix Nation, 2018.

"Messermeisters" (Noble Knives) appeared in *Storgy Magazine*, 2017.

About the Author

Erma Odrach is an author and literary translator living in Canada. Alaska or Bust and Other Stories was published by Crimson Cloak Publishing, Missouri, 2017. Her translation of novel *Wave of Terror* (by her late father, Theodore Odrach, dealing with the Stalinist occupation, WWII) was published by Chicago Review Press, 2008. She won an honorable mention from the Translation Center at Columbia University for a book of stories. Her work has appeared in magazines such as *Connecticut Review, Scrivener, The New Quarterly, Antigonish Review, Yukon, North of Ordinary, Penguin Book of Christmas Stories* (ed. Alberto Manguel), Translation – Columbia Univ. and many more.

Made in United States
North Haven, CT
20 January 2022